S A R A H

NEVER
his MATE

C L A W S   A N D   F A N G S   B O O K   1

CHAPTER 1

Oh, I shouldn't be doing this.

Even as I throw my Jeep into park, I know this is a bad idea. Hell, for all of her instigating, I doubt Trish ever *dreamed* she'd get such a reaction out of me—which just goes to show that none of my new packmates know me half as well as they think they do.

I glare through my windshield, heart pounding like a drum in my chest as my shifter's sight zeroes in on the homey-looking structure tucked along the edge of the woods. My pulse thuds, blood racing through my veins, and if I didn't have ironclad control over my inner wolf, my leather steering wheel would be nothing but shreds courtesy of my claws. Even so, it takes everything I have to hold her back just a little longer.

Just a little longer, girl, because I'm here.

Now, the first time I'm *meant* to step foot inside of the Alpha's cabin is directly after we've performed the Luna Ceremony that would tie me to him for life as his bonded mate. So even though I was brought to Accalia to do just that, I've only ever seen his cabin from a distance.

Until today.

Until right this very moment.

Pack law is crystal clear. The moon might have whispered that I'm to be his intended, but I'm still an outsider until we've accepted the mating bond, done the deed, and received the moon's blessing. The Alpha's cabin is sacred, even more so to the Mountain-side Pack. Since I arrived last month, I haven't been allowed to forget it.

Is that going to stop me from crashing their council meeting?

No fucking way.

Because I'm furious but not a moron, I parked my packed-up car about a half a mile away from the cabin. My trusty Jeep has every single thing I own in it, with a change of clothes sitting on the passenger seat in case this whole thing goes sideways. As a wolf shifter, I can go from skin to fur and back with barely any effort. My clothes, though? They never survive the shift, and I'd rather not flee for my life wearing nothing but my birthday suit, thank you very much.

I glance at the jeans I picked out, broken in though none of my Mountainside packmates have ever seen me in them. The tank top that leaves my arms loose and limber. The sturdy boots should I have to get out and go on foot...

Yeah, I'm pretty sure this is going to go sideways.

And... that's still not going to stop me.

I leave the keys in the ignition. No reason to fear that the Jeep will be gone when I get back. My scent clings to the car, and considering my status in the pack, it doesn't matter that I'm still an outsider. To mess with me is an insult to the Alpha, and for as long as the rest of Accalia believes that, I'm going to use it to my advantage.

Though my wolf wants out—wants to break free and take off into the night, the moon bathing her fur as she outruns the sting of rejection—I tighten my reins on my other half.

Not yet, I tell her. Soon, but not yet.

I don't run, but I eat up the ground anyway. As much as it hurts, I can follow the echoes of the mating bond right to the cabin; even if pack gossip didn't tell me that he was in a meeting with his council, I would know exactly where to find him through the whisper-thin thread stretched between us. From the moment I switched packs, coming to Accalia to stay with the Mountainside Pack ahead of our mating, I've been constantly aware of him.

Ryker Wolfson. My fated mate, and Mountainside's Alpha.

The only difference between his cabin and the rest of ours is its location, its seclusion. Built on the edge of pack territory specifically for the Alpha, its resident is our first line of defense. A non-packmate—human, vamp, or another kind of shifter—would have to go past it if they wanted to reach Accalia. With his impressive senses and overwhelming strength, any threat who hopes to get to the heart of the pack has to go through Ryker first.

Right now, that sounds like a plan to me.

I don't go in through the front. Not because I'm wary of breaking pack law or because I'm trying to be sneaky—growing up the adopted daughter of the Lakeview Pack's Alpha, I know plenty of tricks to avoid being caught—but for the simple reason that I can sense Ryker and his council gathered near the back. Of course. As territorial as we shifters are, he would keep the rest of the pack out of his personal space: his bedroom, his living room, his kitchen. Only his mate is allowed to enter the Alpha's cabin—which, I remind myself again, is precisely why I'm not supposed to be here.

But the den? That's where my dad always held his meetings, a space that was considered a refuge for any packmate in need. How much do I want to bet that Ryker's setup is the same?

It's a loophole. I admit it.

Gonna take it anyway.

Still following the whisper-thin bond leading me toward him, my senses start to ping when I find the closed door attached to the back of the towering cabin. I grab the handle, prepared to snap the lock if I have to; it's bad etiquette and my mother would be ashamed, but she'd understand once I explained myself. I don't have to break it, though. The door's unlocked, an open invitation to all of Accalia to meet with the Alpha.

Gotcha.

I throw open the door, letting the weak moonlight silhouette me against the night.

All conversations stop. There are—through my angry haze, I do a quick headcount—eight other males in the room apart from Ryker. They're all standing, some prowling around the space, others braced with their legs apart, arms crossed over their chests. Ryker's Beta, Shane, has his hip cocked against the desk across the room, obviously in the middle of saying something. I've definitely interrupted them, but I can't bring myself to care.

Only one shifter in the office setup is seated. With a window at his back, a broad mahogany desk stretched in front of him, and his feet propped up on the edge as he leans lazily in his deep, leather chair, Ryker commands the council's complete attention even as he listens intently to whatever it is Shane was saying.

Or, he *did*.

As soon as the door swings open, every head shoots my way. No one says anything, and if they did, I'm not listening. All of *my* attention is focused solely on the Alpha now.

Ryker Wolfson is a young Alpha. Only twenty-seven, he's just coming into his prime, but he's nothing if not strong. Powerful. And, Luna help me, *gorgeous*. He has the dark gold eyes typical to our kind, with a rich tan that makes them pop. Unlike most shifters, though, he wears his hair cropped short; it looks black, but I know it's really a rich brown color when he lets it get shaggy. A perennial five o'clock shadow highlights the sharp edge of his jaw while his lush lips provide a hint of softness to a deliciously hard male.

Those lips are pulled in a tight frown when he realizes that it's me. With a deceptively graceful swivel, he moves his boots from his desk, perching them on the floor as he moves forward in his seat.

Shane Loup is about the same age as Ryker; pack gossip says that he got the Beta position because he's Ryker's closest friend which is surprising considering he's as much of an outsider as I am. Some of the elders thought Ryker should pick someone with more experience to be his righthand wolf, but Shane accepted the nod when Ryker took over the pack at the beginning of the year.

Since Ryker's been too busy for me lately—at least, that's what I *thought* before tonight's unexpected conversation with Trish—Shane's been the one to help me get settled in at Accalia. He's a nice guy. Easy on the eyes, too, with his dirty blond hair and a pair of cute dimples, but I know better than to think he's harmless. He's devoted to Ryker and the Mountainside Pack, and as if he can sense that trouble's brewing, he moves to intercept me.

I tap into my wolf, letting out some of the dominance I rarely rely on.

"What are you doing here?" he asks, brow furrowed as he starts to cross the room before stopping so suddenly, it's like someone has yanked his chain. Yeah. *Me.* Frowning, he says, "You should go back to your cabin, Gem."

Yup. Probably should.

I leave the door open behind me and, bringing a smile to my face, I enter the room.

Except for Shane, the crowd parts easily, just like I expect. These wolves masquerading as men respond to me, even if they don't know why, and it's not like they haven't treated me like this since I arrived on the mountain. A little bit reverence, a little bit respect, and a whole lot of keeping their distance.

Of course they do. I'm an omega wolf. I'm a docile lamb. I'm their Alpha's intended—

7

Ha.

Shame that not a single one of those is true. And, as I stride toward that desk, I'm so far past caring about any future repercussions that I let the old illusion slither down my straight spine. I won't let my wolf out just yet, but I'm done hiding my alpha side.

My flats slap against the tile. As a shifter, I know how to move soundlessly. The noise is purposeful. If the buzz of my aura hasn't snagged their attention already, the anger in my heavy step certainly will.

The other shifters follow my every move—and not because they're picking up on the fact that I might be a threat. They won't. Not yet, at least.

Not until it's too late.

I know what they see when they look at me. Minimal make-up to highlight my pretty honey-colored eyes and my high cheekbones. The flats that make me seem more petite than I really am. I have my hair styled in loose, flowy curls, though I draw the line at a hair bow these days. I'm even wearing a floral-printed sundress putting just the right amount of leg on display for May. And, sure, it gets pretty chilly on the mountain at night, but shifters usually run hot. Me? I run hotter than most even when I'm not this pissed off. Now? I'm burning up, and a dress like this is exactly what they expect from the type of wolf I've spent my whole life passing as.

Everything—from the blonde curls to the dress,

right down to the non-threatening flats—is designed to fool their senses. Even my name was picked to be as gentle as possible. Gemma Swann... who can be afraid of a pretty blonde called Gemma Swann?

I've been doing this my whole life. When I was too young to understand, my mother hid what I was. Now it's up to me. No one can know that I'm not an omega like she is, and even though I'm beginning to have a harder time staying in control, I have to remember that.

Good thing I have a *lot* of practice.

Shifters are unique among supes. We have two souls inside of one form: our human half and our beast. To make their wolves ignore what they can sense about me, I have to make their human halves believe what they see.

I'm a doll. A toy. So very breakable.

By the time they realize I've been hiding in plain sight, it's too late. The claws are already out.

At this very second, I mean that literally.

Now that my steering wheel isn't in any danger of being destroyed, I let loose my claws. Gone are the short nails painted in a prim shade of dusty rose pink. In their place, three-inch-long lethal claws curve around my fingertips, waiting to be used.

But I don't. Not yet. Not until I hear about his betrayal right from Ryker Wolfson's lips.

Like I said. I'm not a moron.

"Gemma." The way that Ryker says my name has always done something to me. He has this raspy voice that washes over me, making me want to curl up and purr like a house cat. "I wasn't expecting you."

Of course he wasn't. After all, this is the first time that I've come to his cabin and every single wolf in the room knows it.

"I need to talk to you."

"We're in the middle of something—"

Ryker lifts his hand. Shane goes quiet.

"I'm almost finished here," Ryker says to me. "We can talk then, unless it can keep 'til morning." He tilts his head slightly. "Can it?"

You know what?

"No. Sorry. I don't think so."

He searches my face. I'm not giving anything away, and he eventually nods. "That's fine. Why don't you wait for me outside and I'll come get you when the meet's done."

Wait for him outside? Luna forbid I get to sit inside and witness what happens when the inner circle gets together. And going into another part of the cabin? Of course that's out of the question since I'm not his mate yet.

If Trish is right, I might *never* be.

I shake my head. "No need for that. I'll be quick. It's about Trish."

Trish Danvers. One of the pack females, she ranks

higher than most of the others—but not as high as me and she knows it. With a sweet smile and hatred in her soft brown eyes, she's had it out for me from the moment I arrived in Accalia.

I can't say the feeling isn't mutual.

Behind me, someone draws a sharp breath at her name. Another of the council members mutters a curse. Since it's not Ryker, I ignore them. I'd rather do this without an audience, but if I have to? Oh, well. I told him I couldn't wait, and I refuse to be sent outside like a trouble-making child.

"Trish?" His tone is neutral. "What about her?"

The tips of my claws prick the fleshy part of my palm. I try to relax my fingers before I stab myself, but just the casual way he says her name like that has my hackles rising. "I'm your intended," I say softly. Softly because, if I don't force myself to keep to a whisper, I'll start shouting. "Is she your chosen?"

Because that's exactly what she tossed in my face moments before I threw her out of my cabin. I tried not to let it bother me, but I stewed over it for hours before I realized that while Omega Gem might take that lying down, I can't.

I just *can't*.

Ryker leans back in his seat. "I don't think this is the right time to have this conversation."

Oh? That's funny. Because I think it's the *perfect* time.

"I told you. It can't wait."

Shane clears his throat. "Ryker. Alpha. This seems like this is between you and your mate. Maybe we can have this meeting tomorrow, leave you two together to hash this out."

"No." My voice is a little stronger. Not a shout since I'm struggling for control, but loud enough for the rest of the room to hear. "As I've been told too many times since I've arrived, I'm not his mate."

Yet is how I always understood it, but I'm beginning to think I was wrong.

Ryker raises his eyebrows. "What do you mean by that?"

How can he ask me that? He has to know that there are more than a few of his—excuse me, *our*—pack-mates who don't think I'm a good match for their Alpha. Trish is just the one who was bold enough to give me the reason why.

"I won't be your bonded mate until the Luna Ceremony," I remind him. "But I'm beginning to doubt that's ever happening. So, tell me, Ryker. Is that something we're actually going to do? Or are you just stringing me along?"

"I never—"

He did. Maybe he isn't aware that that was what he was doing, but he did.

I swallow a growl. "Answer the question." And

then, because I might be an alpha, but so is he, I add, "Please."

Accepting the *please* as his due, Ryker scratches the underside of his jaw. "Are you asking me if we're having the ceremony during the next full moon?" At my nod, he says, "That's three days from now."

No shit. Every single one of us knows the cycles of the moon intimately. As shifters, we can change shapes whenever we want, but we're so much closer to our beasts when the moon hangs high in the sky. Mates will rut like wild animals, young pups might finally trigger their first change, and it doesn't take much for the wolf to take charge.

I know when the next full moon is. What I don't know is if he actually plans on going through with the ceremony.

Despite how they feel about me being Ryker's intended, every new packmate I've met this past month has gone out of their way to assure me that the ceremony is happening during the next full moon even though there hasn't been any planning for it. To a shifter—especially when one was the Alpha—the Luna Ceremony is like a highly anticipated human wedding. There should have been *some* planning involved, right?

Then again, the lack of it makes total sense if he's trying to weasel his way out of the deal he made with my dad. Ryker agreed to bond with me because I'm supposed to be his fated mate. But what good is that if he already has a mate he chose for himself?

I need to know. I need to hear it from him.

"Yes."

"No."

I refuse to let him see how much that simply stated *no* tears at me.

"Because of Trish?" I ask.

His face is expressionless as he thinks it over for a moment. And then—

"Yes."

He's... he's not lying.

And I would know. Deception has a stink of its own, and I've always been able to tell when someone was being dishonest.

Call it a quirk of what I am. I don't know—I *can't* know since I'm the only female alpha I've ever met. My mom figured out that I was different when I was just a pup, and she spent the next twenty-five years protecting me from myself and my kind.

My whole life, it's been drilled into me to keep my true rank a secret. In all of pack lore, there's only been one other female alpha that I know of: the great Luna who is both our goddess *and* the moon incarnated into fur and skin. The stories about her are legend.

Like how she can control any packmate, including the Alpha, with a single howl. Or how any male she took to her lair became an alpha after she gifted him her body whether he was beta, omega, or rank and file wolf before she fucked him. Not to mention how the lucky wolf who she eventually accepted as her bonded mate became a god in his own right...

Is any of that true? Considering I'm still a virgin at twenty-five, I haven't got a clue, and I never wanted to find out the morning after that sleeping with me did something to other wolf shifters. Not that that's the only reason I've stayed away from casual sex, either. Ever since I was fifteen and I saw the seventeen-year-old future Alpha, I knew—just *knew*—that he was my fated mate. Fooling around with any other guy seemed like cheating to me when I'd end up Ryker's forever mate sooner or later.

Damn shame he didn't seem to think the same about me. How could he? He chose *Trish*.

Because he definitely wasn't lying when he said that another pack female is the reason why our mating isn't going to happen—just like how she was being truthful when she said that Ryker told her that he would stay away from me.

I didn't want to believe it. After weeks of dealing with her snarls, her nasty whispers, and her dirty looks, I'd finally given in to my temper earlier when she showed up at my borrowed cabin. It was bad enough that she encroached on *my* territory, but she went a step too far when she smiled as she said that I was never going to be mated to Ryker.

She'd found a weak chink in my armor and gone straight for the kill. I was already a little worried that Ryker was having second thoughts. Getting cold paws, you know? I finally convinced myself that he wasn't in any rush and that was okay—until Trish gleefully confessed that his hesitation had everything to do with him choosing her instead.

Because I might be his fated mate, but I'm not the one he wants. And until he performs the Luna Ceremony, I'm not his fully bonded mate—which leaves him free to be with anyone else.

I spent a decade waiting for Ryker, but he obviously didn't wait for me. I can't really blame him for that, though. It's another one of those rare alpha female things, that I recognized him as mine long before the moon herself blessed the new Alpha with the name of his fated mate.

However, I can sure as hell blame him for letting me believe that my long wait was finally over. The adopted daughter of a pack leader, I always knew that a future Alpha's mating was a pack affair. He wouldn't take a bonded mate until he was installed as Alpha.

Which he was, months ago. And we're still not mated.

Now I know that we won't be.

So, trying in vain to ignore the way my heart feels like it's shattering, I push for some kind of closure.

"You didn't answer me before." Call me a glutton

for punishment, but I need this. "I'm supposed to be your intended. Do you actually plan on mating me at all or is this just some kind of joke?"

If so, I'm not laughing.

No one is.

CHAPTER 2

Again, his loyal Beta tries to intercede.

"Gem, Ryker's right," Shane says calmly. "This isn't the time for this conversation."

"I'm not going anywhere until I hear it straight from the Alpha," I promise.

They could drag me out of here, but I know they won't. Just like I know that Shane is only trying to cover for Ryker, as usual.

When it's obvious that I'm basically daring them to do just that, Ryker pushes his chair away from his desk. But he doesn't stand. He just lounges cockily in the leather seat.

Damn it, but he has good reason to be cocky. His dominance is off the charts, he's good looking *and* he knows it, and now I've made it obvious that he has two females fighting over him.

Ha. If only I could settle things as easily as that.

Trish has no problem taunting an omega, but how would she react if she learned that I'm an alpha? She'd have no chance—and I hate that my pulse quickens at the thought of going for her throat.

Not when all of the blame falls on the handsome bastard at the desk.

"Well." I tap my flat against the floor, glaring at him. "I'm waiting."

"Are you sure you want to do this?"

Any other packmate would back down when they heard the pure alpha dominance in his voice.

Not me.

"I can take it."

The way he looks me up and down tells me that he's not so sure about that. But he answers me anyway. "Then, no. I have no intention of mating you this moon or the next."

Or at all, I bet.

Trying to hide how his answer affects me, I straighten my shoulders as the absolute rejection slithers down the echoes of a bond that began to build when I was still a kid.

I've spent the last ten years working toward the moment when Ryker would take over his father's pack and accept a mate, knowing that it had to be me. Even if some part of me didn't already sense it, during his Alpha Ceremony at the beginning of the year, it was formally declared that I was to leave the

Lakeview Pack, joining with Ryker as fully bonded mates.

But then my arrival kept getting delayed, and Ryker barely spoke to me after I came to Accalia, and I put up with all of it because that's what good girl Gemma was supposed to do. And because I've spent ten years wondering what it would be like to be with the infamous Ryker Wolfson, I figured I could wait a little longer.

It feels like I've already been waiting a lifetime.

I met Ryker, the son of the former Mountainside Pack's Alpha, at one of the grand meets where nearly every pack leader in the country travels for an annual get-together. And I knew from that very first meeting that he was meant to be mine.

At fifteen, it was little more than a schoolgirl crush.

By seventeen, I was smitten with the older shifter.

When I was twenty, after a night spent talking together while we sat behind the Alpha cabin where the pack leaders were assembled, I was enchanted.

Two years later, when a bunch of us younger wolves went for a run together in our fur, I had to admit that I would follow him anywhere.

I hadn't seen him again after that—not until the moment I arrived at Accalia with all my earthly possessions and the new Alpha couldn't even look me in the eye.

Damn it, he's doing it again. Gaze sliding away,

fixed on a point just over my shoulder as if giving the illusion that he's paying attention while, truthfully, he's utterly bored.

I've finally hit my breaking point.

I've been riding an unstable cocktail of adrenaline and heartbreak ever since Trish crowed that she was his chosen. Fate might say one thing, the moon might say the same, but none of that matters. A chosen mate *always* wins—which means that I've already lost everything.

And since there's nothing left to lose...

Before anyone can guess what I'm about to do, before any of the other dominant shifters in the room can react, I leap onto his desk, then pounce. I land on his lap, stretching the skirt of my dress as I straddle him.

His head snaps forward.

Oh, yeah. He's totally looking at me now.

I'm not a moron—but I am a bit of a hothead. And sometimes I know better than to act so impulsively, but that doesn't stop me.

When Ryker became Alpha, everyone knew that he would take a mate. He had to. It's how it's done. How it's always been done. But I had thought, when he arranged with my home pack for me to come to him, that he'd at least felt a little something for me.

Obviously, I was wrong.

I *hurt*. The way I see it, it's only fair that I return the favor.

I flex my fingers, my claws positioned perfectly to attack. And I do. I lash out, stabbing him with every single claw on my right hand. The sharp points slide through the fabric of his shirt, the meat in his chest, as I just about touch his fucking heart.

"I gave you mine," I whisper. "Don't you think it's fair I get to take yours?"

The wolves behind me go absolutely still. Even after watching me stalk in here, they never really expected Little Miss Shifter Barbie to go feral, and they don't know what to do. Their Alpha is in danger, but whether Ryker and I have mated yet or not—whether he rejected me or not—their instincts are telling them this is a battle between an Alpha couple and they can't interfere. Not even Shane speaks up again.

They're half right, too. We're both alphas here— even if I finally understand that I'll never be his mate.

Tonight has made *that* perfectly clear.

Ryker's expression doesn't change one bit. One quick jerk, one wrong breath, and I could rip his damn heart right out of his chest, and he looks as disinterested as if we're discussing the weather.

I want to do it. But that's the bloodthirsty nature of being an alpha wolf shifter speaking, not my more rational human side.

Actually, no. That's not right.

It's the rejected, heartbroken, aching human half that wants to destroy Ryker—but I *can't.*

I can't kill him. I hate him, I hate him for making me want him when I never really had a chance with him, and I hate him for making me love him when I was too young, too silly, too *hopeful* that he could be my savior. If I mated him, it didn't matter what I was or who I was. I would be Ryker's, and maybe then I wouldn't have to hide.

Welp, I'm definitely not hiding now.

But I can't kill him. Even now my wolf is whining, eager to lap at the claw marks I've made in him, tending to the wolf she instinctively knows is her mate.

Only he isn't, is he?

I can't lap at his chest, but I have a better idea. As carefully as I can, I withdraw my claws from his chest. I leave five tears in his shirt, with five perfect puncture wounds deep in his skin that I can't see save for the blood staining the white fabric a rich crimson.

The points of my claws are coated in his slick blood. Still daring him to even breathe, I lift my right hand to my mouth and, with the tip of my tongue, lave each claw clean.

I can't help it. As soon as the tang of his life's blood hits me, I moan.

His eyes widen slightly, the first sign of an honest reaction I've gotten from him this last month. Not even when my claws were centimeters from his beating heart did he show any sign that he gave a shit—until now. Until I cleaned his blood off of my claws with my tongue and felt an answering tug deep in my pussy.

I'm not the only one affected by it, either.

Ryker shifts suddenly in his seat, leaning back as I'm forced to move with him. His eyes flare from dark gold to molten lava as my legs spread a little wider, pressing close to him. In this position, there's no way for me to miss the rock-hard erection just underneath me.

I can't stop what happens next. Between his undeniable arousal and the taste of his blood hot on my tongue, I respond: my eyes flare the same bright golden shade.

Ryker's lips curve. The tiniest hint of a fang plays peekaboo with me. His hand slides up from his thigh, settling like a possessive brand on my hip. Through the flimsy material of my dress, I feel it. I feel the scorch of his palm on my skin, and I feel the rumble low in his chest that makes us both vibrate.

For the last month—for the last *decade*—all I've wanted was to feel his hands on me. But as the color of his eyes fades back to their dark gold shade, I can barely pay attention to his touch.

I'm too busy kicking my own ass.

Shit.

Shit, shit, *shit*.

He knows. From the shocked silence that is just

about screaming at me, he's not the only one. This is understanding dawning, Ryker's pack council figuring out that Gemma has been a naughty, naughty wolf.

What did I expect from my little display? That they'd just accept their newest omega had snapped?

Omegas *don't* snap.

I start to slide off of him. My twisted instincts are telling me to go, to run, to get out before the rest of the pack turns on me for being another alpha, and not just their leader's female. But I've barely gone an inch away from him before Ryker lashes his hand around my wrist, tugging me closer.

His voice has dropped, gone husky as he demands, "Where do you think you're going?"

"Let go of me, Ryker."

"Oh, sweetheart. I don't think so."

I yank but as strong as I am, Ryker is stronger.

Crap.

He *tsks*. "You'll stay here, Gemma. With me. You started this. Let's finish it."

"No."

"No?" His smile widens, but there's no humor in it, only lust and an expectation that I *will* obey him. "You're my mate—"

A lump lodges in my throat at his words. Because, as he says them, it just about kills me that he's telling the truth.

Gee. I wonder what made him change his mind?

My mom always warned me that a male shifter will do anything to make me his if he ever found out I was a born alpha female. I thought Ryker would be different, but I was wrong. He already chose Trish. She told me so, and so did he. No way in hell am I gonna let him change his mind just because I've foolishly let them all in on my secret.

With my other hand, I slash at his forearm. Blood sprays from the gash, covering the both of us. He wasn't expecting me to do that, and I take advantage of the way his grip goes slack to break free.

I'm off his lap and on the opposite side of his desk before he can staunch the blood flow with the edge of his shirt. Thanks to our advanced healing abilities, there won't even be a hint of a scar come morning, but I'm secretly glad he tended to it anyway. I didn't mean to get him so deep this time.

Not like I'll let him know that.

I point a claw at him. "Don't start that shit, Ryker. Not now."

"What? The moon said—"

"Forget the moon," I snap. "I think you've made it pretty clear. I'll never be your mate."

You think I would have succeeded in pissing him off by now. Nope. That sexy little grin from before makes another appearance.

"You will," he says. "You are."

I turn away from him, glaring at the rest of the

council. "Never. His. Mate," I say, making sure to enunciate each word separately so that they can't pretend to misunderstand. He already rejected me with each of them as witness when he said that he never intended to mate me. Welp, turnabout's fair play, right? Now I've rejected him, and it's time to get the hell out of here.

I don't look over my shoulder at him. Instead, I gauge the distance between me and the door that I thankfully left open, and pray that I'll reach it before the rest of the wolves break out of their stunned stupor.

I make it three steps before one of the council members lunges at me. He's a big guy, bulky, with dark hair and meaty hands so I know it's not Shane. I side-step him easily, my claws outstretched in front of me.

I didn't kill Ryker. That doesn't mean that the rest of his council is safe from me.

Right now, no one is.

The air is brimming with tension. One wrong move and I'm poised to shift. As a wolf, there's only one shifter in this room who can beat me—and the Alpha is still sitting at his desk.

The big guy misses me, but I can sense someone else sneaking up on my left. I snarl and drop down to a crouch before—I recognize him—Jace can try to get his paws on me.

Finally, Ryker gets to his feet.

"No." His voice echoes with the command. "Let her go."

"But, Alpha, she's—"

She's *what*?

An impossible alpha?

Ryker's former intended?

His attacker?

This time, all of those descriptors are true. But Jace doesn't get a chance to use any of them before Ryker says in a voice so cold, so different from his husky rasp that it obliterates the last of my broken heart: "She's nothing. You heard her. She's not my mate. Let her leave."

No one stops me after that.

As soon as the cool mountain air welcomes me back outside, I break into a run. The rest of the pack council all stayed behind with Ryker, but I know better than to think that they're just going to let me go. The Alpha's command will only last so long, and I'm not so naive as to believe that Ryker's going to accept *my* rejection of *him* as easy as that.

Give up his very own alpha female? Yeah. I don't think so.

I debate shifting but decide to stay in my skin. I don't want to sacrifice all of my stuff, including my Jeep, and I'm just super fucking grateful I had the foresight to pack it all up before I went to confront Ryker.

I always had a back-up plan. Even as I was

throwing everything I own in the back of my car, I think I knew that this was going to happen. I couldn't stay in Accalia if Ryker was going to keep his chosen mate, and now that the entire pack council knows what I've been hiding, I've got to go.

Going back to Lakeview is impossible. It'll be the first place they check, and I know my dad. Paul will hide me like he did when Mom and me first ran from my bio-dad's pack, and there goes any prospective alliance between Mountainside and Lakeview. I won't do that to my old pack, to my dad or my mom.

And then there's the matter of my sperm donor. If the bastard wolf who sired me ever figured out that I was still alive and that I'm, well, *me,* I don't even want to think about what he would do. My mother spent years trying to shield me from details regarding Jack Walker, but you can't be a shifter in the States and not hear rumors about Wicked Wolf Walker of the Western Pack.

No, thanks.

So, as impulsive as I can be, I do always have a back-up plan. This particular plan might not be a good one, and I'm risking death by fang attempting it, but that's probably better than being forced into a mating that'll leave me even more miserable than I've been lately.

At the base of the pack's mountain, there's an urban city that's controlled by a powerful cadre of vampires. Muncie is a total Fang City, with vamps who rule it ruthlessly. Like the rest of the supernatural world, technically their identities are kept hidden, but in a vamp town like Muncie, there are a few select humans in on the secret.

Walking buffets, I sneer as I hop in my Jeep and quickly start the engine.

For centuries, my people and the vamps have been at war. Claws versus fangs, shifters against vampires. An isolated pack who wants nothing to do with humans looking down on the more integrated vampires who rely on the humans as their sole source of food.

And they call us beasts. Better than being a parasite.

These days, we have an uneasy truce. Shifters keep to their packs, vamps have control of their cities, and we do *not* mix.

Even when I came to Accalia, I had to go the long way so that I could avoid coming within miles of the vamp town. If they caught me on my own, I don't know how they'd react, but I doubt it would be good. As a shifter, I know all about territory. Me going into a vamp town is just asking to be drained.

Which is precisely why none of my former pack-mates will ever think I'd do something so reckless.

I throw my gear into drive and, without a backward look, I take off. Once the roar of the engine echoes across the still night's sky, I figure it won't be long before someone comes after me. They'll expect I've gone down the hidden path located on the far side of the mountain mainly because only a shifter with a death wish would head straight into Muncie.

I try to convince myself that this is my only choice. I couldn't stay behind, and going lone wolf is the only option I have after what just happened at the Alpha's cabin. And an uneasy truce is still a truce, right? I haven't heard of any shifter/vamp skirmishes in years now so maybe I'm just being paranoid.

Or, I tell myself as I slam on my brakes barely a mile into Muncie, I was just in denial.

I don't know where they came from. One second, the road was empty. It's late, and the path into the urban city is more rural as it leads out of the mountain. I was the only car on the empty stretch of dirt road, and the only soul around for miles.

That should've been my first clue. As a shifter, I can sense all living creatures. Humans. Animals. Even insects.

But vamps? Unless they're making noise, they're dead to me. Because, well, they *are* dead, aren't they?

Just because they're dead, though, I know better than to slam into them with my car. Not because it'll hurt the vamps—short of chopping off their heads, they're indestructible—but because of the damage an accident would do to my precious Jeep.

I expected something like this to happen at some point. It's an open Jeep on purpose; my shifter side can't stand to be contained. But I went this way knowing there was a good chance one of the vamps would pick up on my scent and want to investigate it further, especially since Ryker's blood still stains my dress.

Just my luck, I've attracted *three*.

"Look at what we have here." It's a throaty female voice. "The little puppy dog's gotten herself lost."

I decide to let the 'puppy dog' crack slide as I unbuckle my seat belt and slowly ease the strap over my shoulder. Like I know exactly what they are, all it takes is one look, one sniff, even one lucky bite, and these vamps know what I am.

I have one thing in my favor. Because I never shifted, I'm still wearing my sundress and my flats. My blonde curls are windblown, but that just adds to my purposely cultivated air of innocence.

They must think they're dealing with a gentle pack-mate instead of the big, bad wolf otherwise they wouldn't stalk toward me, bloodlust already turning their light eyes a shining red color.

Though this patch of road is unlit, I use the waxing gibbous moon to focus on this latest threat. Three vampires, all of them stunning knock-outs. Tall yet voluptuous, each one has a face that I deem almost unnaturally perfect before I remember what I'm dealing with and, yeah, it's not natural, is it?

They've arranged themselves in a triangle formation, a striking blonde with iridescently pale skin in the lead; she's the one who spoke. To her left, there's a dazzling Black female whose box braids clink softly as she sweeps toward me. To her right, a freckled redhead giggles as she tiptoes toward the Jeep. The three of them fan out, and I wonder how many will be able to get their fangs in me before I can shift.

As a wolf, I can probably take two down at the very least. But in my skin? It's a little dicey.

And that's when another voice whispers across the still night air.

"What's so interesting, ladies?"

Ah, crap. There's not three.

There's *four*.

And I'm super outnumbered.

I can't see him at first—and it *is* a him. His voice makes that obvious. Though it's soft and lyrical, with a noticeable yet faint European accent, it's still undeniably male. I can hear him, but I don't see him until, suddenly, there's a fourth figure in the distance.

"It's nothing, Aleksander," coos the blonde. "We don't need any of the Cadre to step in. We're fine."

Oof. If she had said anything else, I might've been able to try to bluff my way out of this. Be harmless Omega Gem who wouldn't hurt a fly. But after the night I've had, I don't know if I can ever be Omega Gem again.

This alpha bitch is looking for an excuse to make someone else hurt as much as she is.

As *I* am.

"Nothing?" I snarl. My claws are out again as I brace myself, poised to leap out of my Jeep and go for Blondie's throat. "I'll show you *nothing.*"

The redhead bares her fangs, hissing at me while Blondie lowers herself into a crouch.

She might be sizing me up, but she's giving me a perfect target.

Before I can prepare to shift, the male vampire moves closer. "I think that's enough. Find your midnight snack elsewhere, ladies. You're not to feed on this one."

If that's all he thought was going to go down here before he showed up, I've got a bridge in New York that I can sell him for cheap. From one predator to another, these vamps aren't just hungry. They have murder on their minds, and I'm the idiot shifter who appears to be easy prey.

Blondie clearly agrees with me. She slowly rises from her crouch before turning toward the shadow at her back. "What? No. I want her."

"Go on, Gretchen."

"Aleks—"

"You know the rules. No unauthorized biting

outside of Muncie. You wouldn't want me reporting this to Roman, would you?"

"Unauthorized?" echoes Gretchen. "She should've known better than to leave the mountain. This is our city."

The vampire walks out of the shadows. My eyesight is keen—like my sense of smell, it's a shifter thing— and even I can't believe what I'm seeing.

Vamp, I have to remind myself. I'm a shifter, and he's a vamp, and if he's one of the most achingly beautiful males I've ever seen in my life, that doesn't mean we're not mortal enemies. But, coming so close on the heels of Ryker's rejection, forgive me for staring. This vamp is so different from the ruggedly handsome Alpha that it's almost a relief.

Despite his autocratic and gentle appearance, something about him has two of the three female vampires backing away even before he says, "That's not for you to decide. Take Tamera and Leigh with you. You can't have this female."

Gretchen is the only one left holding her ground. She stamps her foot, throwing her hand out toward me as she snaps, "Can't you see? She's a—"

"I know exactly what she is," he announces firmly before turning those eerily pale eyes of his on me. "She's *mine*."

Um.

What?

CHAPTER 3

A YEAR LATER

Like most Friday nights, Charlie's is hopping.

Hailey's running late, so I'm the only one behind the bar. A crowd of usuals lines the counter, a good mix of both humans and supes. Charlie himself is a vampire, so we're fang-friendly here even if most of the patrons are too busy tossing back their shots to notice that the next table over is drinking legit Bloody Mary's.

"Gem?" One of my regulars raps his knuckles on the bar top. "Can I get another refill?"

"Coming right up, Vin."

Vincent flashes his fangs at me. "And if you want to think about my offer, I'm going out on patrol in ten."

I grab a cask of chilled O-negative—Vincent's preferred type—and pour it into a blacked-out shot glass. Some vamps ask for a little whiskey or some rum added to their blood, but not when they're on the Cadre's payroll. The alcohol might give them a little buzz, but the vampires in charge of Muncie expect their patrollers to be one hundred percent sober.

Bringing the glass over to where he's sitting, I tease, "Ten minutes? Is that all?"

He winks as he accepts his drink. "Believe me, baby, it's long enough to make you think twice about your loyalty to Filan."

Almost reflexively, I lift my hand and pat the slight bulge beneath my tight, black Charlie's tee. I don't have my necklace visible while I'm working for a couple of different reasons, but just mentioning Aleksander Filan has me double-checking that I haven't lost it —again.

"Be careful that you don't let him hear you badgering his girl," Jimmy says, nudging Vincent in the side.

Jimmy Fiorello is as human as they come but, as he's told me a hundred times since I started here last year, he was living in Muncie before the vampires moved into town, and he'll be here long after they move along; considering he's probably in his early sixties and vampires are essentially immortal, I don't have the heart to tell him that he doesn't have a prayer. So, like the rest of the supes who frequent Charlie's, I let the old barhound dream. He's harmless, he gets along well with my vamp customers, and he tips well.

Plus, he doesn't flirt with me. That's a win in my book.

If only he could convince Vincent St. James to give it up, too. The first time, I brushed him off. And the second. And the third. These days I just ignore him. If he hasn't gotten the hint by now, he never will. There are only so many ways I can say *never gonna fuck you, my dude* in customer service-ese.

Unfortunately, if there's one thing I've learned living among vampires, it's that their immortality means they're really, really patient. He keeps trying because he has this idea that, one day, I'll take him up on his offer of a quickie in the bathroom. Yeah... that's not gonna happen, and my relationship with one of the most well-known vamps in Muncie has nothing to do with it.

Hey, sue a girl for having some standards.

I dodged the bullet of a piss poor mating once before. I haven't seen Ryker Wolfson since the night I walked out of the Alpha's cabin, and though it took me longer than it should've to bury our would-be bond, I eventually managed it. So what if I'm perennially single? At least I'm not trapped.

I'm a shifter. I need to be free.

Right now, though, I need to take care of the rest of my customers. As soon as Hailey comes in, Charlie told me I can head on out. This is my ninth night in a row and I'm looking forward to a relaxing evening where, for once, I might actually get home before my roomie heads out on his nightly patrols.

Speaking of Aleksander—

With a sly look my way, Vincent sniffs, his fangs lengthening just enough that it might cause an unaware human to take a second peek. "I'm not afraid of him."

Oh, really?

I pretend to spot someone on the other side of the bar. "Aleks, hey. Over here!"

Vincent spins on his stool so quickly, he nearly falls off.

My laugh comes out like a bark. Whoops. You can take the girl out of the pack, but you can't take the wolf out of the girl. "My mistake. That's not him."

As Vincent rights himself, scowling as he tells Jimmy to stop with the laughing, I give the two friends a quick smirk before going to serve another customer.

Just another normal night at Charlie's.

I learned early on that, as a female bartender, I have to toe the line between being friendly enough to earn tips and authoritative enough that my customers know not to push their luck. My first couple of weeks working the bar at Charlie's, I lost track of how many of the guys tried to get me to go home with them at the end of the night, but it wasn't long before they realized they weren't getting anywhere with me. A little meaningless flirting was one thing, but no one's really pushed it too far.

Amazingly, I did it all without relying on rank, pack status, or my wolf. Apart from Aleks, his boss Roman, and Gretchen (plus Tamera and Leigh), no one else in Muncie knows for sure what I am. And I don't mean being a female alpha—'cause I've gone back to deciding to take *that* secret to my grave—but that I'm a shifter. As far as I know, I'm the only one in all of the vamp-controlled city. So showing off my claws? It wouldn't work.

And, despite how grateful I am for Aleks's help, I don't like using him as an excuse, either. Unless I can get a laugh out of it like I just did with Vincent.

Nope, I did it all by being me. The Gem I've always been deep down, the alpha with the sharp tongue and quick temper, but the good humor to blunt my claws. They think I'm a human with an attitude, one who stands up for herself. It didn't take long before anyone I met in Muncie figured that out, and I pulled it off without any bloodshed.

Which is a good thing since, in a Fang City, bloodshed becomes a real "waste not, want not" sitch that I'd rather stay away from if I can help it.

I like my job. It took a bit of getting used to after a lifetime of pretending to be gentle and meek, the perfect omega, but I enjoy myself even if it seems like

I'm always behind the bar. At least the tips are good, Charlie's a fair boss, and I've learned to handle my customers.

For the next hour, I mix cocktails, have quick convos with some regulars, catch up on the Cadre's latest decrees for their supe residents. I play "spot the human" with Jane, always messing up on purpose because a) the arrogant vamp hates losing and b) thanks to my trusty charm, everyone else thinks I'm human, too. One who knows about supes, sure, but nothing supernatural about sassy Gemma Swann.

Nope. Not even a little.

And I work hard to keep it that way.

I'm not just covering my own ass, hiding out from my former packmates and a fate that I'm stubborn enough to ignore. Roman, the leader of Muncie's chapter of the Vampire Cadre, agreed to let me stay in the city after Aleks vouched for me last year so long as I keep up the facade that I'm human. Muncie is decidedly a shifter-free territory, and if Gretchen and her goons had it their way, it still would be.

Thank Luna for Aleks. I don't know how he pulled it off, but he convinced Roman that I might be a wolf, but I won't be any trouble. I never thought it would work—I had every intention of driving right out of Muncie as soon as I could—but Aleks is a determined guy. He not only convinced me that I should stay, but he got Roman to agree to it. I don't understand how, but I've given up trying to. I just accept that Aleksander Filan always finds a way to get what he wants.

Well, I admit to myself, *almost* always.

After Roman gave the okay—on the condition that, if I lose my mind and go feral wolf in the middle of Muncie, then Aleks is responsible for putting me down—my determined roommate even found a way to make Gretchen and her two followers ignore what they sensed about me my first night in town.

Honestly, I didn't expect my secret to last with those three in on it. Call me bitter, but Gretchen reminds me of Trish Danvers. She's as possessive of Aleks as Trish was of Ryker, and both of them act as if I'm not even worthy of talking to either male. So, yeah, I really thought Gretchen would hold my true identity over my head, even if she begrudgingly kept the secret. She hasn't, though. Not really. On the rare occasion that I run into any of them—either as a trio, or separate—the female vamps suddenly have something far better to do than play nice with Aleks's pet.

And if calling me his 'pet' is the price I have to pay to keep my secret? At least it's better than being called a 'little puppy dog'...

No one else knows more than I'm willing to tell them. So I'm Gem now. An easy-going bartender with a quip or a tongue-lashing, depending on what you deserve. A local transplant to Muncie who lives with Aleksander Filan, though we're completely platonic, despite what Vincent and some of the other vamps think.

But a shifter? Me? From the Mountainside Pack?

You must have me mistaken for someone else.

It's easy, too. A year after I put pack life behind me, I don't look a thing like Omega Gem. No more curls for this chick; I wear my light blonde hair in a sheet down my back when it's not up in a high pony-tail. Dresses? Yeah, right. The best thing about Charlie's is its uniform: the black tee, comfy jeans, and my sturdy boots. I've even discovered a love of mascara and wild eyeshadow palettes that bring out my striking eyes instead of always downplaying them. In a town where most vamps have pale irises—blues, greys, greens—my honey-colored eyes are pretty unique. Luckily, most people I talk to think they're contacts, and I'm good with that... until I have to hear for the countless time that I have the most beautiful eyes.

Yeah, my customers aren't the most creative when it comes to their pick-up lines. But if all it takes is a smile and me batting my eyelashes to see them add a couple of singles to their tip, well, okay then. Drown in my eyes all you like, fellas.

I've gotta work with what I got. Unlike some of the other bartenders and waitresses, my boobs are pretty small. My ass? Non-existent. Since I've given up the omega act, I've burned off a lot of excess energy through running and weightlifting, giving me a more muscular physique.

I fucking love it.

For the first time in my life, I'm living what I truly am. I'm an alpha, just one without a pack.

A lone wolf.

And, okay, a human pretender.

Still, I'm finally content.

Yeah. Definitely a win.

HAILEY COMES FLYING IN THROUGH THE FRONT DOOR AT A quarter to nine, waving at me as she dashes past the bar.

"Gimme five, Gem."

I nod, in the middle of tallying up Jimmy's tab for the night. Vincent already left for his patrol, though not before reminding me that he's only on a quarter-turn shift, meaning that he's responsible for a quarter of Muncie's perimeter before he's free to take the rest of the night for himself. Without his buddy, Jimmy nursed a few more drinks before calling it. Good. Once I close him out and Hailey takes over for me, I can go.

Just as I'm cashing out, Hailey appears behind the bar, a flurry of apologies spilling from her lips. I know from experience that, give it a couple of shifts, and she'll be late again. I'm used to it and, honestly, it's fine.

I know where she is before she comes here. Better she gets that out of her system on her own time instead of looking at some of her customers as potential targets.

Speaking of...

"Uh, Hailey."

"Yeah?"

I tap my neck discreetly.

Hailey's big brown eyes go wide as she slaps a hand over her throat. "*Shit*. I forgot."

"Don't worry. I got you."

Underneath the bar, Charlie keeps an emergency kit. A vial of holy water to stun vamps; a silver rod that I'm careful to avoid because, *hello*, shifter; even a Louis- ville slugger for when one of the human customers gets a little rowdy. But because he's been around the block a bit, he also keeps a couple of patches tucked in there.

I grab one and, after slapping it against my hip to activate it, I hold it out to Hailey.

She grabs it with her free hand. "Thanks, babe."

"Don't worry about it."

This isn't the first time I've seen her wearing fresh bite marks. By now, I've almost come to expect it.

She is a fang-banger, after all.

While most of the non-supes in Muncie are completely oblivious that a group of vampires run this city, there are a select few who have been inducted into the supernatural society.

Jimmy's one. Hailey's another.

Hailey thinks I'm like her: a human at ease with vamps because of my relationship with my roommate. And if she's just a little jealous every time she's reminded that I already have my fang, she gets over it because she's determined to get her own one day.

Fang-banger. Not only does she fuck vamps, but she lets them bite her. Anything to convince one of the vampires that she's perfect mate material.

Honestly, she can have them. My days of looking for a mate are *way* behind me.

"You good?" I ask.

She pats the charmed bandage. Created by the Cadre for any human donors in Muncie, the bandage will heal her bite marks while also replenishing her blood supply. By tomorrow, she'll be ready to be bitten again. "Yeah."

Bending low, reaching for the shelf below the one holding the emergency kit, I snag my light jacket. Even though it's early May, it can be a little chilly in Muncie at night, and humans will wonder if I walk around with no coat on. I don't need it, but I'll wear it because I'm expected to.

In so many ways, I have to admit that I'm still playing a part.

Oh, well.

"Good. Then I'm out of here."

"Ah, come on, Gem," calls out one of my more

persistent regulars. "Don't go. I was just about to ask ya to bend over again. That glimpse of your ass was too quick and I need more. You're not gonna leave a guy hanging, are ya?"

Ugh. If I thought Vincent was bad, Rex is worse. At least I know that Vincent will respect my necklace. As a human, Rex doesn't respect anything except a direct response.

I shoot him the bird, shrugging on my jacket at the same time. What can I say? I'm talented like that. "Sorry. Shift's over. Maybe, if you're lucky, Hailey will throw you a bone."

My fellow bartender snorts. I'm not surprised. Unless he has a pair of fangs and the promise of forever, Hailey won't want anything to do with the guy.

I wave as I move out from behind the bar. "Night, everyone."

"Hot date?" calls someone from the far side of the counter.

Yeah, right. My love life has about as much a pulse as my roommate does. And since Aleks has been dead for more than two hundred years, that's saying something.

Of course, that's by choice. As much as I convince myself that any feelings I had for Ryker are long gone, I just can't bring myself to start dating. Not yet, at least. Ten years is a hard habit to break, and it's only been twelve months since I left him behind me.

I've got time. I might not live as long as a vamp does, but a shifter can do one, two centuries easy. I'm in no rush.

I roll my eyes. "You know it."

Technically, it's not a lie. I have a hot date with a cup of tea, the second season of a show I've been binging, and my bed. Wild Friday night for a twenty-six-year-old, but what can I say? I'm a shifter. Being wild—no matter how one defines it—is part of the job description.

Heh.

STEPPING OUTSIDE OF CHARLIE'S, I GLANCE UP AT THE sky. Another habit that I don't think I'll ever be able to break. Even though I can always sense the moon, that doesn't stop me from sneaking peeks up at the Luna as if she might've suddenly sprung a full moon on me or something.

Considering how it affects me, I like to be prepared.

Good news. Tonight she's only a shade past the quarter moon, coming up on her waxing gibbous form. Still, that means I've only got less than a week until she's full again and, for one night at least, I have to deal with being an unmated shifter on her own. Since I'm not looking forward to it, I shoot a smile up at the incomplete moon, then start toward home.

I decided earlier on my way to Charlie's that I wanted to walk. It's been a couple of days since the last time I shifted, and though I'm hesitant to go wolf in case it gets back to Roman, I use the twenty-block walk to burn off some more energy. A full shift at the bar usually is enough to stimulate my wolf, but I only did seven hours today, and that's including the two extra I did for Hailey. This walk will do me good, and I need it.

Even though Muncie is an urban city full of vamps, I'm not worried about walking around by myself. I'm just as dangerous as anyone else that might be out there, and that's not even accounting for my golden ticket in the form of a golden necklace. So when my wolf yips to get my attention? I listen.

I was busy thinking about what I wanted to cook for dinner—as a shifter, food is on my mind most of the time—and I wasn't really watching where I was going. Why should I? When my shifter senses are always open, my wolf constantly aware in the background even when I'm in my skin, I can daydream without worrying about it.

Something in my wolf's warning yip has me suddenly concerned.

I go still. Tilting my head slightly, I sample the scents on the breeze while listening carefully.

The sounds of the city are the same as they usually are. Cars. Chatter. Doors closing, dumpsters slamming.

Rats scurrying in the distance. Vamps lurking around corners. Nothing out of the ordinary.

But... I sniff again.

No way.

I shake my head, but that doesn't do anything to get the scent out of my nose. A very familiar yet, at the same time, *unfamiliar* scent.

A wolf.

I'd know it anywhere. And it's not a wolf wolf. Oh, no.

It's a shifter.

How?

As far as I know, I'm the only idiot reckless enough to call the vamp-ran city my home. But there's no doubt that that's a shifter's scent, even if it belongs to a wolf that I don't recognize.

Who are they, and what are they doing here?

More importantly, how did they breach the borders?

In a Fang City, supes like vampires and shifters are basically an open secret. While most humans are blissfully unaware that the supernatural walk among them, a select few make their living as willing blood donors. As employees—and, well, *food*—they're owed some kind of protection and security. That's why the Cadre —the vampire leadership who govern each individual vamp town—sends some of their strongest on patrol, keeping out undesirables around the clock. A constant perimeter check.

That's what Aleksander was doing the night I fled Accalia. A vamp with some seniority, he spends most nights doing a full-turn, patrolling the entire border of Muncie to make sure that our community is safe and protected.

And if I understand that they're basically protecting the vamps and humans who live here from the monstrous wolves who live in Accalia, I politely try to pretend I don't for the sake of getting to live here myself.

I'm a shifter, yeah, but I'm a lone wolf. I turned my back on the pack a year ago, and I can't imagine what a wolf is doing in Muncie now.

Well, no. I can. I totally can. But I don't want to think that, after hiding out all of these months, they've finally figured out that this was where I ran off *to*. I don't want to meet up with any other shifters, whether they're looking for me or this is just one big coincidence. I also don't want to have to deal with any vamps who might start questioning what I'm doing in town if it turns out one of my former packmates has tracked me down.

So, though I don't often rely on it, there's only one thing to do. Slipping my finger under my shirt, I pull my necklace out, letting it nestle between my boobs.

Just in case.

CHAPTER 4

Aleks had my necklace made especially for me last year, right after I decided to give staying in Muncie a try. He insisted I wear it, and though the wounded wolf I was back then flinched at the idea of accepting jewelry from any male, I eventually relented.

The chain gleams in the moonlight as I pat it. I don't like to make it so obvious that I'm wearing it, but sometimes that can't be helped.

As a shifter, I can't wear anything made of silver, so the chain is pure gold. The links are tiny. Dainty. The shade is darker than I like, considering it reminds me of Ryker's eyes, but beggars can't be choosers. Aleks assured me it best served the charm hanging off the chain, and it was a vampire tradition to use a necklace that suited its intended.

I'm sure he knows best. Because the charm? It's a fang, and, like the gold links, it's very, very real.

It's also one of his.

The first night we met—after he sent the Nightmare Trio scurrying, and I picked my jaw up out of the dirt—my future roommate snapped off both of his canine fangs. It was his way of assuring me he was harmless. It was also completely unnecessary. Despite the way he claimed me with that hissed 'mine', I could sense he was no danger to me. I went along with it anyway since it obviously made my gallant knight in fang-y armor feel better.

By the time I accepted his gracious offer to stay in his apartment permanently—be platonic roommates with our own space and no expectations—his fangs had already grown back. He'd only been without them for three days which was more than I needed to get a decent read on him.

He was a good guy and, it turns out, a good friend.

So I agreed, and he commemorated my staying in Muncie by taking one of his fangs and turning it into a necklace. At first, I thought it was creepy, but it didn't take long before I understood the meaning behind it.

In Muncie, anyone wearing a charmed fang is protected from any other vampire. It's a sign that we have one of their kind looking out for us, that we're not to be messed with. In my case, something that Aleks did to this charm makes it so that my true scent is hidden. It also keeps the other vamps in town from picking up on my shifter nature. So long as I don't shift in front of them, I seem as human as the next chick.

Because, yeah. He wasn't kidding when he told the Nightmare Trio—my name for the three female vamps who tried to attack me my first night in town—that I was his.

Of course, he didn't mean what I initially *thought* he meant. He didn't want to drain me, and he didn't want to fuck me. My roommate has a bit of a savior complex. When he saw Gretchen and her followers ready to attack, it didn't matter that I was a shifter or a female. I was outnumbered and, to his gentle nature, that just didn't seem right.

So he claimed me. And, with his fang, he branded me. Any vampire who saw me wearing it knew instinctively that I was under the protection of Aleksander Filan.

Basically, I'm off-limits.

So I wear the necklace because I know it makes him feel better. At first, he wanted to make sure that no one gave me trouble. And, honestly, this sucker has saved me from getting into more fights than I count. When someone looking for trouble sees the fang, they keep on looking.

Of course, I'm not a complete idiot. I know fangs like these have another meaning. It's why Hailey is desperate to get one of her own. Wearing this fang is a sign that Aleks really does consider me one of his.

And, these days, it's exactly as it sounds.

A few months into our friendship, Aleks confessed that he had feelings for me. By then, I had told him about as much of my past as I felt comfortable sharing, so he knew all about Ryker and the way he rejected me. Because of that, he told me to take my time, and that if I ever decide to return his feelings, he'd be waiting for me.

Like I said, vamps are really super patient.

For now, he's my roommate and my closest friend. I've never really had one of those before, so it's nice. He does so much for me, too, that the last thing I want is to get him in trouble with Roman because I got in a scrap with another shifter.

If I can sense them, they've got to be near. Which means, if I want to avoid them, I've got to be going.

My hand slides up to the fang again, clasping it securely like the pass that it is. I know I'm going to catch the attention of my neighbors if I start jogging the rest of the way so I decide to hold it out, make it noticeable. Humans will think it's a weird accessory, while vamps will recognize it and let me go on my way undisturbed. It's a win-win and—

Crap.

The chain hits my hand with a soft slap. I yanked the damn thing right off of my neck.

One downside to shifter strength, I suppose. With my wolf on high alert, warning me away from the unknown shifter scent, I lost a little control. The golden chain is so delicate, so finicky, and... ugh.

That's the... what? Third time recently that's happened?

I click my tongue and shove the necklace with Aleks's fang into my pocket.

It's one thing to show it off. But if I accidentally drop it, what happens then? I can get the chain repaired—*again*—no problem, but I don't want to have to ask my roommate for another one of his chompers.

He's already done more than enough for me.

———

I can't shake the feeling that I'm being followed the whole way back to my apartment.

Technically, it's Aleks's, but he insisted that I call it mine after I decided impulsively that I'd take the spare room he was offering me. I countered that it could only really be mine if I was contributing. A gentleman through and through, Aleks refused—which led to him getting his first lesson in dealing with an alpha wolf who was finally free to be herself.

I had a job at Charlie's by the end of my first week in Muncie, I paid Aleks my portion of the rent with that first paycheck, and I've happily considered my room my own personal den ever since.

I stay on alert as I quicken my pace, but if someone *is* following me, they're good. The unfamiliar shifter scent always stays just out of reach, and maybe if I were anywhere but in Muncie, I'd follow it back to its source. I can't, though. I've worked too hard to make a life here, hiding in plain sight of the pack's mountain, and I'm not going to let some unknown wolf mess it up for me.

Just in case they're closer than I think, I pass the front of our building, cut through an alley, and approach it from the back. There's a long, steel fire escape that connects the balconies on each level of the twenty-floor building. Each tenant—nearly all of them vamps—owns their own floor. The twelfth floor is Aleks's, and he's lived here for the last forty years.

I try not to think about that. Like, *logically* I know my vampire roomie is centuries old, but it makes my head spin when I focus on that tidbit too closely. I'm only twenty-six, a mere baby compared to him, and I get that I'm a fully mature adult, but it's still a little... weird to me that my bi-centennial buddy is interested in fucking me.

If I didn't think it would ruin our friendship when I can't quite reciprocate his feelings for me, I might take him up on that. But since I'd much rather have a true friend instead of just a friend with benefits, I purposely shove that idea out of my head.

It's eleven flights from the ground level to our balcony. I scurry up them, hoping that no one is watching me go, leaping when I reach the last stair.

Aleks leaves the balcony door open for occasions just like this. Considering this is a vamp building and everyone on our block knows Aleks, we don't have to worry about anyone breaking in. It... it's just not done in a Fang City. But on the few occasions I shift and need to get back inside of the apartment and he's not here, he keeps the balcony door set so even a blonde wolf can shove her way inside.

Since I'm still in my skin, I use my hand to push the door open.

Aleks is sitting on the couch, glasses slipping down his nose as he reads his book.

I wave in greeting. "Hey."

I know for sure that Aleks picked up on my arrival as soon as I set foot on the first rung of the fire escape. Not because of me, but because of his fang. He's in tune with it, and even with it stuffed in my pocket, he can sense it and know where it is. He's not rude, though. Instead of staring at the balcony, waiting for me to pop up, he continued to finish his page until I made my presence known with a greeting.

Once I did, he sets his book aside, lips curving in a welcoming grin that has my stomach going tight—and it has nothing to do with the hint of his fangs biting into the lush bottom one.

I have to brace myself whenever I look at him straight on. He's too pretty and, even after knowing him for a year, I tend to get a little drool-ly when he catches me unaware. Between his flawless pale skin, his carelessly tousled caramel-colored curls, and a stunning pair of light green eyes, he's otherworldly.

It's not his fault. He's a vampire. Snaring his prey is part of the job description. When Aleks turns his attention on you, you feel like the only person in the whole damn world. He can talk you into anything.

A sip of blood? Anything you say, Aleksander...

Good thing he's never tried that on me. I mean, I'd probably let him feed, but when I came around again? I'd rip his dick right off, and since he's hopeful that he'll get to stick it inside of me sooner or later, I'm pretty safe from his vampire lure.

One good thing about being myself with Aleks? He knows I'm a wolf, and he knows I don't bluff. When I threaten his dick, I mean it, and maybe it'll regenerate like his fangs do, but he's not about to test that theory.

I don't blame him.

"Evening, Gem," he says, a smile that's charm-free but still pretty fucking irresistible. I'm glad I braced myself. "Tea's in the kitchen for you. I'm glad you'll get to drink it hot tonight."

His voice is cultured. Relaxed. Now that I know

him, I catch a hint of his accent—Polish, I've discovered—in even the simplest of sentences; around those he trusts, he lets down his guard enough not to consciously work to cover it.

He's in a good mood, I notice, though that's nothing new. On nights that I make it back before he has to go out and patrol for the Cadre, he's always pleased.

I try not to read too much into it. "You're the best."

"Mm." He pauses for a moment. "I noticed you forgot to drink it last night."

Oops.

"I meant to, but I passed out while watching my show," I tell him. "I guess I didn't need it, but I'm looking forward to some tonight."

Aleks's tea is one of the traditions we've built together since I moved in. It's technically a chamomile tea, and the first few times he made it for me, he said it was to help me relax so that I could sleep. Having spent my whole life living in a pack—the Western Pack, Lakeview, Mountainside—I was used to the quiet of a rural setting. Living in a city was a *huge* adjustment for me. If he thought the tea would help, I was willing to try anything—after he swallowed it first, of course.

Even though Aleks has always been honest with me, I couldn't quite shake the feeling that there was something he wasn't telling me about the tea. He brushed me off when I asked, and that just pissed me off to the point that I refused to take another sip.

And that's when he admitted that it was a chamomile *blend*. And that blend? It was designed to help hide my scent so that the other vamps didn't figure out that I was a shifter.

Of course I freaked the fuck out. He said scent, and I started to think he was doing something to my wolf. I shifted right in the middle of the kitchen just to prove to myself that I still could, then shifted back to test that ability next. I forgot that non-shifters treated nudity differently than we did in the pack, and I showed Aleks all of my goods in the heat of the moment.

Surprisingly, he shrugged off his own shirt, giving it to me to cover up since I was in no state of mind to realize why standing in the middle of a stranger's kitchen butt-naked might be inappropriate. I'd only known him for one week at that point, and I was still licking my wounds from Ryker's rejection.

I understood why I needed to hide out even more than Aleks did, but still. I refused to pull the shirt on until he fully explained his blend and I understood that he was only trying to help me.

Since then, I've had a cup of tea every night almost religiously, and Aleks hasn't been able to convince me to get naked in front of him ever again. I used to tease him that he wasted his only opportunity, but when he came clean about his feelings for me, it didn't feel right to joke any more.

Though the fang is supposed to cover me, I'm

grateful that the chamomile tea gives it a boost. In case I forget to wear the necklace or—oops—I break it, I'm still protected.

As I head into the kitchen, grabbing the still steaming cup of tea that he has set out for me on the counter, I feel a bit like a dumbass. So what if I thought another wolf was tracking me on my way home? Even if they were, they wouldn't know I was there; at least, not by scent. If they saw me? Yeah, I'd be screwed, but only if they recognized me. And since I've done a total one-eighty since anyone in Accalia has seen me last...

I got spooked for no reason. Worse, I snapped another chain for no reason.

Aleks knows it, too.

He's wearing a slight frown when I walk back into the living room, carrying my mug.

"Something happened to your necklace."

He's blunt, but I don't think that has anything to do with his being a vamp. Or maybe it does. He's been alive so long that he doesn't see the point in wasting time beating around the bush, and he usually doesn't bother.

The first time he pulled that trick with the fang necklace, I was suspicious. But then Aleks explained that while just showing off the fang acted like my golden ticket, I had to be wearing it next to my heart for it to really work. Some kind of Cadre magic, just like the chamomile blend and the bite bandages. I just went with it because he obviously knows what he's talking about.

With a wince, I pull it out of my pocket with the hand not clutching the mug. "Snapped another chain. Sorry."

"It's fine. I just thought you decided to take it off."

"Nah. It was an accident."

"I'll have another one for you by morning," he promises.

I don't bother trying to tell him that I'll take care of it myself. I'd only offend him, and I know he'll do a better job. Quicker, too. He doesn't like me going without it for too long, and if that's the one thing he asks of me—apart from drinking the tea—I'll do it.

"Thanks," I say, tipping it into his outstretched palm.

"No worries. As soon as I finish tonight's patrol, I'll take care of it."

Vamps own the night. In Muncie, they own everything, but especially the night. It's when the more powerful vamps patrol the perimeter, which is why Aleks is on the dark squad.

Unlike what pop culture would have you believe, he can go out in the daylight, too; slather on some SPF 500 and he's free to step out in the sun. It just weakens him the same way that prolonged exposure to silver does to one of my kind. Without a powerful Cadre-made sunscreen, he'd burn, and it would be a total shame for anything to happen to that beautiful face.

"What about you?" he asks me. "Are you done for the night?"

I nod, blowing on my tea. He must've finished brewing it for me right as he sensed the approach of his fang because it's still too hot to drink. "Yup. Early night because Charlie wants me behind the bar all weekend, but I'm not complaining. I was gonna go make something to eat. You want some?"

Vampires survive on blood, but I've seen Aleks eat real food on occasion. Nothing too heavy, and maybe it's cocky to admit that he seems partial to my cooking, but we usually sit down and eat together when I'm off and he's not needed to go out on patrol just yet.

It's so good to have a meal with a male and not have to worry about the meaning behind it. In the pack world, food basically equals sex. The Alpha couple get first kill, or first pick at any meal when we're in our skin. Courting couples use food to show their interest in one another. I learned from a young age not to accept food from a male in case it meant you were telling him you were into him, too.

With Aleks, dinner is just dinner. I appreciate that.

Not tonight, though.

With an apologetic shake of his head, Aleks says, "I wish I could, but Roman heard from one of the sunset spotters that there might've been a break in the border earlier this evening. He has the full overnight patrol coming in early to check it out. I just wanted to wait until I talked to you first before I met him."

Talk to me? What for?

A break in the border only refers to supes. Humans are free to come and go as they please, but vampires have to be invited.

And, as I discovered last year, shifters never get an invitation.

I try not to look too concerned. "Shouldn't be a big deal, right? Rival vamps are always trying to sneak into Muncie."

Aleks reaches out, laying one of his chilled hands on mine. As a vamp, his body temp runs a lot lower than mine does. I must feel like I'm on fire compared to him, but—especially lately—he will take any opportunity to touch me.

I'm... probably going to have to do something about that sooner or later.

And maybe I would, if it wasn't for the gentle way he pats my hand as if he has terrible news to tell me.

Oh, wait.

He *does*.

"Dominick didn't pick up on a rogue vamp, Gem. He found wolf prints leading into Muncie. Big wolf prints." He waits a moment. "Shifter tracks."

I close my eyes.

Why am I not surprised?

CHAPTER 5

Thank the Luna for Aleks's chamomile tea. Without it, I don't think I would've been able to sleep a wink.

All I keep thinking about is the sensation I was being followed, the scent of an unknown wolf on the breeze, and the wolf tracks leading out of Accalia and into my new city. The Mountainside Pack is the local shifter power, but they're not the only shifters nearby. It's *possible* that the wolf tracks belong to some other shifter, but then Aleks explained that they led straight from the mountain.

Between the Mountainside wolves guarding their territory and the vamps' paranoid patrol, odds aren't so great that a third supe decided to test the Cadre. It has to be one of my former packmates. Makes sense that I wouldn't recognize their scent, too, since I only spent a month living among them a year ago. Packs change, and as the Alpha's intended—plus an omega—I'd been coddled. Out of a pack of more than fifty members, I maybe met half that before I left.

What's an unknown wolf doing in a Fang City? The thought keeps me up until Aleks's tea finally kicks in. I've spent a year hiding out, covering both my scent and my tracks. The only way I could be followed now would be through my whisper-thin bond with the pack's Alpha, and since there's never been any kind of tug from Ryker in the time after I ran out on him, I can't imagine why he'd come looking for me *now*.

He's probably perfectly happy with his chosen mate, I figure. He wouldn't leave the mountain after so long just because of me. I mean, maybe I spent the first couple of weeks in Muncie looking over my shoulder, but when one full moon passed, then another, I had to accept that Ryker's rejection was final.

Still, just because he doesn't want me, that doesn't change what I am. I'm an unmated alpha female who would be a prize to any shifter with ambitions of his own. It doesn't really matter if it's a Mountainside packmate or any other shifter. They can't find out I'm a lone wolf, not if I don't want to lose the life I've spent the last year putting together.

After a lifetime of pretending to be someone I'm not, I've gotten pretty good at bluffing. So when Aleks asks if I'm all right, I act like I could care less that there might be a shifter in town. I even tell him, in as casual a voice as I can manage, that I thought I might've picked up on a shifter's scent on my way back home from Charlie's.

That... was probably a mistake. I should've known better. Not only is Aleks a savior, but he can be pretty overprotective. As soon as I tell him, he has to hear all the details. Where was I? Did I see anyone? Did I recognize the scent? Did the necklace break before or after I caught it?

It's that last question that makes me realize that Aleks isn't thinking of himself as a protector of Muncie. He's worried about me, and he proves it by offering to stay home.

As if I need a babysitter.

No, thanks.

I point out that the Cadre comes first. That Roman won't be happy if he ignores a summons just because he's concerned about me. Even if the wolf is here because they're looking for me, I can deal with it. What about the unsuspecting humans who might run across a shifter who, for all we know, could be feral?

It's a possibility. I mean, no shifter would choose to leave pack territory and head into a city full of our enemies unless they lost their mind. I certainly hadn't been thinking clearly when I sped off the mountain. I expected any vamp who caught up with me might bite first, ask questions later, and I thank the Luna every damn day that I met Aleks that night. Not just because

I ran into the Nightmare Trio first, but because—the mood I was in—I think I would've slaughtered them if I had to and, yeah. I was pretty feral myself.

A feral shifter is the most dangerous creature in our world. The second you pair a beast's strength with a lack of any human empathy, it's a disaster in the making. If I gave in to my wolf's single-minded desire to survive and my human side's bloodthirsty nature, I would've been unstoppable. They'd have no choice but to put me down if I actually let go.

A pack stabilizes a shifter. Like the Cadre has created tight-knit vamp communities in their Fang Cities, living among their own kind keeps a balance between both halves of a shifter's soul. It's why Roman thinks of me like a ticking time bomb.

Technically, I *am*.

But I've put down roots. I've made friends. Unless someone pushes me—and, thanks to Aleks's fang, no one's tried since Gretchen wanted to drain me—I'm not a danger to anyone in Muncie.

Until now. Until there's another wolf skulking around, threatening me and my new life here.

I'm not afraid of the unknown wolf coming at me, though. As an alpha, I don't *get* afraid. But... maybe I'm a little concerned that the wolf will reignite the war between vamps and shifters. The truce between our kinds is shaky at best. If a wolf goes feral in Muncie, I'm screwed.

I need Aleks to do his job. And, if I have to, I'll do mine.

After all, I *am* an alpha.

Though I can tell he's only reluctantly going, Aleks leaves the apartment around eleven, an hour before his shift should've begun. As one of Roman's most trusted guards, he patrols a full eight hours every night no matter what; it's the price of being part of the Cadre, and if I don't understand it, I figure it's a vamp thing and I'm not meant to. Since vamps usually sleep through the day—turns out pop culture got *some* things right—and they only need a couple of hours to recharge, the eight hours isn't really a sacrifice for such a long-lived vamp like Aleks.

At his urging, I drink a second cup of tea with him before he goes. I'm still obsessing over what the sudden appearance of a second shifter could mean when I finally feel drowsy. I let it take me under, hoping that Aleks will be back when I wake up again in the morning.

His scent is renewed when I shuffle into the living room, but a second sniff confirms that it's old. He must have stopped by earlier, but then left again.

A quick glimpse at my phone confirms it. Though Aleks rarely uses his—that one's a two-century-old vamp thing—he'll sometimes send me a message when he's on patrol. The Cadre forbids their guards from talking while they're on duty, but he can spare a few seconds to shoot off a text.

No sign of the shifter, he confirms, and Kellan discovered another set of tracks leading out of Muncie. The consensus is that the wolf high-tailed it out of the Fang City as soon as they could, heading back up the mountain.

Just in case, Roman has called for all of his full-turn patrollers to meet at his penthouse office in the middle of the city. Until they can figure out whether it was a one-off or not, they're increasing the perimeter checks, but they also need to be careful not to draw the attention of the humans who have no clue that they live under the protection of a group of powerful vampires.

They did the same thing last year when I drove into Muncie. I didn't realize it at the time, but Aleks filled me in later. It's how I know that none of my former packmates ever came after me. If they had? The Cadre would've known.

Honestly, a supe can't take a dump in Muncie without Roman Zakharov knowing about it.

You'd think I'd feel a little relief that the shifter had bolted. And I do... kind of. Call it alpha intuition or what, but I can't shake the feeling that there was a reason why they risked death by fang by coming into Muncie on their own.

And, Luna, I really, really hope it's not because of me.

———

I WAIT TO SEE IF ALEKS IS GOING TO STOP IN AGAIN before I have to head out for my next shift at Charlie's. Even though he assured me that the shifter threat is gone, I can't help but wonder if maybe the vamps are underestimating my kind.

If I can hide out in Muncie without being sniffed out, why can't this new wolf? Backtracking, leaving a false trail... even a pup could do it with the right training and instincts. I hope they're going on more than that, and I make a point to remember to ask Aleks when he comes home again.

At around two, I get a text from Carmen, the morning/afternoon bartender; when you cater to a supe clientele, the bar's open all hours since one chick's noon is another's midnight. She needs to cut out a little early, something to do with her kid, and she wants to know if I can cover for her.

I jump at the offer. Waiting for Aleks to get back has me pacing around the apartment. I even shifted to my fur, doing laps around the living room, anything to burn off the looming sense of anticipation that I just can't get rid of.

After leaving a note for Aleks that I headed into

work early, I leave the apartment. My wolf is completely alert as I purposely take the walk to Charlie's. Not that I don't trust Aleks, but I've learned a long time ago to trust my own senses.

Luckily, there's no sign of any other shifter. Even the scent from last night is nothing but a memory. If they're still in town, they're hiding even better than I am, and I decide that so long as they leave me alone, I'm not going to think about it.

Saturdays at the bar are even more hectic than Friday nights. So even though I arrive a little before three, there's a pretty sizable crowd already. I relieve Carmen, and jump into bartender mode.

An hour or two later, I'm taking advantage of our dinnertime lull to do a quick inventory. Between keeping the booze stocked up, the blood casks full, and the garnishes for some of our cocktails prepped, I've got to stay on top of it before the nighttime crowd comes filing in.

All of my customers are taken care of, but my head shoots up when the bar door opens. Not just because it's any other patron, either. As soon as Aleks's scent hits me, I'm already putting my clipboard down and heading for the end of the bar.

I'm not the only one watching him glide toward me. He has the attention of nearly everyone else in Charlie's. Every vamp—and most humans—know exactly who he is, and if they don't? He's so effortlessly attractive that he catches their attention anyway.

He gets the stares while I get the jealous looks when they realize that he's here for me. I don't know which is worse, and I try to follow his lead in ignoring them.

"Hey. What's up? I thought you were still with Roman."

"I was, but he finished the meeting. Since I have a couple of hours until he wants me back on patrol, I thought I'd stop by." Aleks holds out his hand. It's my necklace with a brand new chain. "I have something for you."

I take it. "You didn't have to bring it down here."

"After last night, I felt that I had to. I didn't like the idea of you walking around without it on."

I don't have the heart to tell Aleks that, while his fang might protect me from other vampires, the sight of it won't do a damn thing against a shifter. Actually, if one of my former packmates saw me wearing a fang, they'd probably think it was a memento from a vamp I killed or something.

But he came all this way to bring it down to me after he got it repaired. I know it's important to him, too. The least I can do is wear the necklace.

"Thanks, Aleks. I appreciate it."

"Here." He leans over the bar, gesturing for me to move closer. "Let me help."

"Uh. Sure."

I scoop up the length of my hair, giving him access to my throat as I turn around. It's an intimate position, one that leaves me more defenseless than I like considering he's an apex predator and I'm baring my throat to him, but it's *Aleks*. I'd be more in danger of him kissing my skin than biting it.

He doesn't do either.

As if he wasn't seemingly perfect enough, he really does respect the fact that I want to keep our relationship platonic. He doesn't even linger or accidentally brush up against me. He just loops the necklace around my neck and clasps it together.

"There." I turn again just in time to see a look of satisfaction cross his beautiful features. "Perfect."

I pat the fang. When he heads on out again, I'll stick it under my shirt so it's not so obvious that I've got it on, but for now I leave it. "Want a drink? I've got some Earl Grey I can brew for you in the back real quick."

"That would be lovely."

"Hang tight."

Before I head toward the back, I glance around the bar. Hailey's due in later tonight. Right now, there are a couple of waitresses working the tables, and Tony, the busboy.

I call for him. "Hey, Tony."

"Yeah, Gem?"

"Keep an eye on the bar for me? I'll be right back."

He flashes me a thumb's up, and I head into the storage room. It's where we keep all of the stock that doesn't fit out behind the bar, plus the massive fridge where Charlie stores all of the chilled blood for his vamp regulars. I also have a small electric stovetop, a kettle, and a microwave.

What can I say? Ever since I met Aleks, I've developed a taste for tea.

A couple of minutes later, I've got the tea steeping. I grab the steaming mug in two hands and use my ass to swing the door open again. Aleks swears that his Earl Grey is perfectly steeped in three minutes and anything over that is undrinkable which is why I'm so surprised to find that he's not sitting where I left him.

I set down his mug, frowning. Not only is he gone, but there's no sign of him in the whole bar.

"Hey, Gem. Looking for Filan?"

I know that voice. That's the flirtatious vampire Vincent. He must've sat down at the counter while I was in the back.

I nod over at him. "Yeah, Vin. You see him?"

The vampire nods. "He got a call. Said to tell you he'd be right back."

Huh. That's interesting. Like a shifter, a vampire's hearing is extremely keen. Even with the bar's normal noise level, he'd have no problem having a conversation inside—unless he needed privacy.

77

Like, oh, I don't know. Maybe it was Roman calling him?

Great. Just great.

Well, if he comes back and his tea is over-steeped, I can always make him another cup if he wants. Until then, I reach for a blacked-out shot glass and get ready to pour out Vincent's regular order—but not before I take the opportunity to tuck my fang beneath my shirt.

Just as I'm sliding his drink over to him, the door opens again. Immediately, my wolf lets out a warning yip that has my head jerking toward the entrance. A familiar scent rises up over the alcohol, the fried appetizers, the stink of the rest of the clientele. It's musky, it's spicy, and there's a hint of pine that has my heart starting to pound.

I was expecting it to be Aleks, but despite his natural icy scent, every vamp carries the scent of blood and death with them.

And that scent?

It smells like life.

It smells like hope.

It smells like *mate*.

Holy shit.

Ryker. That's Ryker standing in the open doorway.

And from the way that his dark gold eyes find me from across the bar, I know that it's way too late for me to duck and hide.

CHAPTER 6

What the fuck is he doing here?

He... he's not supposed to be here. In Charlie's. In Muncie. Anywhere near I am. He's supposed to be in his cabin with his chosen mate, not staring at me as if he can't believe that I'm here, too.

That's all right. I'm probably pulling the same face.

Because I can't. I can't believe it.

Did I think that the whole bar watched when Aleks walked in earlier? That's nothing compared to the reception Ryker gets. Even non-supes can sense that there's something different about this male. Between his Alpha aura, his animal magnetism, and his looks... he's almost as dangerous a lure as Aleks, just not so pretty.

That's one thing I can say about the Mountainside

Alpha. He's not pretty, but hell if he's not still the most alluring male I've ever seen.

He's grown his hair out a little since I saw him last. Instead of being closely cropped against his skull, it's shaggier than I remember, though I haven't forgotten what a nice shade of chocolate-colored brown it is when he isn't chopping it all off. Like his lush lips, it's a small hint of softness on such a hard male.

His jaw. The sharp planes of his cheeks. A straight back that looks like it's made of steel.

And those eyes...

Even from across the bar, I can see the immovable force of his alpha wolf peering out from behind those angry eyes.

I'm not afraid. I'm *not*.

Well. Not of him, at least.

I'm afraid of the way my body immediately betrays me. One peek at him and, if only for a moment, I'm that fifteen-year-old girl again, the one who looked at Ryker and saw her forever. I take his scent into my lungs, my knees going weak, my panties going damp, my heart singing out for its mate.

Only he's not my mate. He can't be.

He rejected me.

So what the *fuck* is he doing here?

I've never heard Charlie's fall so quiet before. A hush, a murmur, a few shocked exhalations when the vampires realize that one of their enemy is walking so boldly among them. It doesn't take long for them to peg Ryker as a shifter, but they can also sense that he's not just *any* shifter. He's an alpha, and not someone to fuck with.

Me? I'm fair game, for the most part; at least in comparison, I am. When it becomes even more obvious that his complete focus is on me, the rest of the bar starts sneaking peeks my way. They're following my lead. And since I'm not about to sacrifice my new life in the vamp town for the sake of Ryker Wolfson, I bring the fakest grin to my face as I can, as if he's just another customer and not the bastard who broke my heart.

"Hi, there. Welcome to Charlie's."

The spell breaks. The humans who don't quite understand what's happening just shrug and go back to their drinks, their food, their company. The vampires watch Ryker from the corner of their eyes, but they leave him alone. They might not know that I'm a shifter, but it's obvious that the dark-haired alpha has come for me. Unless I give them some sign that I need help, they're gonna let me take care of it.

Ryker makes a beeline straight for me. As if I expected anything less.

I reach for one of the spare waitress pads Charlie keeps under the bar. Always prepared, he has a bucket of pens and pencils down there, too.

"How're you doing?" After a year working the bar, I

don't need to take down a customer's order. With Ryker, though? I make an exception if only because, if I don't have something to do with my hands, I'm not so sure I can control my claws. "What can I get you?"

He's staring at me. I watch as his nostrils flare, trying to catch my scent, before his rugged features form a deep scowl when his nose fails him.

Thank you, Aleks. It's good to be reassured that his charm and his tea don't just fool vamps. Seems like even the Alpha can't pick up on my scent. Definitely good to know.

I poise the tip of my pencil to the pad. "Well?"

"Aren't you going to say anything?"

His voice is a deep rumble as he continues to stare as if he's thought I've lost my mind or something. Maybe I have. That's as good an explanation as any for how I feel drawn to the prick who cast me aside more than a year ago.

Keep smiling, Gem. "I did. I asked you what your order is."

"Gemma—"

I tap my name tag with the edge of my pencil. "Call me Gem."

He clenches his teeth so tightly, I can see a vein bulging in the side of his neck. It's so big, I decide to name it Duke.

Duke doesn't look happy. Come to think of it, neither does Ryker.

"What?"

His eyes flash. "Don't do this. Not here. Not now. I'm hanging onto my wolf by a thread, *Gemma*. A year. A whole fucking year I've been looking for you and you ask me what I'll have. You. I came here for *you*."

My heart lodges in my throat. Worse, my hand flexes and the pencil snaps into three distinct pieces.

Oh, *hell* no.

Batting my eyelashes, I open my hand, dropping the pencil pieces. As he so kindly reminded me, it's been a year since I walked out on him. A year since I've had to play the gentle omega princess. To my surprise, I can slip into the old role easier than I thought I could.

"Me?" The sweet voice is so unlike anything I've used in so long, some of the regulars at my counter do a double-take. Then they go back to pretending they're not straining to hear every word over the suddenly raucous din. "Now why would you do that? Considering I'm *nothing* to you."

I see Ryker's mouth move quickly, spitting out a word or two that I can't hear over the angry thudding of my pulse—but I can guess even so what he's saying. Too bad I'm more preoccupied by the incredibly loud, cracking sound that seems to cut through the rest of the noise. A piece of the polished wooden curved part of the counter top has smashed and splintered underneath one of Ryker's big paws. Even though he's still wearing skin, it's his turn for his hand to flex, claws slicing out, breaking off a huge chunk of Charlie's bar.

I raise an eyebrow. "Cash or credit?"

Shaking out his hand, letting the wood shards and plastic pieces flutter to the sticky floor, Ryker's brow furrows as his heated gaze flies back to me again. "What?"

"I want to know how you plan on paying for the piece of counter you just broke. Cash or credit? I might be able to convince Charlie to take a check, since I know you're good for it, so I guess that's an option, too."

"Stop that. Look, I don't know what you're doing here—"

"Working. Isn't it obvious?"

He thins his lips. "I don't give a shit. You're coming with me."

The pure alpha demand in his voice is hard to ignore—or, it would be, if I wasn't protected by the charmed fang.

Score another point for Aleks.

So though Ryker expects me to just jump because he says so, I make a big display of pulling my phone out of my back pocket, glancing at the time. "Ooh. Sorry. I've got another five hours left to my shift. Looks like I'm not going anywhere 'til then."

A whisper of shock dances across his face, as if he can't believe that I can refuse him.

Pity he recovers quickly.

"Then take a break."

Hmm... "No."

"Take. A. Break."

There's something in his snarl. I dare another quick look right into his dark gold eyes, not even a little surprised when all I see is the wolf staring back.

I recognize that wolf. Mine calls to his, hoping against irrational hope that he's changed his mind.

Yeah. Right.

A year. It's been a year. If he thinks that he can just storm in here and start giving me orders, he's got another think coming. If I'm nothing to him, he's nothing to me. Not my mate. Not my Alpha. He's just another customer, and since he doesn't want a drink, he's not even that.

"Can't. Sorry. So... nice to see you again, but I've gotta get back to work. I'll make sure to send the bill to Accalia."

Tossing the empty waitress pad on the counter, I turn away from him.

He's behind the bar before I can snap at him to get away from me. The message is pretty clear, though, and I refuse to give him the satisfaction of reacting to the way he invades my space.

But then his hand shoots out. As much as I hate to admit it, I'm aware of every inch of him. From the way his nostrils flare to the twitch of his tiniest finger, I know where he is even with my back turned. He might think he has some claim to me, some right to touch me, but if so?

He thought *wrong*.

So his hand shoots out, but I'm ready. I spin, catching it. The warmth of his skin just about sears mine, and it takes every ounce of self-control I profess to have to keep from pulling back.

Hell if I'll give him the satisfaction.

I'm not the only one affected by our touch. His eyes light up, a deep rumble from low in his chest revving, like he's a freaking machine and I just pressed 'on'.

I realize too late that this was a trap. Like everything else he's ever done, this was planned. It was a pure Alpha move. Somehow, he knew exactly how I would react.

He's quick, too. Before I can pull away, he switches our positions, using his hand to grab mine. With the other, he reaches for my throat. Using the tip of his pointer claw, he hooks the chain looped around my neck and gently eases it out from beneath the collar of my Charlie's shirt.

"What," he says in a voice so icy, it feels like I just walked into the back fridge, "is this?"

"None of your business." I slap at his hand. "And don't break it. I just got it fixed."

He doesn't let go. "It's a vampire fang, Gemma."

"So you *do* know what it is." I quirk my eyebrow at him. "Then why did you ask?"

Another rumble. I'm pushing his buttons, but I can't find it in me to care. If he came here expecting to find Omega Gem, he's wasting his time.

"Let go."

"No. Take it off."

I slap his hand again. "Don't tell me what to do. You're not my Alpha anymore."

"No," Ryker says, "but I am your—"

"Gem. Is everything okay here? Do you need me?"

Oh, shit.

So distracted by Ryker, I didn't even notice that Aleks has returned to the counter until his soft voice washes over me. I can only imagine what he thinks is going on. I've got an obvious shifter male standing behind the bar with me, his paws still holding tightly to the necklace Aleks gave me while I'm slapping at him ineffectually.

This time, I pinch Ryker. He lets go, though I think that has nothing to do with my pinch and everything to do with the politely possessive way that Aleks regards me.

Uh-oh.

Ryker turns his attention on the bigger threat—and I don't just mean that because Aleks is a vampire.

"Who are you?" he demands. He sniffs, his cheeks going suddenly taut as he sucks in a breath. "Bloodsucker." His gaze darts to my necklace, and I can just about see the gears inside of his skull whirring as he puts two and two together. "You? You gave your fang to *my* mate?"

Oh, he's got to be kidding me.

I open my mouth, a "not your mate" already halfway to my lips, when Aleks answers before I get the chance to.

"Yes. Because she's not yours, wolf."

The unsaid *she's mine* hangs in the air. After that? There *is* no chance.

Ryker bends his knees, then leaps. He clears the bar easily, swiping with his claws as he aims right for Aleks.

Aleks holds his ground. A powerful vampire, I'm sure he's earned his reputation—but whether he meant to or not, he challenged an alpha wolf shifter. He has his fangs, but Ryker has berserker strength, killer canines, razor-sharp claws, and the instinct to eliminate *any* threat.

And, for some terrible reason, he's shown up in my life a year later convinced he's my mate.

I don't know why. I don't know how. But there's one thing I do know: that when Ryker just claimed me in front of Aleks, in front of the whole of Charlie's, when he said *my mate* like that... he fucking meant it.

He barrels into Aleks, swiping with his claws from gut to shoulder. Between the force of his hit and his perfectly aimed strike, Ryker knocks Aleks to the floor. Straddling the stunned vampire, he keeps him down while he goes to town with his claws.

It's a show of dominance, and not a single soul steps in to stop it.

My wolf doesn't want me to interfere, either. A mate should be strong enough to protect what he considers his, and watching Ryker slice Aleks open so single-mindedly is intoxicating to my other half. It proves that we were right to think of Ryker as a match for us, that the moon picked the best mate to bond us to.

Only that's my friend he's attacking, and despite my instincts warning me not to get involved until it's over, I can't. I just can't stand by and let this happen.

"Ryker." I lace my voice with as much of a command as I can manage. Sure, I'm probably blowing up my spot if the supes in Charlie's pick up on my hidden alpha nature, but I have to. For Aleks. "Stop this. Now."

He immediately jerks his head over his shoulder, searching for me. "For my mate, I will."

That's all he says before he climbs up off of Aleks, wiping his bloody claws on his jeans before using the back of his hand to swipe at the spray of blood covering his cheek.

I know he's not dead, but that's a small mercy when I see the mess that Ryker has made of my roommate.

"*Aleks*." I race over to him just as his eyes blink open. A sigh of relief escapes me as I help him into a sitting position. "Are you okay?"

He mumbles something in Polish.

That's not a good sign. "What?"

"I said, Roman's not going to be happy about this."

Probably not. The head of Muncie's Cadre is really big on secrecy, and Ryker just turned Aleks's chest into so much ground beef. I mean, that's what it looks like. Chunks of pulverized meat with blood *everywhere*.

"It'll be fine," I mutter. If anything, any unaware humans who made the mistake of an evening drink at Charlie's will just finally figure out why the fang-friendly bar is so different than some of the others in Muncie. We usually have more supes in here this time of day anyway, so it shouldn't be *too* bad.

And if it is? I'll worry about that later. Right now I have to take care of Aleks.

Charlie's got a bona fide blood bank in the back. It might cost me my next couple of paychecks, but I'm gonna make sure that Aleks recovers enough so that he can go out and find a fresh donor himself. A couple of blood bags will seal him up tight.

After that, I'll take care of Ryker. The time for pretending that he's not here because of me is long gone. He proved that by the way he went after Aleks like that. He's a threat to me, too, and I have to handle it.

I use my shifter strength to bring Aleks to his feet, looping his arm around my shoulder to keep him there. Then, as I help him toward the backroom where we keep the blood, I point at Ryker. "You. Stay."

"I'm not your dog," he snarls.

"Yeah? Well, I'm not your mate," I shoot back. "The sooner you get that through your thick skull, the better we'll both be."

Ryker shows me his canines. "Yeah?"

"Yeah."

His eyes go from dark gold to molten lava. "Have it your way, *Gemma*. We'll see about that."

And, though I told him to stay, he walks out of Charlie's, secure in the knowledge that—despite being covered in Aleks's blood—no one will try to keep him from leaving.

Not even me.

Because I recognized that look in his eyes. Ryker's wolf was in charge just then, but he wasn't looking at me with anger.

That was need.

Desire.

Lust.

And I'm in big, big trouble.

CHAPTER 7

The logical side of my brain tells me that I'm reading too much into it. But then I remember the way his alpha wolf stared out at me from behind his eyes and I'm not so sure that's the case.

Because the last time he looked at me like that? I had just licked his blood from my claws and sat with my legs spread, feeling the length of Ryker's erection under my ass.

So, yeah. Forgive me for being thrown a bit.

By the time Ryker's disappeared through the exit, I realize that that... all of that... it really happened. My former Alpha—the mate who rejected me—just showed up out of nowhere, and though he made it pretty clear that it wasn't an accident—

I'm hanging onto my wolf by a thread, Gemma. A year. A whole fucking year I've been looking for you...

—I honestly can't believe it.

I go into alpha mode myself. Though I consider myself a lone wolf, I really am part of a small pack of two. I live with Aleks, I eat with him, and I'm as protective of him as he is of me. I don't think of him as a prospective mate or anything, and he'd probably be insulted that my instincts toward him are more like he's my pup, but seeing him in such bad a shape?

I have to help him.

I don't even tell Tony to cover the bar again. Now that the spectacle is over, the rest of the bar's staff is reacting, too. I can see that Natalie's on her phone—straining my ears, I hear her say *Charlie* and know she's called the boss—and two other waitresses are fielding comments, concerns, complaints from our customers. Tony's moved behind the bar, and maybe he thought it would be a good place to hide after Ryker attacked Aleks, but he can handle anyone who—rightly so—needs another drink.

"Come on, Aleks," I murmur. "I've got you."

I lead him into the backroom. Because it couples as a makeshift break room, there's a handful of chairs. I plop Aleks in the nearest one, tell him to sit tight, and dash over to the massive fridge.

As I go, his voice calls after me. "That was him. Wasn't it?"

I don't pretend to misunderstand. "Yeah. That was him."

Aleks knows about Ryker. At least, he knows what I felt comfortable enough to admit. He knows that I left my pack because my adopted father agreed that I should mate with Mountainside's new Alpha. I arrived at the mountain, the Alpha decided he wanted another mate, and he rejected me. Since I didn't want to go back to Lakeview with my tail between my legs, I moved to Muncie instead.

Aleks, once he made his intentions clear, always marveled that Ryker gave me up. I thought it was sweet, but a little heavy-handed.

So, yeah. He knows about Ryker.

But did I ever confess that he was my *fated* mate?

It... might've slipped my mind.

"I'm so sorry, Gem. He caught me off guard."

My laugh comes out far more hollow than I mean it to. "I didn't think that was possible."

"I didn't want to involve the humans. I didn't want Roman to find out, either." He sighs, shifting in the seat to a more comfortable position. "Guess that's a lost cause. He'll know as soon as the first vamp reports in that we've got another shifter in town."

Another shifter because, like me, his senses would've told him that the wolf who crossed into Muncie last night was different than Ryker.

So what was that about? An advanced guard? Or was it a wolf who got lucky enough to spy Gemma

Swann walking around Muncie and ran back to Accalia to tell their Alpha?

"I don't think Ryker's gonna say 'thanks' for trying to cover his ass," I mutter, grabbing the first blood bag I can reach from the fridge.

"I didn't do it for the mangy wolf. I did it for you."

"Me?"

"I know how much he hurt you. I wasn't sure if you still cared about him even after all this time. But then the way he treated you... I couldn't help myself."

I use my claw to pop the plastic on the blood bag. I hold it out to Aleks. "Here. Drink this."

If he notices that I pointedly avoided responding to his comment, he lets it go. Though he's going to great lengths to act as if he's fine, I watch in amazement as he lifts the puncture in the plastic to his fang. The second fang makes another hole. Seconds later, he's drained the whole bag.

"Let me get you another one."

"Thank you."

He's really got to stop thanking me. It only makes me feel worse that his injuries are my fault.

Ryker might have done this to him, but make no mistake. I'm responsible.

I bring three more bags over to Aleks. Partly because I'm desperate for him to recover, and partly because he can't talk when his fangs are busy with the blood. In the end, it takes six bags before his chest is completely healed and his light green eyes lose that glassy look.

He gets up, swallowing another 'thank you' when I glare at him. I'm stacking the empties so that I know how much I'm going to owe my boss, and I would've willingly replaced six more if it meant that I did something for Aleks instead of the other way around for once.

Even though Ryker's gone, I refuse to leave Charlie's. I don't know what staying at work proves, but when I snap my human teeth at Aleks after he suggests that we head back to the apartment together, he throws up his hands in a silent apology. He then offers to stay, but the idea of him sticking around like some kind of personal bodyguard—or, worse, getting in the way if Ryker does come back—just rubs me the wrong way.

The only way to make all of Charlie's believe that what happened was no big deal is to *act* like it. That means that Aleks has to leave, and I have to return to my post behind the bar before I give Charlie a conniption.

Besides, both of us know that Aleks *can't* stay. He still needs to feed; human blood straight from the source is far more potent than the chilled stuff that Charlie keeps at the bar. And then there's the matter of Roman...

He's not wrong when he says that the story of what happened in the bar will come better from him than one of the vamp customers. Just like I'll have to deal with Charlie, he's got his own boss to answer to.

I give Aleks one of the chef coats they keep in the kitchen since his shirt is toast. A quick splash in the bathroom and no one could tell that he was attacked barely half an hour ago.

With a searching look, he asks me one final time, "Are you sure you want to stay? I can walk you back to the apartment before I go see Roman."

I shake my head. "I'll be fine. Actually, I should probably stay until close to make up for everything. I'll see you later. Okay?"

"Be careful, mały wilku."

Be careful? Now that I know Ryker's in town, he should be the one who's careful.

He caught Aleks off guard. As much as I hate to admit it, he caught me unaware, too, but he won't do that again.

We'll see about that.

Yeah, Ryker. We will.

Bring it on.

———

I GET SUPER LUCKY. NOT TOO LONG AFTER I FINALLY convince Aleks to leave, Charlie calls. He wants to hear about what happened from me, so I tell him that it's handled and he doesn't need to come down tonight. He never comes by the bar on Saturdays since it's his poker night with a couple of Cadre members, so I know that he'll head downtown if he has to but he won't *want* to—and, trust me, I don't want him coming down, either.

Since there's no sign of Ryker when I leave the backroom, I figure that everything's okay for now. I have no illusion that he's gone back to Accalia, but so long as he waits until I'm done with my shift, I can deal.

And if he doesn't know how to find me at home to resume our challenge? Oh, well. That's not my problem.

That doesn't stop me from looking up whenever I get the chance. Now that I have his scent in my nose—and my wolf is prickly from his sudden appearance—I'm sure that I'll pick up on him if he decides to push me by coming back to Charlie's. Still, I can't help it. The sense of looming anticipation has only gotten worse now that I know what caused it.

It's the calm before the fucking storm, and I know it. I just try to act like I don't.

By the time night falls, the bar is *slammed*. I don't know if it's because word got around to the supe population and they're hoping for a rematch between Ryker and Aleks or what, but I've never seen the place so busy even on a Saturday. A majority of the patrons are vamps, too, and I have to consciously tune out the conversations because almost every single one seems to mention the brawl.

There goes any hope that it didn't get out. I just hope that Aleks can keep Roman calm, and that I don't get my sorry tail tossed out of Muncie because Ryker couldn't control himself.

For the first time in ages, Hailey shows up to a weekend shift on time. I can tell from the way she's buzzing that she's heard the gossip and she's dying to ask me about it. And while we are super busy, I make sure to keep myself occupied because I just don't want to listen to a human talk about how amazing it is that a vampire and a shifter fought over me in the middle of Charlie's.

Because I know my co-worker. That's totally what she thinks happened.

And maybe it did? I don't know, and I wish I didn't care.

I throw myself into serving customers, even bringing food out to tables when the waitresses fall behind if only because I need the distraction. Even so, my head pops up every time the door opens before I swallow a snarl and resolve not to do it again.

At around nine o'clock, Jimmy Fiorello walks into

the bar. It's not Ryker, so I just give him a wave as I pour out a Rum and Coke for Jane. A second later, I do a double-take.

His wrinkled face is all scrunched up.

Uh-oh. I don't know why, but that seems like it's a bad sign.

"What's up, Jim?"

"Is Charlie having a cat problem? 'Cause I'm telling you, Gem, it fucking *stinks* out there."

No way in hell does Charlie have a cat problem. Though Aleks's fang keeps my shifter nature shielded from vampires, other animals know exactly what I am. Ever since I started at the bar, there hasn't been a sign of any kind of critter. No mice. No rats. They sense me and stay away. Cats, too. Without the mice to hunt, they're not brave enough to face off against a human-shaped wolf.

But if it's not a cat—

"Don't worry about it. Hailey will get you a drink, and I'll go see what that's about. Kay, Hailey?"

"A whiskey for Jim, and Gem deals with the cat pee. Sounds good to me."

I laugh along with Hailey's comment, though my wolf is already chomping at the bit, desperate to scare off any predator attempting to encroach on my territory.

One step outside and I'm sure that that's exactly

what's going on here. Because the stink? That's urine all right. Straight up piss. But it's not what Jimmy thinks.

Across the street, leaning with his back up against an electrical pole, arms crossed over his button-down shirt, a smug look on his face... there's Ryker.

And unless my instincts are wrong—and I know for sure they're *not*—he's responsible for the piss.

He wasn't wearing those clothes before, I realize. He'd had a black t-shirt on when he first stormed into the bar, and he left with Aleks's blood smeared all over his jeans. Now, he's traded his tee for a white button-down with the sleeves rolled up to his elbows, and a pair of jeans a few shades darker.

And maybe he changed because walking around with blood on him in a Fang City is a bad idea. Considering he's an alpha wolf shifter, though, I think there's a much more logical reason.

On the plus side, that means he was most likely in wolf form when he decided to take that piss...

I fist my hands on my hips, trying to keep back my claws. As soon as Ryker saw me, he pushed off of the pole, lazily moving across the street until we're on the same side. He gives me a crooked smile, as if he's decided that making this whole thing seem like a joke is a better way to approach me.

Only I'm definitely *not* laughing.

"What do you think you're doing?"

"Marking my territory."

Marking his—

I try to stay calm. *Try* being the operative word there. If my claws shoot out and tear open my palms, I'll have a hard time popping the caps off of bottles of beer. Sure, I'll heal pretty quickly, but it'll be a pain in the ass until then.

Stay in control, Gem. You got this.

Gritting my teeth, I say shortly, "You pissed a circle around the bar?"

"The bar, and everything inside of it," he agrees.

"But why? It's not your territory." If anything, it's *mine*. "This bar belongs to Charlie."

"Ah." He holds up a finger. No claws, which means he's still in control of his wolf, too. "But you're inside of this bar. And you belong to me."

My jaw drops.

Oh. He did *not* just say that.

Okay, say I kill Ryker. It's okay because, technically, this is an alpha challenge. He came into my territory, he challenged me, and now he's trying to mark something that is *mine*. Pack law says me killing him would be totally justified, right?

My wolf lets out a chuffing sound. Straight up disagreement.

No. Damn it. She's right. As angry as I am, I still can't kill him.

But that doesn't mean I have to put up with this shit.

"Get out of here."

His eyes are still a lighter shade than normal. They twinkle as his smile widens just enough to stab at me. "Make me."

"Excuse me?"

A liiiittle bit wider. "You heard me. You're an alpha. If this is your territory, protect it."

I'd really, really hoped that he'd forgotten about that. Maybe then I could've convinced myself that he meant it when he said he'd been looking for me for a year. When he said I was his mate.

But it's not me he wants. It's an alpha female.

And if I do what he said, if I *prove* it, he'll never leave me alone.

"Ryker—"

"Come on, sweetheart."

I blink. "*Sweetheart*?"

"You prefer Gemma?"

"It's Gem."

He ignores that. Lifting his hands, he reaches for the first button on his shirt. "Sweetheart it is then," he says before he flicks that top button open.

And then another.

"What are you doing?"

"Making it easier for you."

I know exactly what he means, too. I wish I didn't, but I do.

Wolves show dominance with both fighting and sex. By taking off his shirt, he's signaling that he's open to either; he'll take off his clothes so can prepare to shift, or to mount his mate. Sounds weird to non-shifters, but because we're of the same rank, he's actually showing me a tiny bit of respect right now. Unlike when he attacked Aleks, he's turning this into an official challenge.

I don't *have* to follow along. In fact, I have no intention of it. But between his marking the bar and the way he's undressing himself right now, Ryker is treating me like both an alpha *and* a mate.

Which, yeah, is what I'm supposed to be, but still.

"I'm not stripping down."

"You will eventually."

He sounds so sure that even my wolf is offended. I flash my canines, before spitting out, "You gave up your chance to be my mate when you chose Trish Danvers."

"I didn't."

"Yes, you did."

"You don't understand. I didn't choose Trish."

Bullshit.

It doesn't matter to me that I can scent no deception coming from him. I was there, and I'm not about to let him make me doubt what happened.

I scoff. "You rejected me for her. Don't deny it."

He doesn't. Instead, he says, "That night... you didn't give me a chance to tell you what was going on. You just left, and then I spent... oh, that's right... a whole fucking *year* trying to find you so that I finally *could* explain."

Explain? Seriously?

"'I have no intention of mating you this moon or the next'," I mimic. All these months later and his off-handed comment is still burned in my brain. "Sound familiar? If you can explain that, go right ahead. Otherwise you wasted a year and, sorry, but that seems like a *you* problem."

With a soft *snick*, I notice that he just set free his claws. Ooh... looks like I finally touched a nerve there.

"I couldn't mate you, Gemma. And, yes, Trish is part of the reason why. But it's not what you think."

"Please." Does he think I'm an idiot? Or does he just hope I'll fall for his story? "I heard rumors about you and Trish from the moment I arrived on the mountain. And it wasn't just the pack gossips. Even Shane confirmed you were spending all your free time with Trish."

He definitely wasn't spending it with me, that was for sure.

"Shane?" Ryker echoes.

"Yeah. Your Beta. You remember? The one who got stuck with babysitting duty while you were busy with Trish."

"Omegas need to be protected," he reminds me. "What did you expect me to do?"

Honestly, I expected him to be the one doing the protecting if he really believed I needed it. Sure, I *didn't,* but he didn't know that then, did he?

Ugh.

"Make up your mind, Ryker. You challenged me on my turf. You just admitted I was an alpha. So am I? Or should we go back to pretending I'm still an omega?"

"Omega? Hardly. You're like me, Gemma. Pure alpha, but you're not *the* Alpha. Without a pack of your own to lead, you have no idea what it's like to be responsible for every life, from the retired gammas to the youngest pup."

"You don't know what the fuck you're talking about," I tell him. "I'm not on my own. Muncie is my new pack."

"You belong to the Mountainside Pack. You belong with me."

"You wish."

Ryker looms closer. A spark of temper has the heights of his sculpted cheeks going red as he says in a low voice, "You think this is a challenge. You don't know how right you are. But not like you think, sweetheart. You'll never be my mate? I told you. We'll see about that."

That's it. I don't care if I stab my own hands, I let out my own claws.

Rising up on my tiptoes, going nose to nose with Ryker, I say, "Oh, yeah?"

His eyes drop to my mouth. "*Yeah.*"

I swallow. His gaze follows the motion of my throat before locking back on my mouth. And I know that he's going to kiss me, almost as much I'm absolutely sure that I... I'm not going to stop him.

I tilt my head slightly.

Ryker's so close, I can feel the heat of his breath on my skin.

"Gem— oh. I'm sorry."

I'm not. I swear to the Luna, I'll never, ever complain about Hailey's habitual lateness ever again. Because right now? Her timing couldn't be any more perfect.

I back away so quickly, if it wasn't for my shifter's reflexes, I would've landed on my ass. I recover, purposely giving my back to Ryker while hoping against hope that Hailey didn't realize how close I came to falling under his spell like that.

"Hailey. What's up?"

She tucks a strand of her hair behind her ear, biting down on her lip.

Oh, yeah. She realizes.

"Sorry," she says again, "it's just that Clark has a complicated order I keep messing up on, and Charlie's on the phone again. I thought I'd see if you were done out here."

"Uh. Yeah. Just give me a sec— oh. Never mind. I'm coming."

Because when I turned around again, I saw that all that's left of Ryker is the stink of his piss in the air and a sinking feeling in my gut that I've only just tapped the surface of what he's doing here.

And I was right. It has *everything* to do with me.

CHAPTER 8

After everything that happened last night, Charlie gives me Sunday off.

That's the nice way of saying that, between the fight involving one of the Cadre and the Alpha of the Mountainside Pack—not to mention the six bags of blood I fed to Aleks—he didn't want to risk me bringing trouble down to his bar for a second night in a row.

If it wasn't for Aleks being involved, I'm sure Roman would've had all of our heads for how obvious those two ding-a-lings were. Brawling in sight of that many oblivious humans? Seriously? I don't know how Aleks convinced his boss that we weren't to blame, but he assured me this morning that we were in the clear.

I'm glad. Last night, I drank *three* cups of tea and even that wasn't enough to put me to sleep. I paced for hours, part of me expecting Ryker to show up at the apartment, the other part wondering how the Cadre was going to respond. I was almost convinced that they'd run me out of town before long.

At the very least, I hoped that the vamps forced Ryker out.

When I asked Aleks, he changed the subject. Though I've never told him outright that I can tell when someone is lying to me, he's pretty fucking astute. He figured it out on his own, and has his own workaround. My roommate doesn't lie to me, but if he doesn't want to tell me the truth, he evades the subject.

Fair enough. It's not like I'm completely honest and open with him all the time. And after everything that happened at Charlie's, I'm doing a bit of avoiding talking about it myself.

We come to an unspoken agreement. Neither one of us mentions Ryker, and when I tell him that Charlie gave me the night off, Aleks confesses that he already requested another guard take his patrol. Without saying so, I get the idea that he planned on joining me at Charlie's, just in case Ryker made a third appearance.

I'm actually a little surprised by that, though I probably shouldn't have been. In the year since I've known Aleks, he's only taken a handful of nights off. My twenty-sixth birthday was one, the anniversary of his death another. He insisted we celebrate both nights —even if I thought it was weird to celebrate his death, but, hey, *vamp*—and he brought me to one of the most exclusive nightclubs in the whole of Muncie each time.

Mea Culpa.

Really. That's its name.

It's a vamp club. A fang is your ticket inside: either you have a pair of your own, or you wear one as a charm like I do. Even if Ryker avoided being chased out of Muncie by the Cadre, there's no way he'd be able to track me down at Mea Culpa.

Which is precisely why I ask Aleks if he wants to go with me.

Am I using him? I'd like to think that I'm not. We've gone clubbing together as platonic friends, so it shouldn't be a big deal to have drinks and do a little dancing at the club. Deep down, though, I know a good chunk of my reasoning has to do with proving to myself that I'm over Ryker.

Because while I was pacing last night? I kept thinking of our near kiss and wondering if I really *am* over him.

For the first time in months, I feel the bond stretched between me and Ryker that I've long thought buried. All it took was him showing up, acting like a possessive alpha, and I'm falling under the same spell.

I don't want to, though. And if I have to go out on the arm of a beautiful, generous, kind vampire to prove it? Wow. What a hardship.

Of course, Aleks jumps at the offer. I make it clear

that this isn't a date—I'm not so cruel that I'm purposely going to lead him on—but I don't think he cares. Honestly, I get the idea that, after the way Ryker attacked him, he likes the idea of being seen with me. Like I chose him, and not the aggressive wolf that didn't belong.

I don't blame him at all. His body might've recovered, but I think it's going to take some time before his pride does. Going out to Mea Culpa instead of hanging over at Charlie's is just what he needs.

At least, I think so—until about an hour after we arrive and, with a soft rumble, my wolf warns me that our mate has found us.

What the...

I don't normally second-guess my senses, but I have to be sure. I turn in time to watch Ryker stroll confidently into the club. The music is pumping, countless bodies swaying, and still I can pick him out on the edge of the crowd. The vamps nearest to him give him a wide berth, and after a few seconds, he's standing all alone.

His eyes are locked on me.

I don't blink until I catch the rusty, tangy, meaty scent of blood on the air. *Aleks*'s blood. I jerk my head, following the scent. Holy shit. I must've grabbed at Aleks's arm when I first picked up on Ryker. I don't even remember giving my claws the order to come out, but I obviously did because I've basically stabbed the poor guy. I can already see blood welling up.

"Ah, shit. Aleks, I'm so sorry." I carefully pull my claws out of his arm. "I don't know what came over me."

Aleks isn't even looking at the marks I left in his formerly flawless skin. His jaw tight, his fangs lengthening, I see that he's also spotted Ryker.

Oh, boy. The last thing I need right now is a repeat of yesterday.

Grabbing Aleks by the sleeve, I tug him until he's looking at me instead. "Wanna dance?"

The fierce look in his eyes softens when he glances down at me. "Are you doing this so that I don't confront your wolf?"

"He's not my wolf," I argue, "but yes."

A tiny smile, only one punctuated by the point of his fang digging into his bottom lip. Better there than in Ryker's thick throat. "I'd be an idiot to refuse. Lead the way."

I can feel the heat of his shifter's gaze on my bare back as I take Aleks by the hand, pulling him further into the crowd. If I have to dance with him all night to keep the two of them from fighting, I will.

For a moment, I wonder if I'll get the chance. After the way he tried so publicly—not to mention *failed* so publicly—to stake his claim on me, I almost expect that Ryker's going to chase after us. If he really was an alpha coming to retrieve his mate, he'd never let another male get between us.

He doesn't.

From across the club, I watch as Ryker purposely walks away from the dance floor. He climbs the stairs that lead to the private tables. One of Mea Culpa's bouncers intercepts him, and I'm not sure what happens next, but the vamp nods and brings Ryker to a table that *just so happens* to overlook the part of the dance floor that I'm standing on.

It takes everything I have to ignore him. And when that doesn't work, I just try my best not to let him catch me watching him watch me.

Ah, Luna.

How can Ryker Wolfson make me so crazy by just *being* there?

Well, I came here to unwind and to dance. I might not be able to relax with the weight of his golden stare on me, but hell if I'm not going to dance.

So I do. I already knew Aleks was an amazing partner, and if he throws in a little something extra because he knows we have a spectator, I forgive him. He promised me that he has no hard feelings for Ryker for the way Ryker shredded him open yesterday and, shockingly, he was telling the complete truth.

Doesn't mean he's not going to rub the fact that he's dancing with me in Ryker's face.

I'd probably enjoy myself a lot more, though, if I

could figure out if Ryker cared. He's careful to keep his expression neutral which only riles my wolf up more. That expression... that *expression*! It's the same look he wore right before he broke my heart and rejected me.

At that memory, I move a little closer to Aleks, trying to dance the sting of Ryker's rejection out of my head.

It... doesn't work. And, eventually, I give up on trying—with dancing, at least. Instead, when Aleks offers to get us a couple of drinks, I accept.

I can tell that he's hesitant to leave me on my own, but he's not stupid enough to actually verbalize it. With a quick look over my shoulder to where Ryker's still lounging at his table, he murmurs over the cranking music that he'll be right back.

A few minutes later, he returns, but he isn't alone.

I have to work hard not to let my annoyance flash across my face. Though I rarely have to interact with any of the Nightmare Trio—trust me, we don't run in the same circles at all—there are times when I'm forced to. For Aleks's sake, I play nice.

Gretchen, Leigh, and Tamera are not Cadre, but they're vampires. He's known them for decades, if not longer, and they respect him. Sure, Gretchen would've eaten me happily the first night we met, and I've gotten the vibe that she's barely refraining from licking her lips when we do run into each other, but she's kept my secret.

Just because of that, I'll tolerate her. And, though it isn't often that she's out on her own, she's not *as* terrible when she isn't showing off in front of her followers.

I offer her a tight-lipped smile as she comes strolling up with Aleks. He mouths the word *sorry* to me, so I know it's not his fault, and I accept the drink he holds out to me with a nod.

Gretchen sniffs. At first, I think it's because she's just reminding me how much disdain she has for me—or maybe she's just judging my short, strapless, backless dress and the heels that put me closer to her in height—but then she says, "Like I was saying, Aleksander. I can't believe the Cadre's allowed two of the mutts in our city." Another sniff, then a cool look my way. "One was bad enough."

"Gretchen," Aleks says, almost as a scold.

"What?" The blonde says it so innocently, I'm almost fooled.

My roommate sighs. "Enough."

Whether she heeds him or not, I can't tell. But I do notice that her pale eyes flicker toward Ryker. And, unlike how wary most of the other vamps are regarding the dangerous shifter in their midst, she looks almost... interested.

An idea starts to form in my brain. Probably not the *best* idea, but it's a kernel that begins to go *pop, pop, pop* when Gretchen adds, "Though, I must say, if the

Cadre hadn't passed it down that the Alpha wasn't to be bothered, I might've tried to take a nibble out of him myself."

I don't know what surprises me more: that she knows he's the Alpha, that the Cadre's on Ryker's side, or that Aleks doesn't look like any of that is news to him.

One thing that doesn't surprise me, though? Is how spot-on I was when I thought Gretchen was interested in Ryker. I guess her hatred for shifters only extends to me and not the ruggedly handsome Alpha sitting on his own.

Hmm.

"That's not a bad idea," I say casually. "You don't know Ryker. I do. He's always wondered what it would be like to try a vamp on for size. You should go over there."

Gretchen glances over at him again. "He *is* cute."

He's more than cute, but I'm not about to argue with Gretchen. Not when I might be able to kill two birds with one stone.

Distract Ryker and get rid of Gretchen?

"Go on. Say hi to him."

"Gem..."

I guess it's my turn to be the reason for that warning tone creeping its way into Aleks's softly accented voice as he murmurs my name.

Oops.

I pointedly ignore him. "Hey. What's the worst that can happen?"

Aleks shoots me a look that says he knows very well what the worst that can happen is. He's living— well, not really *living*—proof of how well Ryker gets along with vamps. I can only imagine how many donors he tapped last night to be completely back to normal after Ryker's attack.

But, I tell myself, Gretchen is different. She's always reminded me of Trish, so maybe Ryker will enjoy her company. From the way her pale eyes light up as she zeroes in on him, like a predator sizing up its prey, I know that she's even more intrigued at the prospect of taming the wild alpha than she's letting on. Not only because Ryker is, well, *Ryker*, but because the female vamp obviously thinks that he's mine.

If he is, then she seems more than happy to take him from me. And I'm more than happy to give him away.

Of the three of us, Aleks is the only one who doesn't like what's going on here.

"Gem, I don't think—"

Again, I pretend I don't hear him. Sorry, Aleks. Club's too loud, and my shifter's ears are on the fritz. Whoops.

"You're just his type," I tell Gretchen. "I'm sure he'll be happy to meet you."

"Is that so?" Her tone turns thoughtful. And, unless

I'm imagining it, a little accusatory. "I thought he's crossed our borders to see *you*."

Ugh. Looks like news of his appearance down at Charlie's has spread through the supernatural gossips like wildfire.

I give my head a royal shake, as if I couldn't care less. "And? It doesn't matter what he says, he's not my mate."

Gretchen slants a sly look my way. "Does he know that?"

Aleks clears his throat. Though he answers her, his gaze is locked on my face as he says softly, "You heard her, Gretchen. It doesn't matter what the wolf says."

That cements it for her. She didn't give a shit what I told her, but Aleks basically giving her the 'go' sign? She's taking it.

"Okay." Gretchen flips her long blonde hair over her shoulder. "Why not?"

I fight back the urge to shoot off a feral grin.

Why not, indeed?

I don't know what's in the drinks that Aleks keeps bringing me, but they have me thinking real inappropriate thoughts as the night wears on. And, yeah. That's a cop-out. I'm a fucking bartender, for Luna's sake. I know exactly what's in each one, and like I purposely requested, they've all been virgins. Getting drunk with Ryker within touching distance... bad idea all around.

I'm being ridiculous. Even I admit that. After I sent Gretchen to flirt with him, I get annoyed that he lets her sit down with him for a few moments. She doesn't linger, and I'm not so surprised when she shoots me a loathing look as she sweeps away from his table, but Ryker isn't alone for long—and I didn't send a second vamp over there.

And so begins a carousel of club-goers all trying to be the one that'll snag Ryker's attention. Though I know I shouldn't care, and that I'm just driving myself crazy for no reason, I can't help but keep an eye on his table, waiting for the moment when he chooses a date for the night and leaves.

It'll happen. I know it will.

Which is why I get the irrational idea to beat him to the punch.

Once Aleks realized that I was more interested in paying attention to Ryker than dancing with him, he led me to the edge of the dance floor for good. It's in a spot where we're somewhat hidden, but I angled my body just enough that I still have a line on the shifter as well as some of the male vamps prowling around the club.

They're not as pretty as Aleks, but one of them will do in a pinch.

"Hey, Aleks?"

"Yes?"

"How mad would you be if I brought one of these guys back to my room with me?"

Did I really just say that out loud?

Aleks's eyes go wide for a moment. I don't think he can believe I did, either.

And then—

"Are you asking me as your roommate, or as the male who would much prefer to be the one you use to make that idiot jealous?"

I feel my cheeks go hot. Yup. Instant regret, all right. "Never mind. Forget I said anything."

If only it was as easy as that.

"But I don't want to. I prefer to be honest. And the truth is that I'd take you any way I can get you, Gem. I've made that clear since the beginning."

He did. I'm just the selfish bitch who let the green-eyed monster blind me for a moment to Aleks and his feelings. What the fuck was I thinking, asking him if he was good with me picking up a stranger and sleeping with him in a twisted way to get back at Ryker?

I would regret it. For so many reasons, I would regret such a stupidly, impulsive action. But apart from giving it up to someone who means nothing to me, I know it would hurt Aleks.

"Like I said. Forget it."

"Mm."

I hate it when he does that. I know he has something he wants to say, but he's choosing not to. Normally, I let it go. But I *am* jealous and I *am* frustrated and, hell, it's creeping closer to the full moon than I want to admit which means that I'm full of sexual tension.

It's nothing that I can't take care of myself—I usually do—but with Ryker a tease to my senses and Aleks's offer almost too tempting, I lose what little temper I've been clinging to. It doesn't help that I have to admit my *brilliant* plan in regards to distracting the Alpha has backfired spectacularly on me.

Ryker's not jealous, but no denying that *I* am.

"What?" I snap. "If you've got something to say, spit it out."

When he doesn't say anything, I feel worse—and then, because I do, I growl under my breath. I'm being unfair, I know I am, but I can't figure out how to stop myself.

"Look," I continue, "I fucked up by even mentioning that. I didn't mean it. I'm just—" A harsh exhale. "I don't know what I am. Sorry. Maybe this was a mistake."

Maybe the whole night was a mistake.

I start to storm away from Aleks. I've made it about four steps before I feel the chill of his palm pressed to my forearm as he latches onto me.

Out of the corner of my eye, I see Ryker suddenly get to his feet.

I shake Aleks off. "What?"

"Roman has allowed him to court you."

At that moment, I forget all about Ryker. Ironic, since I know that's exactly who Aleks is talking about, but if Ryker doesn't think I can handle Aleks, then he really doesn't know me at all.

"What did you say?"

"That's what Gretchen was referring to before. It's why he's still in Muncie. Why he's allowed at Mea Culpa. Roman approved it."

Okay. Maybe I'm being an idiot, but I don't get it.

"Approved *what*?"

"He claims you're his mate. I don't know how he convinced Roman, but he did. He asked for permission to court you inside of Muncie when it became clear that you consider this your home."

Supes—whether they're shifters or vamps—respect the mate bond. Like my kind, vampires have their own mates. Some fated, some chosen, but it's for life, just like a shifter's bond. If Ryker showed proof that I was his intended, that would've been enough for the Cadre to back off. And, like it or not, there was an arrangement made between my dad's pack and Ryker's.

That's not even getting into the fact that he's also my *fated* mate...

But he asked? I find that so hard to believe. After all, he *is* an alpha. *The* Alpha. They don't ask.

At least that explains why Aleks didn't look surprised at all before.

"You knew this?"

Aleks nods. "Roman informed me this morning when he warned me not to get involved in a shifter's mating. I wasn't punished for my role in yesterday's... mm... *altercation*, but only because I could plead ignorance. He won't believe that a second time."

And, yet, if I hadn't dragged him onto the dance floor earlier, Aleks would've gone after Ryker as soon as he walked into Mea Culpa.

Hang on—

"Why would you be punished? Ryker attacked *you*."

"And he did so because he believes you're his mate and I interfered. Unless you renounce him and choose another mate, he's at no fault." The look Aleks gives me is so searching, I feel like he can see right through me. "Will you do that, Gem? Or do you like the fact that he's finally chasing after you?"

I gasp. My hand flies toward Aleks's face on its own, and it's just pure reflex that has me retracting my claws before I slap him.

My chest is heaving. My wolf is up and pacing, desperate to be set free as the alpha side of me overwhelms the human I've been pretending to be. Aleks knows what I really am, and he knows how I feel about Ryker, and no matter how thoughtless my comment was, he just took it way too far.

I'm a female alpha. Being a bitch is part of the job description. But Aleks? He's always been such an aristocratic, gentile, mature male that I guess I never expected him to go for the low blow like that.

He's already trying to make his apologies but I'm just not willing to hear him out. Maybe later. Maybe tomorrow. But now?

No fucking way.

After warning him not to follow me, and knowing from the shamed expression beneath the imprint of my hand still on his cheek that he won't argue, I make my escape.

It isn't until I make it to the club's exit that I realize something: I don't remember seeing Ryker in my rearview as I booked it across the dance floor.

It shouldn't matter.

I shouldn't care—

I glance over my shoulder and curse.

Ryker's table is empty.

Reaching out with my senses, my wolf whines when she finds nothing but Ryker's lingering scent. He isn't just missing from his table. He's left the club.

I don't know what's worse: the idea that he's waiting for me outside, or that he took advantage of my little tiff with Aleks to sneak out.

Alone?

As much as I wish I didn't care, I really, really hope so.

And I'm even more pissed that I have no way of knowing.

CHAPTER 9

I 'm glad I warned Aleks against following after me because, as I let myself into the apartment, Ryker's scent is *everywhere*.

It's not as pungent as his marking outside of Charlie's which is good because that means he didn't feel like upping his... whatever he's doing... by peeing in my apartment. Of course, the markers of his scent just tell me that he went with a little B&E instead.

He's been in here. The front door was locked, so I know he didn't break in this way.

Ugh. The balcony.

Of course.

Though his pine-and-spice scent overlays the whole damn apartment, I open my mouth just enough to taste it. In close quarters, I can snuffle my nose, tasting a scent and tracing it.

Why am I not surprised to find that he headed straight to my room?

It's hard to tell if he's still in there. The hairs on my arm are sticking straight up, my entire body aware of his presence. Either he was just here—which makes sense since he couldn't have had much of a head start on me—or he's waiting for me. Neither option really appeals to me, and I can only guess how he found the apartment. To beat me here, no way he followed me... unless he already tracked me to the building.

Just like he tracked me to Mea Culpa.

My hand freezes on the doorknob to my room. How, I wonder. How can he do that? Between the chamomile tea and Aleks's fang, I don't really smell like me so it's not like he can use his snout.

But, as my mate, he wouldn't need to use my scent trail to chase me down. At any time after I became his intended—so after the Alpha Ceremony at the beginning of last year—he could follow the bond stretched between us right to me.

It doesn't work for me, but that makes sense. These days, my half of the bond is a memory.

What if his isn't?

He's never given me any indication before now that he even feels it. Does he?

I wish I fucking knew.

I also wish I didn't have to deal with this.

I shake my head, giving my doorknob a turn so rough, I nearly break it off.

No. There's got to be another explanation. Maybe some alpha skill that no one's taught me because I've always presented as an omega. It has to be that. Otherwise, if I accept that Ryker could've used the bond to find me all these months, that begs the question: why hasn't he?

Why now?

I don't know, and after the night I've had, I'm pretty fucking sure I don't want to.

I shove my bedroom door in.

Then, as if I can't believe what I'm seeing, I stare.

Welp. He's definitely been in here. Not only that, but he's left a couple of things behind.

There, placed neatly in the middle of my messy bed, is a bouquet of wildflowers wrapped with a ribbon the same deep honey color as my eyes. Their sweet scent and colorful array draw my attention, but they can't compete with the second scent wafting its way over to me.

Holy shit. He brought me a slice of sausage and onion pizza. One of those massive ones you get when you buy it by the slice instead of ordering a whole pie. It's spread out on two flimsy paper plates, a pile of napkins tucked underneath it, a plume of smoke rising up from the melted cheese like it's just been pulled from the oven.

My stomach grumbles. As a shifter, I'm always down to eat and, whether he knew or he just got real fucking lucky, Ryker's left me a piece of pizza with my favorite toppings on it.

Shame I can't eat it.

I can keep the flowers. There's no deeper meaning behind them other than they're pretty and Ryker's probably trying to fool me into thinking he has good intentions. But the food? They blow his 'good' intentions out of the water.

No matter his reasons—and, from everything I've learned about Ryker Wolfson over the last eleven years, I'm sure he has his reasons—he's made it clear since he arrived in Muncie that he sees me as his mate. Bringing food to another shifter isn't just a kindness. It's a gesture that says: I will protect you, I will feed you, and you'll want for nothing if I'm around.

If I accept it, I'm basically saying: okay.

Not. Gonna. Happen.

Leaving the flowers where they are, I grab the plate and march back out into the hall. I plan on bringing it to the kitchen and unceremoniously dumping it in the trash. However, as soon as I leave my room, my senses start to ping and, before I think better of it, I let them guide me to my living room.

No. Not the living room.

The balcony.

Peering through the glass door that separates the

balcony and the apartment, I see Ryker out there, back against the railing of the fire escape. His arms are folded behind him, perched on the top bar of the railing. His bare feet are crossed in front of him.

Oh, boy. No shoes. When a shifter takes off his shoes, it's a sure sign that he's preparing to shift. Clothes are pretty easy to replace if you go wolf before stripping down, but a good pair of boots is a waste if you can't kick them off in time.

I should pretend I don't see him. I should just chuck the pizza and go back to my room. I'm almost a hundred percent sure he wasn't out there a few minutes ago, but now that he's back? He's looking for my reaction. He wants to see how I accept his 'gifts'.

That seals it for me. He wants to see?

Sure thing.

Pausing only long enough to kick off my heels, I throw open the door and step out onto the balcony.

You'd think that, after spending the last few minutes with Ryker's scent whirling around me inside my enclosed apartment, I would be able to handle being next to him. That would be a *nope*. The second I get within his space, his scent goes straight to my head.

Luna, he smells so, so good. It's not *fair*.

A tiny, secretive smile tugs on his lush lips, as if he knows exactly what I'm thinking. Then, with a nod at the plate I'm still holding, he says, "Hungry?"

There's a hint of an arrogant tease in the one word

that pulls me toward the surface. I might've been drowning in the Alpha's presence, but the way he seems so sure that I'm going to accept any kind of food from him reminds me what I was going to do with this pizza.

I give Ryker a steely look and, with a quick flick of my wrist, send the paper plate and the pizza flying off the balcony, like it's some kind of delicious frisbee.

Ryker watches it fly, then shrugs his shoulders. "And here I thought you were a fan of sausage. Maybe next time I'll bring the pepperoni."

"Don't bother," I tell him. Then, because I have to know, I demand, "What are you doing here? I thought you'd still be back at the club."

That's a lie. I know he already left, but if I say what I really suspected—that I'd been worried he'd left the club with a bombshell vamp or two on his arm—then he'd just turn around and accuse me of being jealous over him.

And, Luna damn it, he'd be *right*.

Can he tell that I'm full of shit?

Maybe, considering he snorts and says, "Yeah, right. We both know the reason why I was watching you dance with your bloodsucker boyfriend, and it wasn't to pick up a date of my own. Once I sensed you getting ready to go, I was out of there."

"Okay," I say, trying to ignore the way my wolf perks

up at his admission—or how she snorts herself when she hears Ryker call Aleks my 'bloodsucker boyfriend'. "But you shouldn't be here. I already told you, Ryker. This is my territory. Go back to yours. Go back to Accalia."

"Oh, I plan on it." Ryker uncrosses his legs and widens his stance, spreading his arms out along the railing. Getting cozy, is he? "Just not without you."

"Why?" I still don't have the answer to the question that's been haunting me since he first showed up. "You forgot about me for a year. Then, out of nowhere, you're here and you think I'm just going to go along with your courtship bullshit."

Because that's what this is. The claiming, the showing of his dominance as he fought Aleks, the way he marked the bar, then brought food to my freaking *bedroom*. These are all shifter rituals that take place during the mating dance—and they're all a year too late.

And it's not like I expected Ryker to do all of this stuff last year. I didn't. I went along with the arranged mating because I *knew* that he was my fated mate. When the moon said I was *his* intended mate, Ryker accepted it, too, until the moment he didn't. Why would he have to work for such a sure thing? The courtship rituals were for shifters who were trying to convince their mates to accept them. To *choose* them. Ryker didn't have to convince me of anything.

Of course, that was last year. And, no matter what he says, I'm not his mate. Not anymore.

The fact that he's trying to involve me in his one-sided mating dance is proof enough that he knows that. But it's not going to stop this determined alpha from trying.

Why? I just don't get it. Why *now*? The *now* is what counts. The *why* he wants me is pretty obvious. Hello, female alpha here. But *now*? He could've come after me a year ago. Why *now*?

"A year," I say again, hammering home the point. "What? Did you forget about me?"

His shoulders tighten. It's the only sign that he's not as relaxed as he's trying to appear. "No, I didn't forget you. You need to understand this, Gemma. I gave you the first full moon to cool off, then I went after you."

"Bullshit."

"It's not. Maybe I was too cocky, but I thought I could explain. But you were gone. I couldn't find you. No one could find you. It was like you up and disappeared. I could sense you were out of Accalia, and then you weren't anywhere. No trace of your scent, no hint of our bond."

Whoa. That's the first time I've ever heard Ryker mention any kind of bond, especially not one with *me*.

"A year," he tosses at me, sounding far more carefree than the muscle ticking in his jaw reveals him to be. "Do you know how long that is? A year, searching.

Despite what you think happened that night, I didn't reject you. You're my mate. You've always been my mate. Alphas aren't meant to rule the pack alone. Mountainside needs its Alpha couple. So I searched, and I waited, and I hoped that you'd come back to me. Some packmates thought you might be dead, but I thought I would know even if our bond was gone. And then, on Friday night, I felt it. For the first time in a year, I could sense you. I knew where you were. I knew you were down here, so close I could almost taste you."

Friday. I go absolutely still as I think about Friday.

That's the night when I caught the scent of an unfamiliar wolf. When I snapped my necklace so I wasn't wearing it, and I'd neglected to drink my chamomile tea the night before.

Holy shit. Talk about a perfect storm of fuck-ups.

Is that how he found me?

"I made arrangements with my Beta to leave Accalia, but by the time I made it here later that night, it was barely a whisper," Ryker adds, basically confirming my unsaid suspicions. Later that night... oh, about the time I drank the tea Aleks made for me? Hmm... "My wolf's a stubborn bastard, though, sweetheart. I found you, didn't I? And, now that I have, I'm not going anywhere.

"It might not be as strong as it's supposed to be, but I feel our bond. It's here. Gemma, it's *here*." He raps his chest with his knuckles before resuming his lazy pose.

"So tell me you'll never be my mate all you want. I know better. You're mine. Sooner or later you'll agree and come back with me. I'll just have to wait here until you do."

Great. Just what I need. Another patient supe.

"No waiting necessary." I fold my hands into fists. "I'm not your mate, and there's nothing you can do to change my mind."

A small, lazy, *sexy* smile slowly crawls its way over his face.

Not the reaction I was expecting to my heated declaration.

"Know what?" Ryker's a wolf, but damn if that isn't a purr. "That sounds like a challenge to me."

'Challenge' again. And, this time, there's no mistaking it. He's not challenging my position in the pack, or my dominance. He's challenging my rejection of him.

Alphas never back down from a challenge. If I thought Ryker had pushed things by showing up at Charlie's, showing up at Mea Culpa, breaking into my apartment to leave me flowers and pizza... he would only just be getting started. Especially since Roman Zakharov has given him permission to stick around Muncie.

I have to shut this down. *Now.*

"It's totally not."

A bark of a laugh. Ah, there's a bit of the wolf. "Too late."

I back up against the balcony door.

Ryker watches my sudden retreat. His alpha aura, the one that has been reaching toward me, licking out at me, trying to lure me closer... he pulls it in some, just enough to give me the air to breathe.

His voice drops. "I'll never force you," he vows. "It's your choice, Gemma. It's always been your choice. But you've thrown out the challenge. I'm an alpha. You had to know I couldn't refuse."

I swallow roughly. I can breathe, but I'm so consumed by him that it's a struggle.

Finally, I manage to say, "You should probably go."

His eyes dip low, back up, then down again. At first, I think he's openly appreciating the little black dress I wore to the club, but when his gaze skims over my bare thighs, my narrow hips, and the little cleavage I have before landing on Aleks's fang, I realize that it has all of his attention.

And if I'm a little disheartened that the skimpiest dress in my closet barely earned me a once-over, I shake it off. His fixation on my necklace is a bit more of a pressing matter right now.

He looks at the fang as if he's itching to yank it off, but he knows better than to push me that far.

Still staring at it, he says, "The bloodsucker isn't here."

I don't even ask how he knows that. He's an alpha wolf who's never once shied away from who—and what—he is. He embraces his nature in a way that I've never been able to. My senses are keen, but his are unstoppable. He can probably pinpoint exactly when Aleks was last in the apartment, so of course he knows that I'm alone.

And if there's a rumble of pleasure coming from him when he mentions that fact, I do my best to pretend I don't notice.

"So? Despite what you think, he's not my boyfriend. He's my roommate. We come and go as we please, and I'm used to sleeping by myself at night."

"Good answer," Ryker drawls, his eyes flashing so brightly, I have to fight the urge to flinch.

Only when the air turns thick with his sudden arousal do I run my words back through my head and realize what it is I just said—and how he must have interpreted it.

Not that Aleks and I aren't dating, but that I'm not dating *anyone*.

I step toward him. "Ryker, I—"

"I'll watch over you," he cuts in. "I'll stay out here on the balcony, but I'm not leaving you alone. Not now that I've found you again."

From between gritted teeth, I tell him, "I don't need your protection."

His eyes sparkle mischievously. "Oh?"

That should've been my first warning. I haven't seen Ryker this unguarded since the pack meet when I was twenty, he was twenty-two, and we spent the whole night talking under the stars as I fell further and further in love with the future Alpha.

"The parasites that run this city of yours don't want any trouble with the pack," he reminds me. Yeah. Thanks, Roman. "I'm allowed to stay as long as I behave myself. Parading around in my fur? That probably isn't what they expect. What do you think?"

My immediate response—"Don't call the Cadre parasites"—is cut off with a frustrated growl when, before I can guess what he's about to do, Ryker shifts on the spot.

The clothes he was wearing seconds ago rip and shred and just about slap me in the face. I wasn't expecting him to shift so close to me, and I jump away again, landing in a crouch with one hand pressed against the balcony door.

With a smug look on his wolf's muzzle, Ryker settles down. He deserves to be smug, too. Unless I want to physically pick him up and toss him off the fire escape, he's not going to leave that spot until he wants to.

I scowl. "That was a dick move, Ryker."

He cocks his head and, as a wolf, barks out another laugh that isn't so different from the one he has when he's human.

Still, I'll always give credit where credit's due.

As I roll my eyes and stalk back inside of the apartment, I have to admit that he's definitely won this round.

I LOCK MYSELF IN MY ROOM AND PRAY TO THE MOON herself that I can just fall asleep and put this night behind me.

It's tough. I don't want to think about Ryker's wolf acting like a sentry out on the balcony which means, of course, that it's all I dwell on as I toss and turn, waiting to see if I can sense Aleks's return to the apartment. Hours after I slunk into my room, he still hasn't come back which just makes me feel worse about the way everything went down.

Even though I was still pretty ticked off with him, I sent him a text that Ryker was out there since I figured he'd appreciate the head's up. I already knew my roommate wouldn't be too happy that Ryker made himself at home in our place earlier, but after our argument at Mea Culpa, I was doing my part to smooth things over.

Letting Aleks walk into this whole mess unprepared would be a disaster. I hated the idea that he might think that I got back at him for his comment by inviting *Ryker* home with me when there was nothing further than the truth. And, up until last night, I never would've guessed Aleks would even think something like that—but that was up until last night.

I didn't expect him to answer me, and I'm pleased when I get a message back within seconds.

I understand. We'll talk more in the morning.

Can't say I'm looking forward to it, but as quick to temper as I can be, I'm not the type of chick who likes to go to bed angry. Me and Aleks will hash it out in the morning and we'll be okay.

Me and Ryker?

That's a whole other story.

Not surprisingly, Ryker's gone when I peek out onto the balcony the next morning, leaving only the remains of his tattered clothes behind. My wolf woke me up at around three am when it picked up on Aleks finally coming home. If he was really only watching over me while Aleks was gone, he would've left soon after and he obviously did.

That makes me wonder. Since he's staying in Muncie with Roman's blessing, I figure he's not running all the way back to Accalia. He's gotta be sticking close by. Somewhere he can keep an eye on me *and* store enough clothes. At the rate he's going, he'll run out and then he'll be stuck wearing his skin with nothing to cover it.

Mm. Naked Ryker—

No. Bad Gem. Don't think about naked Ryker. That way lays total danger.

Breakfast. Breakfast sounds good. Ever since I had to throw away that pizza from last night, I've been craving sausage. I think I have some of those little breakfast sausage links in the freezer.

And if sausage also makes me think of Ryker, then I just need to get my head out of the damn gutter already.

I'm moving toward the kitchen, completely focused on breakfast, when Aleks's door opens.

I freeze in the hall.

"Gem. Can we talk?"

I turn toward him. There goes any hope that it was a coincidence he was getting up this early. Aleks has already showered and gotten dressed. Unless I'm wrong, he must've been up for a while, just waiting to start this conversation.

"Depends," I say carefully. "What do you want to talk about?"

Aleks lifts his hand, running his fingers through his curls. "I want to apologize."

I raise my eyebrows. "Yeah? What for?"

A soft exhale. "I should've known you wouldn't make this easy for me."

"You've got more than two centuries on me, Aleks. You should be an old pro at apologizing by now."

"Not if I never believed I was in the wrong. I could count the number of times I've said 'I'm sorry' using one hand."

"And I get one? I'm honored."

His lips quirk just enough to shatter his solemn expression. I'm glad. I know we were fighting last night, but it takes two to tango. We both messed up. There's no reason for him to approach this talk like he killed someone.

Unless he *did*.

Only half-joking, I say, "You didn't drain Ryker or anything last night, did you?"

His gaze flickers over my shoulder toward the empty balcony. "Your puppy is gone?" he asks, then he winces. "Perhaps I should apologize for that remark, too."

"Nah. He deserves that."

"Then I'll just apologize to you. I'm sorry. I never should have said what I did last night. When I—"

I hold up my hand. If he repeats himself, I'm not so sure I'll resist the urge to slap him again. "I remember."

"It was cruel and unnecessary. You've made your-self very clear and I… I shouldn't have taken my frus-trations out on you. I know where we stand. But when I think about how much that Alpha of yours hurt you." He gulps, his light green eyes bleeding over to bright red. It's a sure sign that he's fighting his own blood-thirsty nature. "I was there. I watched you get over his rejection. I don't want to see that happen again."

So tell me you'll never be my mate all you want. I know better. You're mine…

"It won't," I say firmly. "And, if it counts for anything, I'm sorry, too."

"It counts for everything." The red staining his irises starts to fade. "Friends?"

I nod. "Yeah."

It's the best I can offer him.

CHAPTER 10

I'm sitting on the couch, mindlessly watching a rerun of one of my shows, when I hear the rap against the glass balcony door.

Ryker was gone when I woke up. Three hours later, when I'm thinking about making lunch, he returns.

I think he likes the fire escape. Either that, or the idea of riding the elevator up to my floor irritates his wolf as much as it does mine. The confinement in the small room always has my wolf pacing, and the way it stinks of vamps is often overwhelming. If I have my choice, I take the fire escape, too.

Ryker's out there now. Wearing a different black tee —one that's tight enough to show off his magnificent shifter's physique—plus jeans and a sturdy pair of boots, a front lock of hair flopping into one of his dark gold eyes, he uses two knuckles against the glass to catch my attention.

And then, when he sees that he has it, he grins.

My stomach goes tight.

Does he have to look that tempting? It would be so much easier to simply ignore him if he wasn't that Luna damned attractive.

Worse, he *knows* it, too.

Arrogant bastard.

I toss the remote and slowly unfold myself from my comfy position in the corner of the couch. Wearing a suspicious expression I don't even bother to hide, I approach the balcony door, though I don't open it.

The glass is strong enough to keep out the full brunt of Ryker's scent. Right now, I'll take any help I can get.

"What?"

"Can you come out here?"

"What for?"

"I just want to talk."

Talk? Really?

He must pick up on my hesitation even through the door because he holds up his hands in a gesture of harmlessness. "Just talk. No tricks."

You know what? Just talk... I think that's an excellent idea. I've got a thing or two I'd like to say to Ryker.

But not here. Aleks went back into his room, and maybe he's sleeping, but it just doesn't seem right to have this conversation outside on the balcony while my roommate is home.

"Go back around the front," I tell Ryker. "There's a park about five blocks away from here. It has a couple of benches and some privacy. Meet me there."

For a moment, it looks like he's going to argue with me. He doesn't, though. He just uses his pointer finger to gesture in both directions. When I tell him to go right, he nods, then disappears down the fire escape.

I sigh, hoping I'm not making a major mistake, and go searching for my shoes.

TEN MINUTES LATER, I STROLL UP TO THE BENCH. I'VE got nervous hands in my pocket, a blank expression on my face, and my long sheet of hair falling forward like a curtain. I don't want to make it look like I particularly *want* to be here, and I'm trying to hide the way my heart just about stuttered in my chest when I saw him sitting alone on the bench.

I think I forgot how big Ryker is. I know he's got at least a head on me, and his body is pure shifter perfection, but it's something about his being an alpha. His aura extends even further than his broad shoulders do, and though the bench is wide enough to seat three, he takes up way more space than he should.

Or maybe that's because of the way he's sitting. Legs spread, arms resting on the back of the bench, he looks like he's content to sit here for as long as it takes.

Comfortable. He seems comfortable.

Me? I'm just about crawling out of my skin with a need to touch him, and he's *comfortable*.

The unfairness of it all has me stomping over to him. "Okay. I'm here. What do you want to talk about?"

"Take a seat, Gemma."

His command rankles. "I think I'll stand."

"Please."

Ugh. I plop myself next to him. "Fine."

A flash of a satisfied smile, then he tilts his head. He's staring openly at me in that way he has that makes me feel like he's looking straight through me.

"What are you doing?" I ask him.

"Just looking at you. That dress you had on last night was nice, but I've seen you in dresses before. This is different. I like different. Let me appreciate it."

I look down. I'm wearing a worn pair of jeans, a dark grey tank top that leaves my toned arms on display, and my favorite pair of boots. It's what I like to wear when I can actually be myself and not act like Little Miss Shifter Barbie, but it's nothing special.

I mean, I do think I look pretty damn good, but it's a shock to hear Ryker agree when it really is so different than anything he's ever seen me wear before.

What's going on here? This... this isn't what I expected when he said he wanted to talk. Another tactic maybe? He tried forceful at Charlie's, he tried sneaky last night, and now he's trying to flatter me.

But he's also being honest and, for some reason, that really puts my back up.

"I don't think—"

"Have I ever told you that you're absolutely gorgeous?" he says, interrupting me. "Even if you weren't meant to be mine, you'd be just the type of female I'd choose. You were a fucking vision in those sundresses and with those curls, but now?" My shock only grows when he drops his hand to his crotch, drawing my attention to the obvious erection pushing against his jeans. "The things I want to do to you, Gemma. Unh. Come on, sweetheart. Say yes. Be mine."

Forget flattering. This is a pure sexual onslaught that I definitely wasn't prepared for.

I stare at the outline of his dick for longer than I probably should. When I hear him take a deep breath, followed by a rumbled groan, my cheeks flame up. No doubt he's picking up on my sudden arousal.

I can't help it. My heart is wary, my head knows to be guarded against this male, but my pussy? Yeah. She's never gotten the message.

I clamp my thighs together, scooting a little further away from him. When I'm on the edge of the bench, inches away from dropping to the sidewalk, I clear my throat. "That's what you want to talk about?"

"Luna, *yes*."

Okay, then. Two can play this game. He knows he

can turn me on thanks to his nose, but there's no hiding that erection from anyone.

I point at it. "Where was that attitude last year?"

"It was there, but last year I had to be careful not to frighten my omega mate away from just how bad I wanted her. Now that I know you're no more an omega than I am, I don't have to hold my wolf back."

Then, as if proving his point, he snaps his canines at me.

I jump and only manage to save myself from landing on the ground by a single claw. Ignoring his chuffing laugh, I shift so that I'm sitting closer to him.

He sucks in a breath.

Ha. Good to see I affect him as much as he affects me.

I cross my legs, the toe of my boot brushing up against the top of his calf. With another groan, he widens his legs so that his thigh touches mine.

It's a dare, and I know I'm only doing what he wants, but I refuse to be the first to move. Instead, I slide my jeans against his, then tell him as sweetly as I can, "You should've come looking for me last year when you discovered the truth. Maybe then I would've still cared."

He stiffens next to me. Not because he's aroused—which, yeah, he is—but because he's suddenly fuming.

I can feel the rush of angry heat from where I'm sitting.

"I *did*—"

I scoff. "Please."

A rumble deep in his chest, before he snaps,"How many times do I have to tell you that I did? It's not my fault it took so fucking long. If you weren't wearing that fang, I would've found you a year ago." Beneath the sunlight, his shifter's eyes flare a brilliant amber color. His raspy voice turns hollow. "Fair play to Filan. He knew exactly what he had to do to keep you away from me. And without you feeling me on the other end of our bond, it's so Luna damned easy to forget that we're made for each other. Ain't that right, Gemma?"

What?

"What are you talking about? Our bond died the night you rejected me." At Ryker's scoff, I raise my voice a little. "Aleks didn't even know that I was running out on you when I first met him. I don't even think I mentioned your name the first few weeks I was in Muncie. If he hates you now, it's just that he's protective of me. You did a number on me, Ryker. I'm not gonna let you do it again. Aleks has nothing to do with that."

"Oh, sweetheart. You can't be that naive."

"What do you mean?"

"You know he's in love with you, right?"

It's one thing to know that. But to hear Ryker put it out there like that?

I shake my head royally, knocking the curtain of

hair out of my face. "He's... he's told me he has feelings for me. But I told him I don't feel the same, and he gets that."

Ryker gives me a look of pure disbelief.

"*What*?"

"Do you really know Aleksander Filan?"

"I've lived with him for a year—"

"That's not what I mean." His brow furrows, his gaze narrowing as he gives me a once-over. It's different from before. Colder. Calculating.

Now *this*?

This is the Ryker I remember. Not the seventeen-year-old I crushed on, or the twenty-two-year-old I fell for. This is the twenty-eight-year-old Alpha of the Mountainside Pack, the one who rejected me wearing an expression just like this one.

"You think he's a good guy," he announces at last.

Of course I do. "So what? He *is* a good guy."

"He's fooling you, Gemma." When I begin to argue, he cuts me off. "He let me kick his ass."

"Ryker—"

"Listen to me. I know it's hard for you to do that, but just listen. I'm strong. I'm alpha. I know how to take down my prey, and that bloodsucker? He's no easy kill, even if he's already dead. He let me attack him. At that bar. With you watching. He never even once tried to fight back."

"But why would he do that?"

Even as I'm asking him, I think I already know the answer.

Ryker's not wrong. Aleks *didn't* try to fight back. I remember thinking that was so weird at the time, that he just stood there and let Ryker slice right through him. Since he wasn't in any danger of being killed—you can't kill what's dead unless Ryker went for his head—he had to know he'd recover eventually.

But would my opinion of the alpha wolf who attacked my friend?

Yeah.

I don't want to believe it. Ryker has every reason to be making this up. I'm sure he'd love it if Aleks turned out to be just another guy willing to manipulate me to get what he wants.

Maybe it isn't a shifter thing, but a male thing. Especially after the way he basically accused me of secretly liking Ryker's attention...

"No. You're trying to turn me against Aleks." It's the only thing that makes sense. "He was there for me when you weren't. I might not be in love with him, but I *do* love him. He's my friend. He wouldn't do that."

He *wouldn't*.

Ryker taps his fingers against the back of the bench. When I hear the *click-click-click*, I know his claws are out.

He's quiet for a moment, before he says, "Ask him about his fang."

What for? "I already know about the fang."

"Yeah?" It's a dare. I know it is. Still, when he says, "Tell me about it, then," I fall for it anyway.

"No one in Muncie knows I'm a shifter. Well, except for the first vamps that I ran into after you rejected me—"

"Gretchen. She told me all about you. She's not your biggest fan. Funny that she tried hitting on me when she hates you for being Pack, but I got her to tell me about your life here before I sent her on her way so I guess she has her uses."

I shouldn't be jealous at the casual way he mentions the leader of the Nightmare Trio. I should be pissed off that he grilled her about me, but I'm not. I'm jealous, and it seeps into my voice as I say drolly, "Oh? Is that what the two of you talked about over drinks?"

"Yes."

A simple answer.

Yes.

Okay, then. I wasn't expecting that.

Shaking my head, I tell him, "Well, Gretchen and two of her goons wanted to drain me because I was a shifter, and if it wasn't for Aleks coming along when he did, they might've. Don't know if you noticed, but shifters aren't very popular in Muncie. So, yeah. Aleks gave me his fang to show everyone else that I was under his protection. Plus, it has a charm in it that covers my scent so no one else knows what I am. They think I'm human, and I'm okay with that."

"You can't mean that."

"Why not? It's no different than pretending to be an omega," I toss back. "I had to do that for more than twenty-five years, Ryker. A year as a human? That's nothing."

"You're an alpha," he tells me. Like I forgot. "You should be proud of that."

I *am* proud. But I'm also not going to let the truth of my ranking be a death sentence or, even worse, a jail sentence in a loveless mating.

I tap the bulge beneath my shirt. "This fang protects me so that I can hide in plain sight. For the first time in my life, I *can* live like an alpha. I know I'm a shifter. That's all that counts. Let the other supes and humans think what they want. I don't give a shit. I'm finally free."

Ryker leans forward, clasping his hands, letting them swing in the gap left between his braced feet. Cocking his head slightly, his amber eyes shining on me like a pair of high breams, he says, "Because of that fang?"

"Yes."

"I asked you if you knew that he loved you. Did you also know that he's marked you?"

"Don't start—"

Ryker is suddenly so serious, there's not a single

sign remaining of that flirtatious male from before. He shifts in his seat, all focus on me—and not in the same way from before when he was appreciating my outfit.

"I'm not," he says, cutting me off. "If anything, I'm here to finish this. He marked you without telling you, sweetheart."

An accusation like that is rich coming from him.

"What about you? Pissing in front of Charlie's? Breaking into my apartment? Sleeping on my balcony? Claiming me in front of everyone I know in the city? What do you think you're doing?"

"I'm being an alpha," he says simply. "You know that. Just like you know, whether you want to admit it to yourself or not, that I'll never force you. I'll never use my rank to overrule you. It's your choice. I won't make it for you. But by giving you that fang, making every vamp you encounter believe you belong to him, he has. It's not a protection thing. He claimed you as his mate, and you *let* him."

No.

A mate gets to choose.

Fate has a say, sure, but in the end, *both* mates have to choose. That's where me and Ryker went wrong last time.

I chose him.

He chose Trish.

And here we are.

But Aleks...

"You don't know that."

"I don't? I'm sure he's told you that I met with Zakharov. The Alpha of these parasites. I told him you were my mate, that I'm here to convince you. I could already sense that other bloodsucker using his fang to mark you—"

"How?"

"How what?"

"How can you sense it? It's only supposed to work against other vamps." Because sudden nerves have my heart racing, I cover it up with a purposeful sneer. "Something you're not telling me, Ryker? You part vamp?"

"You'd like that, sweetheart, but nope. I'm pure alpha and..." His voice comes to a sudden close as he sees something in my sneer that I couldn't hide. "And, *shit*. You really don't know, do you? Gemma... your scent."

"What about my scent?"

I hate that he can pull back any hint of emotion, closing off like that as if he has some kind of internal switch. He did that that night in his cabin, and he's doing it now.

At least he actually deigns to answer me this time.

"It's not that you don't smell like you. I think that's what you've been told, that that fang covers up your scent. And it does, to a degree. But, more than that, it's how much you smell like *him*."

I'm suddenly reminded of Saturday, when Ryker appeared in the bar, flaring his nostrils and staring at me in disbelief. I thought it was because he couldn't pick up my scent. But if I wore Aleks's scent instead... well, no wonder his first reaction had been to attack.

Mates wear each other's scents so innately that it lingers. That's all. I *know* that, and still I try to argue with him because I *have* to.

"Of course it does. I live with him."

Ryker's not buying what I'm trying so desperately to sell him. "Don't play stupid, sweetheart. It doesn't suit you. You know as well as I do what I mean. His bloody scent clings to you the way that mine will once we're fully bonded and it's that fucking fang's fault."

He has to be wrong. "No."

"Don't believe me, but you know I'm telling the truth. The head parasite told me what the fang really means, so maybe you'd rather take his word for it instead. Filan's keeping you from me because he wants you for himself. And, by wearing that fang, you're agreeing to it. You're his fucking intended, Gemma, when you're already *mine*."

"No, I'm not." It's a knee-jerk reaction. I can't help it. "Not yours. Definitely not Aleks's. It's just a necklace, Ryker."

"Yeah? And who told you that? You have a sit-down with Zakharov, too?"

Me and Roman? Of course not. I've actually never

met the leader of the Cadre. It was always Aleks who stood between us—

"Aleks. Aleks told me."

Ryker gives me another disbelieving look. "Oh. Right. I'm sorry. I forgot that the vamp who's actively trying to steal you away from me might be a trustworthy source. Of course he wouldn't lie to you."

He doesn't lie to me.

I almost snap the denial right back in Ryker's face. I'd know. If Aleks was lying, I'd *know*. But, in the back of my mind, I think of how easily he avoids committing to anything that isn't the exact truth.

He told me what the fang stood for. That doesn't mean that he mentioned every last detail.

And... I should've figured that out long before now.

I think of Hailey's jealousy whenever she's reminded that I have Aleks's fang hanging off of my golden necklace. And then there's how Vincent and some of my other vamp regulars always regarded me as Aleks's courtesy of the necklace I wore. It makes sense, doesn't it?

The reality of my situation doesn't keep me from arguing back anyway. Because if I don't? Then I have to admit that he's right, that Aleks has been lying to me this whole last year, and, yeah. There's no going back from that.

"You don't know Aleks. He's a good guy. He's been here for me this last year when you haven't."

Ryker grits his teeth, the same vein from Saturday bulging.

How ya doin', Duke? Good to see you again.

Oh, wait. No, it isn't.

"Yeah? Do me a favor, sweetheart. Why don't you ask him about that? Your precious fucking blood-sucker. Ask him why he took care of you and I couldn't."

"Ryker. You're being ridiculous."

"I'm not. And this isn't over, either. Push all you want, but I'm not going anywhere. So, when you're willing to talk to me... willing to listen, take that chain off. Throw it away. See what happens. I'll be waiting for you."

What is *that* supposed to mean? I've taken the fang necklace off more times than I can count. Usually because I snap the chain and it falls off, but still.

Then again, if I'm not wearing the necklace, I'm drinking the tea. And, as much as I tried to ignore it, it's only when I forgot to drink the chamomile tea on Thursday, then the necklace broke on Friday, that Ryker was finally able to track me down.

But... no. It can't be.

Aleks has spent the last year keeping me safe from the vamps in his Fang City. He hasn't been purposely hiding me from my fated mate, has he?

Has he?

Oh, Luna.

No.

THOUGH THE STUBBORN SIDE OF ME WANTS TO PRETEND that none of what Ryker said has gotten to me, I can't. It's impossible. Too much of what he said makes sense for me to act like it doesn't, and now that he's riled up my wolf, there's only one thing for me to do.

So, abandoning him on the bench, I take off for the apartment. I have to work hard to fight my urge to shift, though I do break out into a jog that quickly becomes a sprint before I'm bolting toward the back side of our apartment building.

I'm in no mood to take the elevator, and I head for the fire escape. If Aleks is still home, he'll sense me heading back, his fucking fang a beacon that I took for granted for way too long.

But not any longer.

I don't even try to offer an explanation for the way I come flying in here. I just shove open the balcony door, gaze zeroing in on Aleks. Just like the other night, he's sitting in the living room, reading his paperback. I absently notice that he's nearing the end of it before I put the damn book out of my head.

A moment later, he does the same. After finishing his page, Aleks puts his book to the side before glancing up at me. "Gem? Is everything okay?"

No, Aleksander. It is *not*.

His nostrils flare just enough to be noticeable. Of course. His sense of smell is as strong as mine, but he'll never admit that he relies on it the same way that us shifters do.

Oh, no. He's too *civilized* for that.

"You were with the wolf," he remarks.

I don't deny it. "Yeah. He wanted to talk to me. And, now, I want to talk to you."

"Of course." He waits a moment. "Is this about last night? Because I thought—"

"It's not," I say, interrupting him. "It's about the fang you gave me."

"Oh."

Oh.

I don't like that. He sounds resigned, like he's been expecting me to bring it up sooner or later.

"I know what you told me it means. I know what you told me it does. But, and forgive me if I'm wrong... but I just listened to Ryker try to convince me that there's more to it that you've never said."

"And you believe him?"

"I don't want to. That's why I'm here. I need to hear it from you. Your fang... tell me it doesn't mean what Ryker says it does. Tell me that I haven't been walking around all of Muncie wearing a fang that marks me as Aleksander Filan's mate."

"Gem. You have to understand—"

I don't have to understand shit. I just need an answer.

"It's a simple question. Tell me. I have to know, alright?"

Aleks removes his reading glasses before pinching the bridge of his nose. A soft sigh, followed by an even softer, "It's a vampire tradition. You wouldn't understand, would you?"

At my angry curse, he lifts his head, meeting my stare. "You needed time to see that I was the better choice. I told you, I'll wait for you. I... I've just been waiting longer than you thought."

"Oh, *come* on."

I dig beneath my shirt, grabbing the fang between two trembling fingers. Ryker was right. That sucks almost as much as how blind I was to Aleks's intentions.

I show him the fang. "Let me get this straight. When you gave this to me, you already planned on making me your mate?"

"Gem, we don't have to do this now. I don't know what that wolf told you, but you can trust me. I only want what's best for you."

Trust him? I did. For a year, I did.

"You want me to still trust you? Then answer me. Have you always thought of me as your mate? Yes or no." When he refuses to respond, I let my wolf rise to the surface. It echoes in my voice as I say, "If you don't answer me, I'm leaving. I'm not going to Accalia," I add, because I know that's exactly what he's thinking, "but I won't stay here if I can't trust you."

"No matter the answer?"

I nod.

Aleks says something under his breath in Polish, then he straightens his shoulders. "Then, yes. I've thought of you as mine since you first drove past the perimeter of my city."

His admission seems to hit me like a truck. I actually stumble, though maybe that's just because I need to put some space between us.

"But... that was May. You didn't tell me until fucking *September* that you thought you might have feelings for me that were more than friendship."

"I had to," he insists. "If I told you in May, you never would've stayed with me. You never would've accepted my fang."

Would I have?

"You're right. I wouldn't have."

The weight of his fang hanging off my neck is absolutely unbearable. I'm not so ticked off that I snap the chain, but I do reach behind my neck and unclasp it.

"Gem, please—"

Nope. Not listening.

I shove my hand at him. The chain hangs off my pointer finger. "Take it back."

His jaw goes so tight, I can see a muscle ticking there. "I won't. It's yours."

Luna, does he have to be so *stubborn*? I'm the wronged one here, and he's looking at me like I'm ripping the heart out of his damn chest.

He's getting off lucky. With Ryker, I almost did —*literally*. At least, in Aleks's case, the threat's only a figurative one.

"Fine." I slam the necklace down on the coffee table, biting back another curse when I hit it too hard and the glass in the center cracks upon impact before spidering. "Leave it there. The table, too. I'll fix it when I come back."

"You are coming back, aren't you?"

I said I would. No matter Aleks's answer, I said I wouldn't leave. At least, not for good.

"Eventually."

He rises up from the couch. "Where are you going?"

I throw up my hands. "I don't fucking know, alright? But right now? I want to be anywhere that you're *not*."

CHAPTER 11

Well, Ryker. You said to take off the necklace and see what happens, I think to myself as I jump down from the last step on the fire escape. So what now?

Honestly, I didn't expect anything to come of it except for missing the reassuring weight of Aleks's fang against my chest. But, right when I'm about to scoff and maybe take a trip to Charlie's even though tonight's my regularly scheduled day off, something happens.

My hands flex, claws shooting out. I feel my canines lengthen, the muscles in my forearms, my calves, my thighs bulging for a moment until I can force back the partial shift. My wolf wants out. Not only that, but she wants to chase.

To follow.

To run.

Where? I'm not so sure, and that denial lasts for maybe five seconds before I realize she wants me to find Ryker.

And, holy shit, if I give her control, she can. She's caught his scent, and she can follow the imaginary thread that ties us together. For the first time in almost a year, our bond is pulsing, Ryker calling me to him.

You know what? I've spent so long denying the call of the wolf that I just don't want to anymore. Ryker wants me to come to him? He might not like the alpha who answers his call, but okay.

Let's go, girl.

Somehow, I'm not surprised when my wolf brings me back to the park where I left Ryker. Even though my whole world seems to have shifted since I turned away from him, it's probably only been about twenty minutes since I was sitting on the bench that I just passed.

He's not sitting there anymore, but he didn't go too far from where I left him. Instead of resting against the bench, he's sitting on a patch of grass with his legs stretched in front of him, ankles crossed, hands perched behind him. His head is hanging back a little as he watches the sky.

"Full moon's coming," he tells me.

Thanks, Ryker. As if I need the reminder.

I follow his stare. He doesn't say hi, I notice. Doesn't rub it in that I've come back to him, especially since I really wasn't gone for long at all. Still, even though I'm looking up at the blue sky—no sign of the moon, but I know instinctively where she'll be later tonight—I can see him out of the corner of my eye. He looks over his shoulder, his gaze dipping to my chest. As much as I'd like to think he's checking out my boobs, I know better.

He's looking for Aleks's necklace, humming to himself when he can tell that I left it behind.

I stiffen. Okay. Now he's going to say something. He's not going to let that slip by him without making some kind of comment, right?

Wrong.

I brace myself when he opens his mouth, absolutely stunned when all he says is, "You want to go for a run with me? My wolf's getting antsy with the full moon coming soon."

It's a shifter thing. We have so much excess energy that one of the best ways to burn it off is with physical activity. Fighting, fucking... running. I guess I should be happy he picks that over the others. But the way he asks? It's so casual. No dares. No challenges. Just a simple offer.

And I want to say yes more than I probably should.

"What, now?"

"Tonight. Tomorrow." Another gaze skyward. "There's time."

Not much, but there is some time.

"Maybe later," I tell him.

He looks back at me again. He can tell from something in my expression that, while he's happy not to mention our earlier discussion, I'm obviously not willing to just drop it. I should. Rehashing it is only going to be a strain on me, but that doesn't stop me. He had some kind of point to prove, telling me about the meaning behind Aleks's fang. Well, he made it.

Let's see what happens now.

His eyes dip to my chest again. "I take it you believe me now."

"You kinda left me with no choice there, Ryker."

He shrugs, then slowly climbs to his feet. His movements are still careful, as if he's trying not to trigger me into bolting or something—or like he's gone back to treating me like an omega. "Hey. All's fair in love and war."

"Yeah?" I snap. I have this irrational urge to prove to him that I'm as much of an alpha as he is. It's the damn challenge, I know it is, but I fall for it every fucking time. "Which one is this?"

He smiles, but he doesn't answer me. At least, not with words.

Instead, he reaches for the hem of his shirt. His intent is obvious. He's totally about to take his shirt off.

And, yet, I still find myself demanding, "What are you doing?"

"Showing you something. You stopped me last

time, so I picked a shirt without buttons this time. That way I can do this"—he pulls the tight black tee over his head before I can squeak out a protest— "before you get the chance to stop me again."

Swallowing that almost-squeak, I turn it into a scowl. "You'll take any excuse to start stripping in front of me."

His eyes seem to spark beneath the sunlight. "Any fucking excuse. But I think I've got a good one," he says, tapping his chest.

What the...

At first, I'm not sure what I'm supposed to be looking at. His chest is so sculpted, it looks like it belongs in a museum as the work of one of the masters. Though he's an alpha, he's completely hairless. His arms have black hair like his fur, but his chest is completely bare.

Well, except for—

No.

No, no, no.

Maybe.

I blink.

Now, shifters heal almost as quickly as vampires. While Aleks had to replenish with six bags of Charlie's blood after his fight with Ryker, if he'd actually fought back, Ryker would've just needed a little time to recover. We have great regenerative properties. Someone can stab me, and unless it's with a silver blade, I'll be one hundred percent by morning. I won't have a single mark, single scratch, single scar on me.

It should be the same for Ryker—but it isn't. Or, at least, one time it *wasn't*.

Because that's what I'm looking at. That's what's there.

A scar where there really, really shouldn't be one.

Forming a circle around his left nipple, I see five perfectly spaced, perfectly even scars that would indicate where his heart is. And unless he goes around pissing female shifters off on purpose so that they'll threaten to tear the heart right out of his chest, I know exactly how he got those marks.

I know when. I know who.

And I know that those marks should've been healed a year ago.

"What... where did you get those?"

"Don't you remember, sweetheart?"

Oh, I remember all right.

"Why are they still there?"

"You gave them to me. I kept them."

The only way to preserve a scar like that is on purpose. It's a weird male thing, usually. When they want to show off some wound, like say from a particularly fierce fight they got into, a special blend of silver and some other herbs slapped into the mark will create a reminder. They call it a shifter tattoo, and most females go crazy over those types of markings, no matter how crude they are.

But this one isn't crude. In fact, it almost looks like—

No. He wouldn't have. No way.

It's impossible.

Isn't it?

I goggle up at him. I won't know unless I ask him. "But *why*?"

His smile widens. I'm not so sure why, since I feel like I've just had the earth pulled out from under me for the second time today. He's smiling. I'm probably staring at him in ill-disguised horror.

He taps his chest again. "When you figure out the answer to that, then you'll know exactly why I'm not going anywhere until you say yes."

———

I DON'T GO BACK TO THE APARTMENT AFTER I LEAVE Ryker in the park the second time. I tell myself it's because I'm not ready to see Aleks again, but that's the thing when it comes to being a wolfish lie detector: I'm not so great at lying to myself, either.

I don't go to Charlie's, mainly because I know for sure that that would be the first place that Aleks would go to look for me. Since I'm off tonight, I didn't bother taking my phone with me earlier. I left it on my charger, and I'm glad since it means that without it—and without Aleks's fang—I'm basically off the grid.

Only basically, though, because if I can feel my way back to Ryker, it has to be the same for him. He can follow me all of the way across Muncie, especially since Aleks's fang is back at the apartment. When he doesn't, I try generously to think that he's respecting my obvious need to be alone.

And then I pull my head out of my ass and realize that this is just the next part of his obvious challenge.

I'm an alpha. Staying away from him is a coward's move, and we both know it.

I'd like to believe that I would've held out. Call it being determined instead of weak, I could've spent the evening walking around town, daring any vamp with a death wish to confront me now that I'm not wearing Aleks's fang any longer. A dirty fight would help take the edge off the clawing need I'm feeling.

Fighting or fucking, it's the wolf's way.

The approach of the full moon's not usually *this* rough for me; Ryker's casual reminder that she's coming is making it worse. I don't even have to hear my wolf's constant, keening whine for its mate to know exactly why I'm struggling. No matter which way I walk, she keeps trying to re-orientate me so that I'm following that same invisible tether from before.

And maybe I know what's going to happen if I do, but I finally give in.

I almost expect it when she leads me right back to the park.

In Muncie's urban setting, Ryker's wolf is drawn to the only spot of greenery. And maybe if I hadn't been wearing Aleks's fang the whole last year, mine would've been, too.

I thought it was the chamomile that made me relax, that helped me get attuned to the city. Could've been.

Doubt it.

What I don't expect, though, is that I actually find his wolf. This isn't the first time I've seen Ryker in his shifted form, but I take a few moments to appreciate it all the same. Alphas are just built differently than most wolves. He's big—that's the shifter size—but his legs are powerful, his muzzle pointed, his amber eyes intelligent.

As he swings his snout my way, I don't just see a knowing look. I see *relief*.

It's my turn to smile at him.

"I thought I'd take you up on that run," I tell Ryker.

He cocks his head. Shifters don't speak when they're in their beast forms, but I can tell from that simple gesture that he's asking me if I'm sure. Because, at that moment, I think we both understand that, if I join him for a run, if I strip down to my fur before shifting back to skin, that with the full moon so close... what happens next will be inevitable.

And it is.

We're wolves.

We fight. And we fuck.

And even if I'm never his mate, I'm willing to give that up for just one moment in time with Ryker.

"Yes," I whisper. "I'm sure."

I'm not accepting him as my mate, but I'm accepting him if only for tonight.

WE RUN. AND WE RUN. ON SOME LEVEL, WE'RE JUST free to be our wolves, eating up the ground, running together while also racing each other. Sometimes Ryker's in the lead, sometimes I am, but we never get out of sight of one another.

It doesn't take long for him to realize that he can't catch me unless I *want* to be caught.

We also don't forget that we're in a Fang City. As if our wolves are leading us somewhere safe, somewhere private, they take the lead, pushing us through the park, down empty side streets, and past some quiet residential roads. I almost expect to be guided toward the mountain, but as much as my wolf just wants to be with her mate, she's still a part of me. And going back to Accalia? No. No way.

So we don't. Ryker bumps into my side, trying to steer me one way, but I snap at his ear before choosing a different path. With the moon closing in on us, shining her light on my pale fur and his midnight-colored scruff, my nose is more powerful than ever. Over the fuel and the exhaust, the garbage, the humans, the vamps... over all of it, I catch a hint of mud and water and trees and tear off in that direction.

Ryker races right behind me. When he pours on a burst of speed, overtaking me, I guess that his wolf has finally picked up on the same scents.

Forest.

Earth.

Trees.

It's a wooded area, more densely packed than the park where Ryker spent the afternoon and early evening, and on the outskirts of Muncie. If we hope for any type of privacy—and, with my wolf riding me to just do this already, getting some privacy isn't really a dealbreaker for me right now—this is the best spot that we could've chosen.

I'm a shifter. Even before I realized that Ryker was mine, I always knew that I'd have a mate one day. Whether they were a supe or a human, I didn't care, but if they wanted to, they had to tangle with an alpha female.

So renting a hotel and having some sweet guy deflower me on top of a soft queen-sized bed? Yeah, right. Even the idea of a fumbling, grasping, underwhelming one-night stand in my room at the apartment would never be quite right.

Wearing only the moonlight with the grass at my back and dirt in my claws?

Sign me up.

Once we cross into the woods, it becomes real. My heart is pounding almost as loudly as my pads hitting the packed dirt between patches of wild grass, but I'm determined. It's another alpha quirk, I guess. Once I make up my mind, nothing can change it.

Except, it seems, a stubborn alpha who swore he'd get me to say yes.

I try not to think about that as my wolf stops short. If she thinks this is the right place to entice her mate to fuck, I'm going to go with her because hell if I know what I'm supposed to do on my own. She's taken me this far, my wolf and my instincts, and if Ryker rejects me here and now after everything he's said and done these last few days, I might just rip his heart out for real this time.

Ryker has continued to run, but his wolf throws on the brakes when he senses that I'm no longer behind him. By the time he wheels around and backtracks his way to me, I've already shifted, trading my fur for skin.

His wolf gets one look at my naked human body and lets out a howl.

Is that a good howl? I fucking hope so.

I'm shivering. My skin is so hot, it feels like I have a

fever, so I know that the chill from the woods has nothing to do with the minute quakes. No, that has everything to do with how an apex predator is looking at me like I'm Sunday lunch.

Maybe this was a bad idea. Maybe I'm being too forward. I'm an alpha, so naturally I would take the lead, but Ryker's an alpha, too. Maybe that's why he chose Trish. She wouldn't just throw herself at him naked like this, would she?

Well, no. Remembering the rumors I've heard about Trish Danvers, she basically did, so maybe this is one way to seduce Ryker Wolfson.

Luna, help me—

Before I can shift back to my fur and run away like my tail's on fire, Ryker shifts back to his two-legged shape.

For the first time, I get a good look at him in his skin. I've seen his chest and, as mouth-watering as it is, it's nothing compared to the rest of him. I always thought he was a big guy in his clothes, but now I see that I was right. He's built huge everywhere.

And I mean *everywhere.*

I look at the club jutting out from between his legs and start to have second thoughts. *That* thing is supposed to fit inside of *me*? You've got to be fucking kidding. I'm not even so much worried about the length as I am about its girth.

It's *massive.*

He's already hard, so even if I can pretend like this wasn't on both of our minds, that erases any doubt that he didn't understand my wolf's not-so-subtle signals. But he doesn't reach for me. Instead, he stays back, his eyes locked on my face.

How nice. I stare at his dick, and he's gracious enough to keep his eyes up here. The one time I want a packmate to see me naked and actually *see* and he couldn't care less.

And then, as if he's hit his limit of being a respectful kind of guy, he turns on his high beams and scans me hungrily, eyes taking in every inch of my naked body. Like he's memorizing it.

"Fucking *gorgeous*," he whispers reverentially. "I knew it."

That makes me feel a little bit better about myself. "You like it?"

"I *love* it."

I turn around, showing off my ass. Just in case, I give it a little wiggle. It just feels right. "How about this?"

Peering over my shoulder, I watch as Ryker lifts his hand, wiping at the corner of his mouth.

Holy *shit*. Is he drooling?

I... I think he might be drooling.

His voice comes out like a croak. "Even better. But you know what I'm dying to see?"

I lift my eyebrow, hoping my expression makes me

look like the fucking seductress I feel like. "What's that?"

He swallows the lump in his throat. His big paw reaches down, giving his erection a slow, easy stroke, almost as if he's afraid that he'll go off if he adds any more pressure than that.

"Knees," he rasps out. "On your knees."

I expected that. While shifters mate in as many positions as humans do—double, actually, since some of the more kinky wolves will mate as their beasts— going at it with the female on her knees, her male taking her from behind... well, it's a classic for a reason.

On my knees. It's not an alpha command, though it easily could've been, but that's not Ryker's style, I'm discovering. He wants me to choose.

Thing is, I don't think I've had a say in the matter since I was fifteen.

Just once, I promise myself. Just to get it out of my system.

I drop down on all fours, turning slightly so that he can't help but focus on my full moon instead of the Luna shining down on us.

"Like this?" When Ryker makes a strangled noise in the back of his throat, I laugh. "I'll take that as your yes. Come on. Come over here."

He doesn't move. I can tell it's taking everything Ryker has to keep his distance, but he's doing it for me.

Because it's my choice—and because, one way or another, there's no going back after this.

There's no taking it back, either.

"And you're sure? You're really sure?"

"Don't I look sure? I'm on my fucking knees for you, Ryker."

"Yes." Another croaking sound. "You damn well are."

The unsaid *but why* hangs between us.

It hits me then why *he's* so unsure. And, I guess, it's my fault. If I believe him—and I don't want to, but I'm starting to—then he's spent a year looking for me. A year wanting to take me as his mate. Whatever his reasons for it, there's no denying it.

And then all I've done since he's found me is tell him that there's no chance he can have me.

But I'm not offering to be his bonded mate. If only just this once, I want to feel him inside of me. I'm not even all that apprehensive about his size. Shifter males are usually hulking beasts compared to their more delicate counterparts. It's how we're made. If my five-foot mom can mate my six-five dad, then I can take Ryker.

Probably.

Hopefully.

Claws crossed.

CHAPTER 12

He's still hesitating more than I thought he would and I realize that, if I really want to do this, I have to find some way to convince my alpha that I actually *do*.

Deep down, I think *he* still thinks of me as an omega. I don't know how many virgins he's deflowered in his time—and good going, Gem, because that's exactly what I want to think about while I'm naked in the woods with an equally naked Ryker—but with a dick that impressive, I wouldn't be surprised if he was worried about hurting me.

I'm an alpha, too. So, yeah. I can totally take it. It's biology, right?

Fighting and fucking. Maybe if I want to get to do one, I have to do the other first.

He has no clue what I'm about to do. Good. That works in my favor. Before he can stop me, I dash around him, jumping on his back. My canines are extended and, with a rumbling growl, I go for his throat.

I wasn't going to bite him. At least, not *hard*. Just a nibble, if anything.

Ryker's reflexes are amazing. When my canines are barely an inch away from his carotid, he flips me onto my back. He doesn't slam me into the dirt, though. He uses his arms to cradle me, shifting me at the last moment so that I'm back on the grass, belly down, perched on my hands and knees as he hovers over me.

He's panting.

I'm panting.

And then it happens. He takes a deep breath, his body forming a sudden cage around mine as the musk from my wet pussy knocks him past the last of his insecurity.

"Yes, Ryker," I say, rising up on all fours again. "*Yes*."

He moves. I want to demand to know where he thinks he's going, but before I do, I feel the tip of his claw softly tracing the line of my spine. I arch my back, swallowing my moan.

Ryker moves again. He must've retracted his claws because he uses his fingertips to knead my ass cheek with a little more force. I squeal, and I know he's lowered his head closer to me when I suddenly feel his breath on my bare ass. He breathes in deep again, letting out a soft groan.

"Just remember," he rumbles. "You did say yes."

"Just... just this once."

"If once is all I get, I'm going to make it count. You had your chance to get away, sweetheart. Now you're *mine*."

He's right. I am.

At least, for now.

Luna, I can't fucking *wait*.

I brace myself, sticking my ass as high as I can while I rest on my forearms. My instincts tell me to stay loose, to stay ready. I can feel my pussy dripping, so I know that my body's doing everything it can to prepare me for—

I squeal again. "Ryker!"

"Mm. Yes?"

I try to squirm away from him but he's holding my hips tightly, I can't get away. Not that I want to. Whatever just happened felt *amazing*, but it definitely wasn't what I was expecting.

"What was that?"

"Oh, sweetheart. You didn't think I was just going to stick my cock in you without any foreplay, did you?"

Kinda. Yeah.

"If that's not your dick, what was that pressing against me?"

From the way his laugh sends shockwaves straight to my clit, I have a pretty good idea. Hey. I might be a virgin, but I'm a twenty-six-year-old shifter with needs.

Between my vibe and my computer, I know the mechanics.

I just had no idea what *that* would feel like that.

I push back. He wants to lick my pussy from behind? Okay, Ryker. I'm not going to stop you.

And I don't. Even when he dives back in, using his tongue to lick my slit before inserting the tip of his tongue inside of me, fucking me with that magical thing as he goes back to clutching my ass with his claws, I let him do whatever the hell he wants to me. He knows what he's doing, and I know I don't have anything to compare him to, but *fucking* Luna.

If this is mating, I should've agreed to this ages ago.

I also finally understand why Ryker was so turned on when I stuck my claws in him last year. The way he uses their points to anchor me to him has me going wild. A little pain mixed with a whole lot of pleasure. It kicks me into overdrive, my legs starting to shake as my orgasm begins to build.

I'm used to gentle O's. A little pressure, a pop, and some relief. Nothing much, just a little something to take the edge off whenever the need gets to be too much. But what I feel building in my loins right now? It promises to be bigger than anything I've ever experienced before.

And I'm eagerly looking forward to it.

Just when I'm on the cusp of coming, I dig my claws

into the dirt, rubbing my pussy all over his face as I moan out his name.

I might've moaned something else. I... I'm not so sure. If I did? It was probably due to the heat of the moment, and my mindless wolf willing to say just about anything to reach that elusive orgasm she's been chasing.

He heard me, though. I'm almost positive. Either that or he can, I don't know, *taste* that I'm so close. Mindless is a good word for what I am. As I arch my back, desperate for something to fill me, Ryker moves. He pulls his tongue away from my sensitized skin, ignoring my poor clit.

I snarl at him, more wolf than woman, and the last thing I hear is Ryker's satisfied grunt before he replaces his tongue with something hard and long and so deliciously thick.

I realize in an instant what he's done. He's used his tongue to get me ready for him. I'm so hot—so *wet*—that he slides his monster dick in a few inches before I even know what he's planning.

"You okay, sweetheart?" he grunts.

I arch my back again, wordlessly begging him to feed me a few more inches. I can tell that he's only partway in, so why the hell is he stopping. "I'll be better," I pant, "when you start to move. I can take it."

"Yeah?" Another push. "How's that?"

I scoff. "Aren't you an alpha?" I dare. "Prove it. Take me."

Wish granted.

Ryker slams the rest of the way home. I felt a pinch, like something's torn inside of me, but as I said before, it's a little bit of pain and a whole lot of pleasure.

A *whole* lot of pleasure.

Hours later, he cradles me, laying with me on the tufts of grass below us.

We're still in our skin. Completely naked, my hand settles on his pec. I don't mean to find the marks I left on his chest, but like a moth drawn to a flame, my fingertips keep returning to the same place. I can feel his burning flesh, his hardened nipple brushing against the meat of my palm, my blunt fingers tracing the five scars. They're visible, but not raised, so it amazes me that I instinctively know where they are.

Our scents—pine and cinnamon and raw sex—lingers in the air. Now that I'm coming down from the last round of rutting, I feel the cool breeze of the midnight sky blowing against my overheated skin and think that maybe I should go searching for our clothes.

Then I remember that I didn't strip, I shifted, and even if I wanted to leave Ryker's embrace to go searching for my clothes, they're in no shape to be worn.

Oops.

We can't stay out here much longer. It's a miracle that no one's ventured out into the wooded area, looking for the animals making all of that racket. Though we ran pretty far, I'm sure we're still in Muncie, so even if the humans would believe the howls belonged to a pair of mating wolves, the vamps on patrol will know better.

And since the only two shifters in all of Muncie are me and Ryker, no way they won't figure out what just passed between us.

I can't really figure it and I was the one being mated.

While I'm using Ryker's chest as a pillow, he's lazily stroking his hand up and down my bare back. I can hear his heart beating like a drum in there, my pillow rising and falling, rising and falling as he draws in breath after breath.

I smile into his skin.

Yeah. I did that to him. I brought the big, bad wolf to his fucking knees behind me. First as he ate my pussy, then as he took my virginity.

And then, because I'd been dying to know what it was like for longer than I care to admit, I sank to my knees in front of *him* before returning to all fours and letting him fuck me a second time.

Then a third.

No wonder he's out of breath. The first time was a shock. The second time an experience. The third time a fucking a *revelation*.

And it's not even the full moon yet. If we ever do that when the moon's at her height... there's a reason why, during the full moon, mated pack members turn in early. It's for the same reason why my battery-powered boyfriend gets a workout and I try to ignore my need by shoving my face full of ice cream. Sex and fighting. It's the shifter way.

For once, I glad I'm not fighting Ryker. What just happened... it was perfect.

As he presses a quick kiss against the top of my head, I'm sure he feels the same way.

On a shaky exhale, he says, "Wow."

"Got that right, big guy."

"I just..." His voice is husky, a little raw from the shout he let out the last time he came, but I can still hear the wonder in it as he tries to get his words out. "I didn't know it could be like that."

With a laugh I don't mean, I tease, "I bet you say that to all the girls."

Beneath me, Ryker goes still. "What girls?"

I fist my hand. Suddenly, petting his chest isn't as appealing as it was a few seconds ago.

He's not really pulling this stunt right now, is he? I might've lost my head and let my wolf take charge. I might've forgotten just how much it hurt to be rejected by this male. But to act like I didn't know about him and Trish? I can't control who he was with before me, or who he'll be with next, but it's insulting for him to do this with his scent still on me.

I pull myself into a sitting position, gazing down at him. The fact that he looks confused just makes it worse.

"Come on, Ryker. You don't have to pretend."

"Pretend? What do you mean, pretend?"

When his heavy-lidded eyes drop to my bare tits, I cross my hands over them, hiding them from his view. I can see that his dick is already stirring, going hard again, and if my hussy of a wolf has her way, I'll climb right on top of it again and forget what he just said.

"You already got me to agree to fuck you. You don't have to try so hard anymore. Hell, if you're ready for another round, just let me know. But don't act like I'm the best you ever had just because I'm still here and you're still horny."

He blinks that lazy, sated look away. His lush lips tug down into an obvious frown. "Is that what you think happened?"

"No. It's what I *know* happened. Why? What do *you* think happened?"

"Me? I finally got to claim my mate."

Oh, *hell* no.

So he has the marks.

So I slept with him.

That doesn't mean anything until we *both* agree. And, newsflash, I don't.

"I'm not your mate. We just fucked, Ryker. That's all. Just some sex between two consenting wolves. Don't turn it into something it's not."

Because when he rejects me again or, worse, just uses me as a way to increase his own status, it'll *kill* me.

All I wanted was this one memory to hold onto. This one time with Ryker that I can save for myself.

Too bad he won't even let me have that.

"We mated." The confusion flees, replaced by pure, unadulterated determination. "We're mates. No fucking involved."

Still covering my chest with one hand, I use the other to pat his shoulder. "Call it what you want, but you're right. It wasn't even that. We rutted. Plain and simple. You put your dick inside of me and it felt good—"

"It felt amazing."

"Whatever. But that's all it was. Lust. Hormones. Need. To be my mate, there's gotta be love."

And, though I'm pretty sure I murmured *I love you, I love you, I love you* more times than I can count while he was pounding away inside of me, the most I heard from Ryker was my name, his grunts, and a repeated refrain of *mine*.

But not once, I'm realizing now, did he say *I love you* in return.

Why would he? To Ryker, a mate is an arrangement. Someone to have at his side, and someone to keep in his bed. Love doesn't figure, does it?

I'm not regretting a damn thing we just did. I wanted him as much as he wanted me, and I did something about it. But I'd be an idiot to read anymore into it than that, and Ryker acting like he does is a Luna damned insult.

"Look. We got it out of our system." I give him a wry smile that has him scowling. "Congrats, Ryker. You said you'd get me in the end and you did. We had sex. Whoo!" I wave my free hand around. "But if you think that changes anything…"

"Oh, sweetheart. It changes *everything*."

Quick as a flash, he lunges for me. But if I thought I was aware of Ryker before this? Still revving from the orgasms he gave me, this male is a part of me. I know what he's going to do a split second before he does it. I dodge him easily, jumping to my feet and whirling around in time to see him crouching in front of me.

For just a heartbeat, my eyes dip down to his dick. That sucker is rock-hard, pointing right at me as Ryker growls softly, eyes tracking my every movement.

Damn it. I feel myself growing wet again, getting ready for him, my wolf scratching away at the inside of my chest, desperate to worship this male with everything she has.

But not me. Not when I've given Ryker everything I am, and it's still not enough for him.

"Stop it," I snap, holding my ground. "It's gone far enough. Get the hint. What just happened was sex, okay? Call it biology if you want, or blame it on the full moon. I don't care. But I'm not your mate. We both know that. You can have anyone, Ryker. Just because the Luna picked me for you, that doesn't mean we have to listen."

His eyes flash. "You think I'm going through all of this because the moon told me to? *I* chose. My *wolf* chose."

"Yeah. Trish."

"Fuck Trish," he snarls.

"No, thanks. But feel free to go to Accalia and do that again if you like."

His mouth falls open before he quickly rearranges his features into that same old emotionless mask. "You really believe that. It's not just your way of keeping me out. Of rejecting me instead. You really think that I picked her over you."

"I don't have to think anything. I was there." I gesture at the marks on his chest. "Remember?"

He slowly rises up from the crouch.

In an instant, I can see this scene playing out. He'll move toward me, I'll stubbornly stay where I am because an alpha will never back down, and then he'll do whatever he can to distract me. It's what he's always done when we get too close to the night I walked out on him. For all the talking he wants to do, he never once made it seem like he actually cares about me. About Gemma Swann. The woman, not the alpha.

Fuck him. Let him keep his secrets.

Ryker's body shifts, putting all of his weight on the balls of his feet. Just like I expected, he's preparing to leap at me.

Not if I can help it.

I drop my gaze. I fold my fingers, hiding my claws, then clasp my hands together. I shudder out a breath that, unless you know better, sounds suspiciously like a sob.

He just about stops breathing.

Gotcha.

I have a lifetime of experience playing the omega. Doesn't matter that Ryker *knows* that I'm an alpha. With the right posture, and just a hint of salty tears, I can play his damn wolf like it's a piano.

"Gemma, no. Don't cry. I—"

—never should've underestimated me.

My head flies up, hand already swinging as I throw all of my body weight into the punch. Luna *damn*, does he have a hard face. It's like pummeling rock, I swear, but I get three good hits in before he realizes that I've attacked.

My claws stay sheathed. I don't even realize it at first. I went after him with human fists instead of wolf claws because, whether I want to accept it or not, something changed between us after that first mating.

He doesn't swing back. I expected that. Omega or alpha, he'll never attack his mate. And, sure, maybe I took advantage of that, but what did *he* expect? I might've accepted him once, but not again.

I get him on his back, and the way his hands shoot up to my naked waist just tells me that I was right. I only won that fight because he let me, and because we're in the perfect position to mate again.

No. Not mate.

Fuck.

Not this time, Ryker.

He can tell. I don't even have to stop him. The animal might lose control during a rutting, but the human half knows better than to try. So, instead of lifting me up and pressing me against his length, knowing that our instincts will take over next, he gently sets me down on the grass.

"Your choice," he grounds out, chest heaving again, a trickle of blood coming from the corner of his mouth from where I hit him. "It's always been your choice."

And that's when I realize something.

I fucked him. I put his dick in my mouth, and he put my pussy in his. And, yet, our lips have never touched.

While I can still blame the impending full moon for being out of control, I drop to my knees and grab his face in my hands.

"Then I choose this," I murmur before bringing his mouth to mine.

I don't know if I did it wrong. Can you kiss wrong? I had the same thought when it came to mating about two seconds before Ryker pushed himself into me, and we managed to mate just fine. Maybe kissing's the same way. You just rely on a mixture of passion, desire, and instinct as you smash noses, clash teeth, and stroke each other's tongues.

At least, that's how it seems to me. I still want him, and he's not even questioning how easily I've returned to his embrace. Almost as if he knew I would.

No.

I pull away from him. Ryker follows me, nipping my bottom lip with his canines as he tries to initiate a second kiss, but I'm in control now. I still have his face in my hands and I maneuver it until my lips are next to his jaw.

"You were my first," I whisper in his ear. "My first love. My first heartbreak. My first fuck. And now? My first kiss. Pity the order was all wrong, huh?"

The corner of his mouth hasn't healed yet. The blood is still trickling its way to his stubble-covered jaw. Some of it's smeared from our wild kiss, but a small bubble wells up.

I dart out my tongue, swiping it across his skin, capturing the blood before savoring it.

He's just as delicious as I remember.

While he's too stunned to react, I shove him away from me and, before he can recover—or pull me close to him again—I go full wolf.

And if my girl could almost swear she heard his murmured, "Mine, too," chasing after me, it's better than the massive black wolf himself.

CHAPTER 13

Call me a fucking coward because, well, I am.

Because it's a choice between walking through Muncie naked or being a wolf, of course my wolf wins out. I take back alleys, trying to avoid getting spotted by any vamps or humans. I don't want to have to explain what a one-hundred-and-fifty-pound blonde wolf is doing stalking her way through the Fang City, especially since I smell more like Ryker than I do myself now.

The first few blocks, I throw looks over my shoulder, checking to see if Ryker's following me. I tell myself that it's a good thing that he isn't. He's giving me the choice, just like he's said for days that he would, and right now I choose to be alone.

Unfortunately, when my wolf scrabbles all the way up the fire escape, I realize that that isn't possible. Though I'd hoped that Roman put Aleks back on patrol and I'd be returning to an empty apartment, I can feel his powerful aura prickling at my fur even when I'm still a block away.

I've never really noticed how easily I was able to sense Aleks until the one time I don't want to see him. Isn't that just my luck?

Well. Walk of shame, here I come.

He's not in the living room. For all of about two seconds, I hope I was wrong. That I only picked up on the scent lingering from before he left.

And then I enter the hall, trying to make it to my room, and Aleks steps out of his.

One sniff. That's all it takes. One sniff and he knows where I've been and what I've done.

Who I've done.

"Oh, Gem."

I refuse to apologize. Mainly because I'm still a wolf, but also because I never let him think that I wanted him like this. And maybe Aleks was right the other night. Maybe some part of me did crave Ryker's attention, but I've had it now and, hopefully, I was right when I said that we got it out of our system.

Claws crossed again.

Still, just because I never promised him anything, that doesn't mean that I wanted to hurt Aleks. And he *is* hurt. I can see it on his face, taste it in the way his icy scent changes. Somehow, he goes even colder, which is such a contrast to the heat of an alpha shifter, it makes my wolf let out a soft whine.

Then, purposely looking away from him, I pad the rest of the way to my room. I push on the door, walking in as a wolf, before shifting back to my skin.

I stick my head out. I probably have grass in my hair, dirt on my skin, but I don't give a shit.

"If he comes here, don't let him in. I don't want to see him."

That's all I have to say. It doesn't matter that Aleks clearly knows that I've been with Ryker. It's my choice. Even my vampire roommate is always saying that.

And now I choose to pretend it never happened.

He nods, still frowning though I notice his eyes have bled over to red, almost as if he relishes the idea of standing between Ryker and me.

"Whatever you want, Gem."

I close the door and, putting my back against it, turn the lock.

It won't keep either supe out, but I feel better for it anyway.

It's a start.

———

My first thought is to hop in the shower. If it's not bad enough that I can still feel the ghost of Ryker's hand on my skin, the fact that his scent is embedded in every pore has me wondering if I overreacted. But then my wolf snaps at me, warning me against showering off her mate, and I don't have the strength to fight my other half.

Staying naked isn't working for me, though. With a sigh, I push off of the door and shuffle toward my dresser. I'm reaching for my underwear drawer when I notice Aleks's fang attached to the golden chain stretched out on the top of the dresser.

During my walk of shame before, I also noticed that he had repaired the splintered glass coffee table in the time since I left.

Peace offerings from my vamp roommate. That's got to be what they are.

Lovely.

I won't put that necklace back on yet, but I won't rebuff his attempts to repair our friendship. Maybe it won't be as easy as changing out the cracked glass in the coffee table, but it's another start. So, after I yank on some clean panties, I pull on a fresh pair of jeans and shove the necklace in my back pocket.

Since I don't plan on leaving my room anytime soon, I skip putting on a bra. Instead, I just grab the nearest shirt I can find, then reach for the phone I had left on the charger before I went searching for Ryker what seems like a lifetime ago now.

I've been putting off this call for too long. I probably would've called my mother on Friday when I noticed it was getting close to the full moon, but I hadn't, and since then I've been avoiding it. I saw I had a missed call from her yesterday, but I ignored it.

I can't keep on doing that.

If Mom doesn't hear from me before tomorrow night—before the full moon—then she'll have Paul send one of his enforcers into Muncie to find me, and that's the last thing I need.

It's the agreement we made when I told her that I left the Mountainside Pack. When I moved to Accalia, it was the first time in my life that we were apart, and she only let me go because Paul convinced her that me mating Ryker was a good thing. And while she understood why I had to leave after he rejected me, she couldn't accept that I wouldn't go back to the Lakeview Pack until I reminded her it would be the first place they looked.

Of course, then I had to tell her that I kind of, sort of let Ryker's pack council discover I was an alpha, and that put the end to her arguments. So long as I check in every month, she lets me live on my own. She's so worried that another wolf will force me to become their mate. The Luna Ceremony only takes place during the full moon, though. If I survive it, then I don't have to worry about her worrying about *me* until the next one.

So I call her every month like clockwork. The conversations aren't overly long. She tells me about my old pack, and I tell her about Aleks and the bar. We don't talk about me being a lone wolf. And Ryker? He's number one on the no-no list.

I insist. I know she keeps hoping I'll go back to Accalia, if only because having an Alpha for a mate is an added layer of protection, but after he rejected me? I couldn't. And when Mom saw how much it hurt me to confess that, she dropped it. If I ever wanted to mention my old intended mate, it would be up to me.

For a year, I refused to bring up Ryker—until now.

She's my mom. As soon as she answers, I feel tears well up in my eyes. I don't expect her to pat my head, fix my mistakes, or tell me that everything's going to be okay, but just hearing her voice makes me feel like it will anyway.

She can immediately tell that something's wrong.

"Gemma, baby. You don't sound like yourself. Is everything okay?"

That's all it takes. It's like holding back the wind. One hint of her concern and I'm spilling my guts out to her.

From the moment Ryker walked back into my life all the way until I confess what I just walked away from, I tell my mom everything.

She doesn't judge me. Honestly, she doesn't say much at all. She listens, which is what I need, and she offers soft, nonsense replies that make me feel so much better as I struggle to work through my emotions.

"—and he says that I'm his. And that's the thing, Mom. I was. I always thought I was. He's my fated mate, but what if I'm not his?" There. The dark, secret fear I've grappled with for too, too long. "He didn't choose me. How could he reject me like that if he's my fated mate?"

"Ah, baby. Haven't you figured it out by now?" My mom has never lost the hint of her midwestern drawl. Though we've lived on the East Coast ever since we left my birth pack out West—and I don't even think I have one—Mom's accent is the same as it's always been. I close my eyes as her words wash over me. It's home. "Fated mates are a wonderful thing, but they're not everything."

My eyes spring open again. "I know."

And I do. Mom's relationship with Paul is proof of that. Jack Walker is her fated mate, but that didn't stop him from taking his frustration out on her when she was forced to live with him. A powerful Alpha, my omega mother should've been able to temper his lusts, but the Wicked Wolf isn't just any alpha. He's a fucking sociopath, and it wasn't fair for anyone to think that my sweet, gentle mom could save him. When she was still trapped as his mate, she could barely save herself; the most she could do was avoid the Luna Ceremony every full moon.

Until I came along. And, omega or not, you don't mess with a female's pup. She put up with his cruelty for years but, the first time he picked me up by the scruff and threatened to drown me for snapping at him, my mom showed that even an omega wolf shifter can turn feral.

She saved me. She sacrificed so much, too, and if she could survive that, I can survive Ryker Wolfson.

But do I want to? That thought has been beating at my brain since I ran from him. Why am I putting up a fight? Sure, he rejected me once upon a time, but I'm fighting too hard against something that was put into motion more than eleven years ago.

And then I hear my mom sigh.

My wolf perks her ears up. "Mom? Everything alright on your end?"

"Your dad's here. He wants to tell you something. Is that okay? It's about Ryker."

Honestly, at this point, I'm not sure there's anything anyone could say about Ryker that would surprise me.

"Uh. Yeah. Sure."

"Hold on." There's some static as she hands him the phone before a deep voice booms, "Hey, Kitten."

I swallow a laugh. Only Paul Booker would think it's funny to call an alpha wolf shifter *kitten* as a nickname. "Hey, Dad."

"Sorry for overhearing, but you know how your mom is. She had you on speakerphone—"

From behind him, I can hear Mom explain how it bothers her wolf to keep the phone pressed to her ear. I get it. If I didn't live with another supe with crazy good hearing, I might do the same.

"It's okay. What's up? What did you want to say?"

"Janelle?" he says, calling for my mom. "Is it alright if I tell her?"

My heart aches a little to hear how he consults my mom with such respect in his voice. Paul might not have been Mom's fated mate, but she chose him and he chose her and for twenty-odd years they've been a perfect Alpha couple for the Lakeview Pack.

So even though I hear my mom click her tongue in annoyance before she agrees, I know she's only doing so because she can get away with it.

"Kitten?"

"Yeah?"

"Your mom says I'm good, but if you change your mind, just tell me to stop. Okay?"

I have no idea where this is going. "Okay."

"Now, you know how Ryker Wolfson sent for you to be his mate after his father's unfortunate accident? Yeah?"

Uh, *yeah*. How can I forget? I knew from the first moment I looked into Ryker's eyes and saw his wolf that he was my fated mate. But, because he was a future Alpha, I also knew that he wouldn't announce who his intended was until after they performed the Alpha Ceremony. The moon would whisper to him who his fated mate was, and he could either accept her as his intended or choose his own mate.

When my name was announced, he told Paul that he would take me as his mate because the moon said so. Of course, I was thrilled, and it wasn't until I arrived in Accalia that I found out about Trish Danvers. I know that there are some Alphas—my sperm donor being one—who keep their fated mates at their side while fucking whatever female they want; Jack's greedy nature and untamable lust was how Mom was able to avoid the Luna Ceremony for all of those years. I'd always hoped I'd have my bond finalized when Ryker claimed me during the Luna Ceremony, but if I had to share him with Trish, I could've dealt.

But then he rejected me for her outright, and even my sliver of hope of a happily-ever-after with Ryker disappeared in a heartbeat.

Why is Paul bringing this up now?

"Yeah. I know."

"There's something you don't know, though. Your mom and I agreed at the time there was no reason to tell you since you were so young and no one knew for sure when Ryker would take over as Alpha. It could've been decades from now if Henry Wolfson hadn't had his accident, and we didn't want you feeling trapped."

"Trapped?" I echo. I don't understand. "What are you saying?"

"I'm saying that Ryker asked me if he could take

you as his mate at the pack meet four years ago." Paul hesitates. "He said you were meant for him, and he'd wait if I wanted him to, but that he intended to have you. He considered you his intended even then, though he'd wait if I thought he should."

Four years ago... that's the pack meet where I ran with Ryker as wolves, and then I never saw him again until the day I arrived in Accalia when I was twenty-five, he was twenty-seven, and he acted like our mating was just another box he needed to check off since following his father as Alpha.

"What? He wanted me back then?" So what changed? And, more importantly, "How did he know that I was meant for him before the Alpha Ceremony told him so?"

"Well, Kitten. That's the rub of it all, ain't it? Maybe that's something you should ask Ryker."

My dad has a point.

I stew on that for the rest of the early morning and the whole next day before I wonder if I should do something about it.

Because Ryker? Unless Aleks figured out a way to lie to me, he never followed me home. He never tried to get to see me, and there's no sign that he even approached the apartment at all.

211

It's the first full turn of the moon I've gone without seeing him since he suddenly appeared in Muncie and it has my fur feeling like it's been rubbed the wrong way. I keep hoping that maybe he was avoiding Aleks —I know, right—and that maybe he'd show up at Charlie's when I head in for my next shift.

When two hours go by in a flash and there's still no sign of him, I can't help but wonder where he is and what he is doing.

Wonder? Ha. Try *obsess*.

It got so bad that I topped off Jimmy's glass while it was still full, then knocked it over when I grabbed a rag to mop up some of the whiskey I spilled. The liquor splashed everywhere as the glass hit the countertop. It didn't shatter, but the spray hit Jimmy and Vincent.

I must've looked so rattled, even Vincent kept his mouth shut.

I blame it on the full moon that seemed to blossom out of nowhere; even though it's still light out, I can sense her in her full glory, prepared to ruin my evening. I always get a little twitchy, but you think I'd be better since I definitely took the edge off of my sexual need with Ryker. Then again, that might just be the problem. I'm not mated, but after our night together, my wolf won't accept that I don't have a true mate out there. She's convinced that I do, and she wants him.

Luna damn it, so do I.

I must be really bad because, around eight o'clock, Hailey offers to cover the bar herself if I want to head out early.

I'm sure she thinks I'm going to go home and sleep it off. Though I've been careful to keep my shifter identity under wraps, after twelve months working with her, she started to notice I'm always on edge during the full moon. She told me once that she thought it had something to do with my cycle. She's not wrong, so I didn't argue. It is my cycle—it just so happens to be my reaction to the moon instead of my period that gets to me this time of the month.

Still, I struggle to convince myself that my desperate desire to talk to Ryker has nothing to do with the moon. After everything my mom and dad told me, I want to sit him down and hear his side of the story. Plus, the way he seemed to up and disappear after our night together has me notably on edge.

Before work, I stopped by the park, searching for him; it was the only lead I had, but it didn't pan out. My wolf snapped at me until I gave in, letting her take the reins, but even she couldn't find him.

I don't know what to think. My instincts—and my abandoned wolf—tell me he's not hanging around my apartment or the park because he isn't in Muncie any longer. But did he take off because he got what he wanted? Or for some other reason?

Did something else happen to him?

It's driving me nuts. Eventually, I realize that I'm doing more harm than good trying to force myself through the rest of my shift. And since it's still early enough that, if I go to the apartment, I'll have to face Aleks—who I'm still avoiding, though I know I won't be able to do that forever—doing my best to hunt down Ryker again is my only real option.

It isn't until I step outside of Charlie's, the last lingering remnants of Ryker's piss still stubbornly clinging to the cement, that I realize something. Though I used my whisper-thin bond with Ryker to follow him to the park before, it was all too easy to fall back into the habit of pretending it wasn't there.

I take a deep breath, hoping that I'm not making a big mistake, and reach for our bond. If he can follow it, I should be able to, no matter how weak it's gotten over the past year.

And it is weak. It's a tiny spark, but one I can find when I'm specifically searching for it. I clutch it with both hands and give it a tug. I'm not even a little surprised when there's no answering tug in return since I can sense he's nowhere nearby, but that's okay.

I think I've finally figured out where Ryker has gone.

CHAPTER 14

I shouldn't be doing this.

Déjà vu is a bitch as I push my Jeep up the narrow mountain path. This is only the second time I've ever gone this way, and the last time had been when I was fleeing toward Muncie more than a year ago. Tonight? I'm heading back to Accalia—and, yeah, this is just another in a long line of Gem's impulsively bad ideas.

I blame the moon. It's already hanging heavy in the dark sky, a yellow beacon luring me toward Ryker. Following the thread of our fledgling bond that grows a teeny bit stronger the further I get from the Fang City, I know he's retreated back to pack territory.

I just don't know *why*.

Especially now that he's told me that he considers me to be his mate, his instincts should have him scratching at my door. That's how it works. Add in the undeniable truth that I actually fucked him already, and I don't understand why he left me behind in Muncie.

Not that I want to be his mate. I... I don't really know *what* I want anymore. But for Ryker to disappear so soon after I let my guard down, after I let him in... I barely survived his rejection the first time around. And then I stupidly started to think *maybe,* and what happens? He's gone.

It took months before I could ignore my bond with Ryker. Between the magic in Aleks's fang and my own stubborn nature, I eventually was able to shut it off. But since he showed up at Charlie's a few days ago, my tie to Ryker has become an itch I can't scratch. A nagging sensation that only eased up when I stopped pretending it wasn't there.

Right now? I focus on it, trying to use it to guide me toward Ryker. It's not as easy as it should be. Though it is getting strong, it also feels kind of hazy the closer I get to Accalia. Like, I know he's somewhere nearby, but pinpointing his exact location just isn't working the way it did when I found him in the park.

That's okay. From the moment I sped out of Muncie, I think I always knew where I would end up again.

I can't really explain it, but it doesn't feel right just driving up to Ryker's place—and not only because it's so secluded, the road doesn't quite reach it. I've got a pretty sturdy vehicle and I know my Jeep could make it. Even so, I stop when there's about a half a mile to go.

Maybe I'm really buying into the whole re-do thing tonight because I park my Jeep in about the same spot as I did the last time I invited myself over to the Alpha's cabin. Hopping out of the car, I pocket my keys instead of leaving them in the ignition. I abandoned the pack more than a year ago. Just in case, I don't want to make it easy for one of my former packmates to trash my baby out of some kind of retaliation.

I'm still trying to think of a way to explain what I'm doing here when I reach the edge of the trees that border the isolated cabin. Telling Ryker that I was worried when he seemed to vanish will only work against me, and when I think about how I tracked him down to his home, I feel like a stalker. Just because we had sex in the woods, it doesn't mean that we're mated now. I don't own him. He doesn't have to explain himself to me.

Then again, he's the one who promised that he'd do anything to get me to change my mind. He could start by being honest and open with me for a change. Ryker wants to be my partner? That means an equal in my book.

And I hold onto that fantasy for, oh, maybe three seconds before I pick up on someone approaching the front of the Alpha's cabin—and it's not Ryker.

I freeze, stunned.

It's her walk that makes me recognize her even before her scent drifts on the breeze back to me. It's in the way she swings her hips, the skirt of her dress swaying just like that. When I first met Trish, she seemed more comfortable in jeans and a blouse. As soon as she got a good look at the sundresses I habitually wore back then, her style changed overnight. Now, a year later, I see she's still pretending to be a knock-off version of me. I mean, hell. Even her light brown curls —the same hairstyle I used to wear—bounce as she strides confidently toward the cabin.

I watch, expecting her to head toward the back. I don't think Ryker is hosting any pack meets tonight, not with the full moon out, but any packmate has the right to visit the Alpha in his den.

Only that's not where she's going.

Holy *shit.* My heart drops right as my adrenaline spikes. Because Trish? She's letting herself in through the front door of the Alpha's cabin like she has every right to be there.

The *front door.*

Like she's his mate.

Ryker's mate.

No.

I want to snarl, but I swallow it angrily. My claws shoot out and I slash at the air, wishing I could slice right through her instead.

No, that's not fair. I should know better than

anyone how irresistible Ryker Wolfson is. After all, I've fallen for him *twice* now and he's made a fool of me both times.

How the hell can I blame her for going back to him? I did, didn't I?

He told me he didn't choose her. He told me that he had his reasons for staying away from me, and he refused to discuss Trish whenever I brought her up. Still, he told me that she wasn't his mate, chosen or otherwise.

So what the fuck is she doing walking into his house?

I don't know and part of me wants to pull the same stunt I did last year to find out. With my head held high and my wolf ready to attack, I want to follow Trish inside of Ryker's cabin and confront the two of them. Maybe if it wasn't the full moon, I would've. With the Luna urging me to find Ryker, if I walk in on him with another female, I won't just mark him this time.

I really will kill him.

My wolf yips in agreement. Since that's all I need to hear to get that going in there would be a decision I'd eventually regret, I start to step away from the cabin; she's never wanted to go after Ryker or his wolf, but now she's as bloodthirsty as I am. I've got to get out of here before hotheaded Gem takes over.

Turning my back on the temptation, I start to sprint to my car.

I'm so fucking furious—furious *and* distracted— that I don't realize that someone is standing next to my Jeep until I'm only a few feet away from it. Then, when I do, only a lifetime of playing the omega keeps me from turning on her.

Just like with Trish, I recognize the shifter female. She's a few years older than me, her hair a darker shade of blonde though she wears it much shorter than I do. I don't know what she's doing prowling around my Jeep, but I guess that's all right since she probably picked up on my scent and was curious.

She gasps when she sees me, as if she had doubted her own nose. "Gemma? Is that you?"

"Audrey, hi. Yeah. It's me."

"I can't— ah, jeez. I can't believe it's you! I can't believe you're back!"

Yeah, well. Considering I swore to myself that I'd never set foot on this mountain again, that makes two of us.

Not that I can tell her that. Apart from Shane, Audrey was the most welcoming of the Mountainside Pack when I first arrived last year. As Ryker's Beta, it made sense that he'd keep an eye on his Alpha's promised mate. Audrey was just a sweetheart in general. She seemed to honestly want me to be accepted if only because she believed a happy pack began with its Alpha couple.

Too bad that's not me and Ryker. And, after seeing

Trish making herself at home inside of his cabin, I have to accept that it'll never be.

My stomach goes tight. I have to fight against the partial shift, another wave of fury and hurt washing over me. My wolf wants out, and only the fact that I'd have to either abandon my Jeep or drive back to Muncie butt-naked keeps me from following through with the full shift.

I have to get out of here. Coming back to Accalia was a bad, bad idea. I've gotta go.

Before I can make my excuses and try to put an end to this conversation, Audrey darts a glance up at the sky. A whisper of a frown crosses her lovely face. "It's a full moon," she points out. "Shouldn't you be with the Alpha?"

Oof. Now that one really hurts.

A year later, and I show up on the full moon. Of course she'd assume that I finally came crawling back to Ryker. And, well, I guess I did.

I gesture behind me. "I was just at his cabin," I admit before I shove my hand in my back pocket, searching for my keys, determined to make my escape. Audrey's nice, but I'm on the edge of my control. It would be a dick move to take my anger out on her just because she had the piss poor luck to stumble upon my Jeep and be curious about it.

And that's when she cocks her head slightly. "Why would you go there? He's not at his cabin."

I pause. "He's not?"

"On the night of the full moon? Luna, no."

"What? Then where— wha...? Oh. Hang on."

I had been reaching for my keys, but the crook of my finger snags on something else first. It takes a second before I realize what it is: the slender golden chain of my fang necklace.

I haven't been wearing it, but it didn't seem right to just stick it on top of my dresser or hide it away in my sock drawer. So I shoved it in the pocket of my and then completely forgot about it.

The very same jeans I'm wearing now, I guess.

A sinking suspicion slams into me. I don't know why I didn't think of this before—probably because I honestly *did* forget I was carrying the necklace in my pocket—but I suddenly remember just how strong my senses were the second I took Aleks's necklace off when Ryker was in Muncie. After a year of ignoring him, it was impossible to continue to do so, and he was convinced it was because of this fang.

Know what? I kind of think he's right.

Guilt kept me holding onto the necklace instead of hiding it in my room. I might not want to be with Aleks the same way he wants to be with me, but I love him. Tossing aside his gift would be worse than slapping him in the face.

But what if its charm is still working on me, even though it's tucked in my back pocket? I remember how, the one time I slammed it on the coffee table and left it behind, I was able to track Ryker easily. Aleks always said it had to be next to my heart to really be activated, but what if it still did something stuck in my pocket?

Audrey says Ryker's not at the Alpha cabin. If not, then where is he? How can I find him when I can sense him on the mountain, but he could be *anywhere*?

Would she tell me? Ryker's her Alpha, and the Mountainside Pack is known for their loyalty. I abandoned them a year ago. Friendly as she is, there's no reason why she would help me track down the Alpha who publicly rejected me in front of his pack council before I took off.

What if I don't need her to?

What if—

"Hey, Audrey. This might be a little weird, but can you do me a favor? If you don't mind."

I'm careful not to lace my question with any hint of a command. As an alpha, if I use my higher rank against her, she'd never be able to refuse me. She'd always have this compulsion to obey and that's not fair to her when I'm not her pack Alpha.

I'm not sure if I failed miserably or if she's just that kind-hearted of a wolf, but she quickly agrees. "Of course."

I pull out the necklace. "Hold this for me?"

Audrey's nose wrinkles when she sees what's hanging off of the chain. "Is that a vampire fang?"

"Long story," I say, adding just enough dominance to my words to keep her from asking without making her too suspicious, "but yeah."

"Not your kill." She says that like she can't imagine me being responsible for any kind of death. "Not a sweet, little omega like you."

I blink. She... she still thinks I'm an omega. After what happened last year, I thought the whole pack discovered what I really am. Ryker definitely knows, and the shock on the faces of the rest of the pack council made it pretty clear that they knew, too.

So why doesn't Audrey? Her brother is the Beta, her mate one of Ryker's trusted advisers. Both Shane and Grant were there that night.

I decide not to worry about it. That's not important right now. Ryker... I wait until Audrey holds up her hand before tilting the fang and its chain into her palm.

Almost immediately, I have to admit my mistake. Ryker told me once before that Aleks's fang was charmed to keep me hidden from him. Why is it only just hitting me that it works both ways? The reason why our bond seems so hazy *is* because of that fang. I wasn't wearing it over my heart, so it didn't cut off the bond entirely, but carrying it in my pocket? Yeah. That wasn't my brightest idea.

As soon as Audrey's holding the fang, my side of the bond flares to life. What was only a flicker before is like an explosion. Though I could tell earlier that she was being truthful, I know now that she's right. Ryker's not behind me—but he is on the mountain.

I track Ryker to the center of pack territory before Audrey gives Aleks's fang back to me. The second it touches my skin, it's like a switch has been tripped. He's near, but it's a hum instead of a beacon now, all because of the fang.

I almost want to drop it to the dirt; only knowing that I'll have to explain where it went when Aleks inevitably asks has me closing my fingers around the charm. I don't put it back in my pocket, though. Instead, with a gentle toss, I throw it inside my Jeep.

Audrey watches silently as I do, but when I go to climb in after it, she speaks up again.

"Where are you going?"

Good question. There's no denying that Trish has gone inside of the Alpha's cabin, but if Ryker's not there, then what does that mean? Two seconds ago, I was ready to turn tail and head back to Muncie.

But now?

The pull toward Ryker is hard to resist. Especially now that Aleks's fang isn't holding me back, I'm sure I can find him. Should I? I don't know, but I've come this far.

"To find Ryker."

Audrey's eyes light up. "Then come with me. I know where he is."

I offer to drive us, but Audrey insists on walking. Since my wolf is still riled up after seeing Trish act like Ryker's cabin belongs to her, I agree. Maybe a good walk is just what I need to burn off some of this aggression.

Audrey yammers on happily, catching me up on all of the pack gossip I missed since I've been gone. I get to hear about new pups and the latest mated pairs and what packmates have moved on in search of their own mates. She innocently mentions Trish—I change the subject as soon as she does—and she tries to ask me about Ryker, but that's a big no-no, too.

Except for where he is which, pretty conveniently, Audrey promises to tell me once we get there.

It doesn't take long before I begin to suspect I've been duped. I mean, unless he's hiding out at the cabin Audrey shares with her mate because, look at that, that's where she brings me. And since I left Aleks's fang back with my Jeep, I can tell that he isn't anywhere near this cabin.

I want to keep on going, but it's been too easy to fall back into the role of omega around Audrey. She expects me to be soft and kind and accepting. Even though I don't consider her a packmate any longer, I don't want to disappoint her.

She leads me inside her home, offering me a seat

on the comfy couch in her living room. I promise myself I'll only stay for a few moments, then I'll go look for Ryker on my own.

Audrey is still beaming at me as she asks, "Thirsty?"

"Um. Yeah."

She leaves me in her living room, disappearing into the kitchen. She comes back a few moments later carrying two glasses. It looks like Coke, and I can scent the sugar and the carbonated bubbles even before she hands me one.

I'm not a big soda drinker, but I don't want to be rude. I guess I thought she would offer me water. Oh, well. Bottom's up.

I start choking before I even get the first sip down. Maybe she served me Diet or something but it doesn't taste like any soda I've ever had before. It's harsh, almost metallic, and it burns the back of my tongue and the length of my esophagus as I force myself to swallow.

Audrey finishes her sip before an expression of concern crosses her pretty features. "Are you okay?"

My eyes are watering and I just manage to resist the urge to wipe the moisture away with the back of my hand. Instead, I blink a few times, then give Audrey a shaky smile. "Yeah, yeah. I'm okay. Just went down the wrong pipe."

"If you want something else, I have lemonade. Water. Beer. Whatever you want, Gemma."

"No, no. This is fine."

It's not fine, but my mom spent twenty-five years drilling manners into me. Might as well use them.

Her smile widens. "Good. Drink up. As soon as you're done, we'll take you to Ryker."

We? What does she mean, *we*?

Before I can ask, another shifter joins us. I stiffen when I notice the male, only relaxing when I realize that the dark-haired shifter is Grant, Audrey's mate. This is his cabin. Of course he's here.

Still, unless I'm imagining it, something's not right.

Setting my drink down on the coffee table, I slowly begin to get to my feet. "What's going on, Audrey?"

She exchanges a look with Grant, and I *know* I'm not imagining a damn thing. "It's time."

Excuse me?

"I don't know what's going on," I say, "but I think I'm going to be going now."

"But you came all this way to see the Alpha," Audrey reminds me. "He's waiting for you."

"Yeah? Well, Ryker can wait a little longer. I'm going home."

Grant shakes his head. "Your home is here."

Honestly, it never was. My home is in Muncie, and that's exactly where I'm going—and neither one of these shifters is going to stop me if I can help it.

228

"Back off," I warn them. "You don't want to do this."

Forget not using my rank against my former pack-mates. There's a fanatical gleam in their matching golden gazes that has me dropping the old illusion for once and for all tonight.

Grant takes a step toward me. "It'll be okay, Gemma."

The fuck it will. I had put enough of a command into those two statements to have even a beta backing down. I purposely made eye contact, too.

Why isn't it working?

I lift up on the balls of my feet, ready to bolt. The mated pair are glued to my every move.

What the hell is going on here?

I do have one other thing working in my favor. Audrey obviously still believes I'm an omega. Maybe her mate does, too. It's obvious in the way they're treating me, and their inexplicable immunity to my alpha commands only adds to it. Neither of them approaches me like an alpha wolf with her back up against the wall which is *their* mistake.

Grant lunges at me. He's quick, but sloppy. He bends his knees just enough to telegraph his move so I'm expecting it.

Not only that, but I'm ready, too.

As soon as he gets close enough, I shoot out my hand. Tapping into my wolf, I put as much force into the hit as I can as I pivot on my heel. Grant slams into

229

my fist, my momentum flinging him over the couch and into the wall behind it.

The shifter crumples on the floor. I know better than to think that my strike will stop him, though. If anything, it'll only slow him down for a few seconds before he's back on his feet.

It's up to me to make those seconds count.

I take off. I push past a visibly horrified Audrey—oh yeah, she didn't expect Omega Gem to react like that, did she?—and make it to the front door before she starts shouting for her mate.

He'll live, but hopefully he'll think twice before trying to come after me again.

Claws crossed.

CHAPTER 15

As I book it away from Audrey's cabin, heading toward the woods again, I regret letting her convince me to walk back to her place. My Jeep is on the other side of the mountain and while I could shift and get back to it sooner, that still leaves me with the whole "driving while naked" problem.

Now, if only that was the sole problem I have to deal with...

I thought something was wrong before. Know what? I was totally right. I never should've doubted my gut. Something tells me now that the night of the full moon is far from over, and I believe it.

I pour on the speed.

Halfway back toward where I left my Jeep, I notice that my nose... my nose has stopped working, like I've developed a sudden cold or something. I can't scent a single thing—not the woods, or the earth, or anything else—and hell if I know why it's failing me for the first time ever. At least my eyes and my ears are working because, without them, I wouldn't have realized I was being tracked until it was too late.

And, honestly, it just might be.

I'm an alpha, but I'm not invincible. As I stop short, I count three different hooded figures surrounding my front half. Whirling around, I find another four waiting at my back. Picking up on the echoes and the shadows in the distance, I'm sure even more are lurking in the woods. Audrey must've sent a call out to the pack when she caught me outside of Ryker's cabin, because this seems... planned, almost.

And it's not just the way they form a circle around me that has me on my guard. It's the hoods. I see the black hoods hiding their faces, like they don't want me to figure out who they are—with my sense of smell out, I *can't*—and I know that I'm not just in trouble.

I'm in deep, deep shit.

"Remember what happened at the council meeting," rumbles one of the faceless shadows. A big guy, and I'm suddenly thrown back to the night I left Accalia when one of Ryker's larger enforcers tried to stop me from going. "She's more dangerous than she looks."

"A female alpha," whispers another. "Can it really be true?"

"Doesn't matter." I know that voice. That's Jace.

"Ryker will only accept her as his mate. This is for our Alpha."

"For Ryker," echo the others.

Hang on—

They can't honestly think they can force me into mating Ryker, right? I mean, sure, it's the full moon, and it wouldn't take much to perform the Luna Ceremony that ties us together forever, but he promised that he'd get me to change my mind. That he was up for the challenge.

That he'd never use his alpha status to make the choice for me.

Only Ryker isn't. It's the rest of the Mountainside Pack that's turned on me.

That's my cue. I don't care what they're doing, or why, and maybe I'll eventually ask Ryker about it one day, but right now? I'm out of here.

There's no time to return to my Jeep. If I have any hope of escaping whatever Ryker's pack has in mind for me, I'll have to rely on my wolf outrunning them.

One problem: it's not just my nose that's broken. I... I can't shift.

Panic flares up inside of me. It's an unfamiliar feeling, and one I really, really don't like; it's right there with being afraid. Ever since I started shifting as a young pup, there's never been a moment when I gave my body the command and it just didn't work... until now.

It's supposed to be instantaneous. When a few terrifying seconds tick by and I'm still stuck in my skin, I back up, looking for a different escape, but I can't find one. The circle is closing in on me, my wolf anxious and scared, and I don't know what the hell is wrong with me.

I don't even have my claws. I'm more defenseless than I've ever been in my entire life and I *hate* it.

So when Grant suddenly appears behind the circle, I want to go after him again. He's someone to fixate on, someone to blame, but as much as it sucks, I have to accept that I'm no match for him in my current state.

Audrey's mate isn't wearing one of the hooded cloaks like the others, but he's obviously on their side. I get a perverse jolt of pleasure to see that he's rubbing the heel of his hand against his sternum, wincing as he joins the circle. He moves carefully, like he's still recovering from my attack. Considering how hard I hit him, there's a good chance I cracked a couple of his bones, maybe even a rib or two.

Good. He fucking deserved it.

Once I can tap into my wolf again, he'll also deserve what happens next. They all will.

"What are we waiting for?" He gestures at me with his chin. "Audrey put a few drops of quicksilver in her drink so even if she doesn't go down, we'll still be able to handle her. But it won't last long. Let's do this."

My jaw drops.

You've got to be kidding me.

Quicksilver?

Mercury.

Luna *damn* it!

Mercury's not as fatal to shifters as pure silver, but it has a profound effect on our kind. Ingest some of the stuff and it can act as a sedative, and maybe the single sip I took isn't enough to knock me out, but how much do you want to bet it's the reason I can't shift?

"Ready on three," says Grant. "One."

"Two..."

"Three!"

That's the last thing I hear before my former pack-mates surround me. In a last ditch effort to escape, I use my blunt human teeth and my short nails against them, but Grant was right.

With the mercury poisoning me, I might not go down, but they overpower me pretty easily.

Bastards.

I DON'T FIGHT THEM. MAINLY BECAUSE I KNOW IT'S pointless, but also because they made it even harder on me. As if the mercury wasn't enough, they weren't taking any chances. They yanked a dark hood over my head that leaves me blind, and I'm slung over one of the bigger shifters' shoulders like I'm a sack of potatoes.

The meaty shoulder digs into my gut with every step, bouncing me as he carries me through the woods. It doesn't take long for the nausea to kick in and I have to clamp my jaw together to keep from hurling. It would serve him right if I puked down his back, but with the hood over my head, I'd probably choke on it.

So, gritting my teeth, I ride it out, waiting for the moment I can retaliate. I keep hoping my claws will shoot out. I might not be able to shift to wolf with the mercury working its way through me, but I can do a lot of damage with my claws.

Too bad it never happens.

It's not just my nose that goes. All of my senses are dulled, like the hood over my head has wrapped around all of me, cutting me off from the rest of the world—except for that Luna damned shoulder digging into my gut. Everything is muffled, too. Either the shifters are being quiet or my ears are reacting as if they've been plugged up with cotton because I can't hear shit, either.

It's so frustrating. I kick my foot at one point, but when a massive paw with a grip made of iron grabs my calf, holding me tight, even that outlet is taken from me.

When the whisper of the night's wind dies down, and the air seems to shift, going still, warming up, I realize that they've brought me inside. Inside where? No clue. We haven't been walking long enough to be out of pack territory, so that's a plus, but being moved to a second location?

Yeah. Not ideal.

The big guy carrying me has been lugging me around like I'm a package and not a person this whole time. I'll give him some credit, though. When he shifts me in his arm before setting me on my feet, he does so gently, easing me until I'm standing, holding tightly to my arm so that I don't drop from being disoriented.

His voice is a deep rumble. "You good?"

At least I hear that.

I nod.

"She's good, fellas."

"Open the door," orders Grant. "Be careful. We don't want to piss off the Alpha."

Piss off the Alpha? What about me?

I hear something. It kind of creaks, and I'm betting that's the door they mentioned. Someone hooks their hands under my pits, lifting me up so unexpectedly that I can't swallow my soft cry of surprise before they move me forward, then plop me down again.

A door slams behind me.

I rip the hood off of my head.

It takes a second for my eyes to adjust, but even quicker for my ears to pick up on the sound of grunts coming from below me.

It's dark. I'm standing on a top stair, a closed door at my back. Though I know damn well it's going to be locked, I give it a jangle anyway. A quick jerk reveals that it's shifter-proof. Even if I was at full strength, I'd never be able to snap it.

Great. Fucking *great*.

So my choices are stay on the stairs until someone is stupid enough to let me out, or go downstairs and see who is making that awful noise.

Morbid curiosity wins out.

"Hello?" My heart is pounding so loudly, I hear it echo against my eardrums. "Is someone here?"

The grunting stops, but it's followed by a harsh panting sound. Human. The grunts were canine, but the pants belong to a man. So a shifter. Even if his scent didn't hit me the second I inched down the first few stairs—still so recognizable despite my busted sniffer—it doesn't take a genius to put two and two together and figure out who's locked in this cellar room with me.

For the Alpha...

"Ryker?" He still doesn't answer me, and maybe if I had my claws I could try to dig my way through the thick door and maybe escape, but I can't. Since that's out, they had to know I would go down the stairs if they left me trapped in a room with him. "Are you down there?"

I hear a snarl, followed by a raspy voice that I know all too well.

"Gemma, no! Stay away!"

Oh, Ryker. You can't honestly believe that an order like that would work on me without the power of your wolf's stare behind it?

I ease down the stairs, just in case. My instincts tell me that I have nothing to worry about—in fact, they're screaming *mate, it's your mate* at me—but I've been poisoned and wolf-napped so far tonight. Sue me for being a little cautious.

"Ryker?"

A muffled curse, then a sigh. "Luna damn it. You never fucking listen to me."

Nope. I don't.

Not about to start now, either.

I keep going, freezing when I reach the last step.

"Holy. Shit."

Not surprisingly, the first thing I see is that Ryker is just about naked. He's not wearing any shoes or a shirt, and the hems of his loose pants are shredded. A sign of a partial shift, where the wolf pushes against the human form without fully shifting to fur.

He's not standing, either. He's slumped on the ground, looking at a point just past me as if he can't bring himself to witness the horror on my face as he demands in a voice too weak to be his, "What are you doing here?"

Honestly, I have no fucking idea other than that the packmates who tossed me in here seemed to think they were doing this for their Alpha.

The very same Alpha who is chained to the wall behind him.

I fly toward him.

"What am I doing here? What are *you* doing here? Who did this to you?" I grab the length of chain he's trying to hide from me. Right. As if I don't see two sets bolted to the cinderblock wall. The chains aren't silver, but that only means that they're not burning Ryker. Oh no, the chains are just keeping him trapped down here. "What the fuck? Why are you chained up?"

"Who did this to me? I did. I had no other choice."

Is he kidding? "No choice but be chained to a wall like an animal? What's going on?"

"Like an animal? Oh, sweetheart. I'm full feral right now." His laugh is hollow. "It's my fault for being such an arrogant prick. I dared the Luna, and she's making me fucking pay for it."

"What are you talking about?"

"I'm a wolf. I worship her, and I'm a slave to her phases just like we all are, even if I thought I could pretend I wasn't."

In a way, I know exactly what he means. When I look at Ryker... the moon picked the perfect mate for me. I'm just the one who let my instincts get in the way. Plus his initial rejection, and how he all but tried to make my choice for me when he finally found me in Muncie again.

And now, almost a year and a half after she whispered that we were supposed to be together during Ryker's Alpha Ceremony, we're not—not really—and he's clearly suffering because of it.

Feral.

Chains.

Weak.

And I thought I felt queasy before.

"Your turn. What are you doing here?" Ryker says, turning the question back on me. "You're supposed to be in Muncie. You're supposed to be *safe*."

If he was vulnerable enough to open up to me, the least I can do is return the favor. "I came looking for you. I... I thought we could talk."

"I think we talked enough. If you want, we can talk more after the full moon. Now, though? You have to go."

"I can't."

"You can, Gemma—"

He doesn't understand. "No. Really. I *can't*."

As quickly as possible, I tell Ryker all about what's happened to me since I arrived in Accalia, starting with running into Audrey. From her sweet nature to the doctored Coke all way to members of his inner circle bringing me—

I pause. "Where are we?"

"My basement," Ryker tells me. They're the first words he's said since I started talking aside from his growled, "I'll kill them. I'll kill them all. They shouldn't have done that to you."

He's not wrong, but I think killing them is a little drastic. Now that I've seen what the full moon does to Ryker, I can't blame them for hoping I'd help him out somehow. Even if they did trap me in his—

Hang on.

"Your basement," I repeat. "In... in the Alpha cabin?"

He slowly shakes his head. "No. Those idiots might think this is Alpha business, but it isn't. It's mine. This is my cabin. The one I had before I took over for my dad."

Oh.

Welp.

Didn't expect *that*.

Is it worse that I'm here? I wasn't meant to enter the Alpha cabin until I became his bonded mate, but now I'm in his personal home and... I don't know what to think about that.

Later, I tell myself. I'll think about that later.

For now, all my worry is for Ryker.

He's sweating. It drips down his face, plastering his dark hair to his forehead. That only means one thing and, Luna help me, I hope I'm wrong.

Even so, I can't resist the urge. Dropping to my

knees, I reach out to him, aiming to push one particular lock of hair out of his face.

His voice is hoarse as he warns, "You shouldn't touch me."

"You don't want me to?"

"I do. Luna, I do. But it's taking everything I have to restrain my wolf. These chains… they had to know that they weren't strong enough to keep you from me. Especially with the fever…" His words trail off, but both of us know exactly what he was about to say. He shakes his head, and I have to admit that I was *right*. "Maybe if you'd stayed behind in Muncie, you might've been safe from me. But this close…" Ryker's cheeks ripple, fighting the shift. "Just… just stay on the other side of the room, Gemma. *Please*."

Holy hell. He's *begging*.

Fisting my hand, I awkwardly scoot away from him. Once there are a few feet separating us, I climb up from my knees and shuffle as far away from him as I can get.

When there's some space between us, Ryker calms just enough. He slumps against the corner again, head bowed into his chest. His panting goes from rough gasps to a gentle wheeze. If I didn't know better, I'd say he's passed out.

He hasn't, but if that's what he wants me to think, I'll give him his moment. He didn't ask for this. Obviously he didn't want me down here with him. That was all his council's brilliant idea.

Since I don't want him to worry that I'm still staring at him, I look around the basement. It's not overly large, maybe as big as the living room back at Aleks's apartment. Apart from the chains screwed into the wall and its unfortunate guest, there's nothing else down here. It's obviously rarely used, and I can see why.

The walls are made of cinderblock, but there are deep gouges in each brick. Scratch marks, claw marks cover the place. I see smears of old blood, and though my senses aren't what they're supposed to be, I know it belongs to Ryker.

There are no other scents down here except for his.

I can't help myself. I have to ask.

"Ryker?"

His head shoots up, proving that I was also right when I thought he was faking. He shifts as close to me as he can without tugging on his chains. "Mmm?"

"How long?"

He's finding it hard to focus on me. Or maybe he's trying hard to resist the urge to crawl over to me.

'Cause, yeah. I'm having a hard time leaving him by himself on the other side of the basement.

"How long for what?"

"How many times have you been chained down here?"

Because I know for damn sure that it's not the first time. If he's blaming the moon... there's been a lot of moons for Ryker.

"You want the truth?"

I don't tell him that I'll know regardless. "I always want the truth. I thought you figured that out by now."

"Then this is my twelfth."

I gulp. "That's every full moon since I left."

"I was a shifter without his mate. I didn't know where you were. No one could find you. I was a danger to the pack... and to anyone who stood in my way to track you down. I could control my wolf every other phase of the moon. But when it's full, this is the only option I have."

I know why, too. Moon fever. When the Luna is at her strength, our wolves come to the forefront. Our animalistic instincts become almost undeniable. It's why I always get lonely during the full moon, and why I run a few days leading up to it. You get itchy, too, and pretty fucking desperate to find someone to scratch that itch.

Mates rut. It gets easier after you're in a committed, bonded mating, but two unattached shifters working their way through the mating dance can spend the entire full moon banging away.

Two alphas with a bond? No wonder he's chained up. I've heard stories about shifters who fell prey to moon fever. They'll chase their mate across miles so they can ease their lust.

And the pack council thought it was a good idea to throw me down here with their feverish Alpha.

Well, hell. We already had sex once before. If it'll stop his suffering, I'll take one for the team.

"It's not the only option."

CHAPTER 16

"**W**hat did you say?"

"Not the only option," I repeat. "I'm here. I can help you."

And help myself too while I'm at it. Watching him sneak hungry looks at me just now, like I'm a fancy cut of steak and he's been without meat for ages, I can't help but notice how achy *I* feel. How empty. Now that I know what it's like to be skin to skin with Ryker, I'm starved for his touch. I want him inside of me more than I've wanted anything else in my life.

It's just sex, I tell myself. A biological urge.

Too bad Ryker doesn't see it the same way.

"No. I can't."

"Sure you can. If you're worried about the chains—"

"It's not the chains I'm worried about," he bites out. "It's how you'll react come tomorrow. You'll run."

I try to make light of it. "How can I? I'm locked down here with you."

"So? You'll still run. And I'll chase you again, like I've been chasing you this whole last year. Only you won't be able to get away from me."

"You can chase me all you want," I scoff, some of my nerves from earlier tonight returning. I've never once thought that Ryker would hurt me—for Luna's sake, he didn't retaliate even when I had my claws stuck deep in his chest—but I have to remember that I'm still pretty defenseless. Sure, he's chained, but I don't even have my claws right now. Still, I'm an alpha, and we both know it. "You can't catch me unless I let you."

"You don't get it, Gemma. Listen to me. For once, just *listen* to me. If I fuck you, I'll mate you. You won't be able to get away from me because you'll be mine. For good. Forever."

I blink. "You don't mean that."

He drops his head again, like he's too weak to hold it up. "Tell yourself that if you have to, but I'm not lying. You know I'm not."

He's right. I do.

But it doesn't make *sense*.

"It's just sex." With Ryker, it'll never be just sex, but he doesn't need to know that. "I know it's the full moon, but couples mate all the time during the moon fever. We're down here. We might as well make the best of it, right? I want you." No denying that after our last time together. "I'm pretty sure anyone will do for you right now in your state. Unless—"

I'm looking at Ryker, but in my mind's eye I see Trish walking boldly inside of the Alpha's cabin. Maybe she got the wrong message. Maybe she forgot that Ryker would be in his old cabin tonight instead of the one belonging to the Alpha.

I shake my head. "Forget it."

He's miserable, but he's still an alpha. Peeking up at me through the fringe of his eyelashes, I look into his eyes and see his wolf simmering below the surface. "Unless what?"

It sucks. You'd think that, as a fellow alpha, his command would roll right off of me like water down a duck's back.

Nope. Not when he uses his pack Alpha stare.

"Unless there's someone else you'd rather have relieve your need."

His muscles bunch. It's the only warning I get before Ryker pulls against the chains in the wall, making them creak. Cinderblock dust explodes from the point where the chains are anchored. He's not loose, but I get the feeling that it's only because the powerful Alpha restrained himself just in time.

Okay, then.

He grits his teeth as his predator's gaze locks on me again. "Let's make something clear. I want no one else but you. You are my mate. My wolf will accept no other, and you'll only provoke him by saying otherwise. Do you understand?"

I'm speechless.

He snaps his jaw at me. "I said, do you understand, Gemma?"

"Uh. Yeah. I get it."

"Good." He stops pulling against the chains, sinking back down to his corner.

"So... does that mean we're going to do this?"

Poor guy needs something to calm him down. He just about ripped free from his chains, and if a quick lay will keep him from wolfing out entirely... well, he did say that he doesn't want anyone else.

"No."

And then, just like that, he puts another crack in my fragile heart.

"You... *don't* want to mate me."

"No. And if you're smart, you'll stop offering. I asked you to stay as far away from me as you can. Do it."

I almost do. He put enough command in his words to have me drawing away from him, but only a spark of fury at his renewed rejection has me holding my ground.

Damn it, it's last year all over again, isn't it?

My eyes are drawn to his bare chest. It's slick with sweat, heaving as he fights a battle with both of his halves. The wolf that wants to claim me, and the male who gave his word that he'd wait for me to come to him—until I did and he rejected my offer outright.

I don't understand. I can sense it, and it's... it's different than his first rejection, but stronger, too. Undeniable. He means it. I just offered to mate him and he said no.

I can feel it through the bond—but it's a bond that should've shriveled and died when he rejected our mating at the Alpha cabin last May. A bond that's only grown in the days since he reappeared, and that seemed unbreakable following our first mating.

So while he's pushing me away now, pushing me away again, the bond lingers.

What the hell is that about?

Biting my bottom lip, I stare at the marks covering his left pec. The five pale slashes settled right over his heart. The first time I saw them, I was convinced he had to have used silver to keep them burned into his skin. Why? Because the other way he could've kept them just seemed so... impossible.

But now?

Watching him suffer so obviously, I have to admit that maybe it's not so impossible after all.

See, to perform the Luna Ceremony, to turn a casual relationship into a permanent mating, it takes three conscious steps.

One: Accept your mate.

Two: Mate. Obviously.

And three: Get the moon's blessing.

To a shifter, that's the part that makes the union unbreakable. Sure, accepting your mate—saying *yes*—is the most important step, but if a mated pair sleeps together during the full moon, you'll know immediately whether the moon's blessed your mating or not. I've never heard of any union where she *didn't*—which was why my mom was careful not to trigger the ceremony while she lived with my bio-dad—and *that's* why the actual performance of the words, the promises and the vows so similar to a human's wedding, is what a pack really looks forward to.

Especially for the Alpha couple.

The act of performing the ceremony is a spectacle. A scene. It shows their fellow shifters that the two mates are choosing each other with the pack as witness. Later, when they're alone with the Luna, it's cemented.

Done.

I could fuck Ryker right here and we'd be bonded mates only if we accepted each other first; otherwise, it really is just sex. Honestly, I think that's exactly what his pack council expects us to do. Why else would they snatch me and bring me here during the full moon of all nights?

I don't think it was planned. At least, not for tonight in particular. How could it be? Ryker told me that he's spent the last year trying to track me down, oblivious that I was living in plain sight only a few miles away from Accalia. I was promised to Ryker during his Alpha Ceremony. The way those other wolves probably see it, as soon as I came back, it was my responsibility to fulfill that arrangement.

And look at me. I showed up on the full moon.

Fucking fate or what?

But in order for us to do that, the first step is in accepting the bond. I always intended to once I knew for sure he would take me as his, but I gave up on having a fated mate when Ryker rejected me. As for Ryker, I thought he made himself pretty clear last year —until he showed up with all of that 'mine' bullshit.

Maybe... maybe it wasn't bullshit, though.

I can't stop staring at his chest, and not for horny reasons, either. Well. Not *entirely* for horny reasons.

"You didn't choose to keep those scars."

That... might've been the wrong thing to say.

Ryker's head snaps up. "Like hell I didn't. You marked me. They're *mine.*"

"That's not what I'm saying." How to explain? "I always thought you were holding those scars over my head for what I did to you. I don't know... like you used silver to make sure they stayed so you could remind me I lost control."

A spark of recognition lights up his shadowed face. "You thought they were battle scars."

I *did.*

It's an alpha thing. On the occasion that one puts on a show of dominance over another, whether it's a challenge to lead the pack or to claim a mate, there's usually a bitter battle. Sometimes fatal, always blood-thirsty, the only marks I've ever seen left on a shifter came from a fight—or their mating nights.

If I accept Ryker as my mate, he'll bite me. That's what we do. He'll leave his mark on my skin, warning every other male that I'm taken.

And if Ryker accepts me as his mate, it works the same way. If I mark him—whether with my fangs or my claws—the mark would stay, a clear sign that he's been taken by another wolf.

A year later, the five puncture wounds from when I threatened to rip out his heart are still there.

They could be battle scars. A handmade shifter tattoo filled in with silver and magic. I'm an alpha who was seconds away from delivering a fatal blow to him. They could be—but they're not, are they?

"Ryker—"

"They're not battle scars."

No. They're not.

"But *why*?"

"You've always been mine, Gemma. I was just waiting for you to realize that. Then, and only when you accept me in return because you want to, will I take you as my bonded mate. Because once I do? There's no going back."

He's not wrong.

Once a shifter takes a bonded mate, it's 'til death do you part with no way out.

I learned a long time ago that supes don't do divorce. If I mate him, even in the heat of the moment, I'll be stuck with Ryker for the rest of my very long life.

His pained expression softens. "Shit. I didn't mean to scare you."

"You didn't." Luna knows what I look like to make him think so, but I'm not scared. Not of him, or when I'm with him.

But I *am* thinking about what he just said.

You've always been mine, Gemma. I was just waiting for you to realize that...

Clearing my throat, I scoot out of his reach. When did I get so close? "Um. Maybe I'll go sit over there again."

He exhales roughly. "Yeah. I think that's a good idea."

———

Since mating's off the table and we're going to be locked down here until the full moon finally loses her hold on us, we eventually come to an agreement. I'm going to stay on the far side of the basement, Ryker's going to stubbornly hold tight to his chains, and we can revisit the whole "mate" issue when the pull of the Luna isn't working against us.

It's a good plan. I know that, come morning, I'd only regret mating him tonight. Sleeping with Ryker is one thing. I spent more than ten years wondering what it would be like to have sex with him, and if it surpassed my wildest expectations, the upside was that there were no strings attached. It was a mating, but we weren't mates. I could live with that.

But with the moon out and Ryker's confession that he consciously accepted our bond the night I left the pack—otherwise he never could've kept my claw marks on his chest—I finally understand why he seemed so convinced that we were *this* close to completing our bond. On his side, at least, he chose me, he accepted my mark, and the moon blessed our mating when she made me Ryker's intended. If we mate down here, all it will take is me saying *yes,* him marking me, and that's it. We're bonded for life.

A year ago, that's all I wanted.

Then again, a year ago, I didn't know there was a world out there where I could be Gem. Not Omega Gem. Not Alpha Gem. Just plain ol' Gemma Swann. I sling whiskey and I roll my eyes at the barhounds' outrageous attempts at flirting and I like it.

Now? Now I'm stuck in Ryker Wolfson's basement,

the moon doing a number on the both of us, and I don't know what the fuck I'm supposed to do.

I just hope that they'll let me go when the sun replaces the moon in the morning. The Luna won't be so powerful tomorrow night, but after the way the pack treated me already, I wouldn't put it past them to leave me trapped with Ryker until we're officially mated.

I want to ask Ryker more about this basement setup. Call me a wimp, though, but I decide it's safer *not* to. He's right. I think we've done enough talking tonight.

I don't know how long we've been stuck down here together when, all of a sudden, my wolf rouses herself. I'm feeling a lot less queasy—which just makes me notice that I'm starving, for food, for Ryker, I'm not picky—and my senses are a little stronger. For example, I can just about taste Ryker's arousal for me in the tension-filled air, and the blood seeping from the cuts left behind from his chains.

Someone else is here, though. I'm almost sure of it.

Up above, I hear the door open before slamming shut again. A shadow falls against the cement floor as boots thunder down the steps. It grows taller and taller as they get closer.

I sniff, hoping that my senses are back to full strength as I burn through the poison in my veins. Unfortunately, all I can get is *Ryker*, and since he's resting fitfully against the wall, I know it's not him.

He's resting—but not asleep—as he proves a second later when he jerks his head up. "Shane." It's a guttural snarl that puts me immediately on edge. "Get the fuck out."

Shane? Shane Loup?

Ryker's Beta?

What is he doing here?

He wasn't there with the others. I would've recognized him for sure. He wasn't there—is he a part of this? Did he know what the other packmates have done?

One shocked glance toward me as he sweeps over the basement and I know that: No. No, he did not.

"Gem, I... when I caught your scent, I couldn't believe it. And when they told me you were with Ryker—"

He shoots his head over his shoulder, finding Ryker. As Beta, he's careful not to challenge the Alpha, but it's gotta be tough. Shane's fully dressed, wearing boots and, oh yeah, *no chains*. The full moon makes him look bigger, stronger, while it has Ryker more like a beast. Ryker's definitely more dominant, but his Beta has the control.

"Ah, buddy. I didn't know it was this bad."

"Get. Out."

That should've been enough to have Shane dropping his gaze, turning tail, and heading toward the stairs. But it's not.

Weird.

I think it has everything to do with that control. Ryker said he was a slave to the moon, but it's his wolf that's fighting against him. Instead of being a combined soul, they're ripped apart and, because of that, his alpha strength isn't enough to command this beta to do anything.

Thank the Luna.

"Let me out of here," I tell Shane. I'm already scrambling to my feet. "I want to go home."

"Gemma, *no*."

I'm careful not to look at him as I throw my words toward his corner. "Make up your mind, Ryker. You want me to leave, you want me to stay. You want to fuck me, but you won't mate me. I... I can't do this right now. The moon fever isn't just affecting you," I confess, glancing at him out of the corner of my eye. "I'm not as bad, but I've got to get out of here."

His heavy-lidded gaze is locked on Shane, but when he speaks, he's definitely talking to me. "Go. But not with him."

Seriously?

"He's your Beta."

"He's a male."

Shane steps between us. Brave wolf, considering we're two alphas trying to fight against the pull of the moon.

"The others don't know I'm here. If they catch Gem

on her own, they'll just throw her back to your wolf. Is that what you want? You're a strong Alpha, Ryker. Are you strong enough to resist her again?"

"Shane..."

He quails just enough that I know he's not completely unaffected by Ryker. "She can't go on her own. But, if I leave her with you, can you swear she'll be safer than if she's with me?"

I open my mouth. He makes it seem like I have no say in the matter. Like he can stop me if I decide to bolt past him and fly up the stairs toward freedom. Okay. Maybe he *can* since I'm still recovering, but he doesn't know that.

Unless they told him about the mercury...

I look from Ryker to Shane and back in time for Ryker to let out a frustrated chuffing sound.

"Take her," he rasps out. His shifter's eyes are gleaming, but he sets his jaw and points toward the stairs. "Protect my mate as if she's your own."

I don't know what's my strongest knee-jerk reaction: tell Shane that I don't need his protection, or remind Ryker that I'm not his mate. Not yet, at least. Not officially.

Before I can say anything, though, Shane loops his hand around my upper arm, giving my bicep a gentle squeeze. I think he knows exactly what I'm struggling with and, like always, he's being loyal to Ryker.

I get it. Ryker's clearly having a hard time of it, and

Shane is right. Me staying down in the basement with him is both a taunt and a tease and if I don't take this chance to get away, I don't think the chains'll hold much longer. We don't have to do this now. It can wait, and I'd much rather finish giving our earlier conversation another shot when I have more control.

Ryker, too.

So, instead of shaking Shane off, I stay quiet.

"Don't worry, Alpha." He bows his head in Ryker's direction. "You can count on it."

CHAPTER 17

Shane stops me when we get to the middle of the stairs. He gestures for me to wait, then disappears out onto the next floor of the cabin. I take a deep breath, stubbornly trying to filter out any other scents from the basement. No surprise now that I know this is his place and I'm more attuned to him than I want to admit, but it's still pure *Ryker*.

Even if I couldn't rely on my gut to tell me that he was being truthful, I'd know from the layers upon layers that permeate this place that he's spent a year's worth of full moons chained up in the basement. Those chains... they're not new. The wild scratches that cover the walls... yeah.

It's true. It's all true.

Too bad I'm not sure what that *means*.

Shane comes back after a few minutes. Pressing his

forefinger to his lips, he warns me to be quiet before gesturing for me to follow him out of the basement.

He keeps going once we've entered the main floor, but I pause.

I can't help it. Apart from the night I barged into his den at the Alpha's cabin, I've never been inside of Ryker's personal territory unless you count his basement and I don't. I can *feel* him in this space, almost as if his fingertips are caressing my overheated skin instead of just the way he imprinted so totally on the room.

Though Shane kept the lights off, after the gloom of the basement, my sight's recovered enough that I can pick out some of the details from the shadows. I see a leather couch, and a coffee table carved from sturdy wood; no glass like Aleks's fragile furniture. He has a fireplace, too, and an empty mantle trapping it in its grate.

The mantle is empty, but the wall right above it? It's covered in at least ten different photos, all different sizes, each one rimmed in a dark frame. Squinting, annoyed that my sight's still a little wonky thanks to the mercury, I try to get a peek at the subjects of the pictures. I recognize Ryker's dad, the former Alpha who passed at the end of last year. The striking woman with the dark hair's gotta be his mom; she's in more than a few of the pictures. Ryker as a pup... fucking *adorable*. No other females, I can't help but notice.

That's not all I notice, either.

There are two missing. I might have thought it was just a stylistic choice, the way that Ryker hung the frames haphazardly over the mantle, if it weren't for the nails still jutting from the wall. Who removes the pictures and their frames but leaves the nails and the empty gaps?

Weird.

I find myself drawing closer to the wall of photos. It's Ryker's family, and I even see a candid shot of Ryker and Shane that looks pretty recent based on the hairstyles. All people who mean something to him, I'm guessing… so who was in the pictures that he took down?

My stomach tightens. Could it be—

"Gem?"

At Shane's call of my name, I give my head a clearing shake.

What the hell is wrong with me? I'm supposed to be sneaking out to make the pull of the moon easier on Ryker, not spying on the guy.

There will be time to obsess over the missing photos later. When Ryker's not suffering from moon fever, and I'm not sweating out mercury. I still can't shift. Though I can sense my wolf stirring deep in my chest, the mercury has left her feeling heavy and drowsy and detached. I can't tap into her, not yet, but knowing she's still with me is a bit of a relief.

Soon, girl. Soon.

"Coming!"

———

SHANE DID A PERIMETER CHECK BEFORE HE TOLD ME IT was clear. It seems as if the rest of the pack was either too preoccupied with the full moon to run a patrol, or they respected their Alpha too much to set a babysitter on him. Either way, Shane had no problem letting himself inside of Ryker's cabin or waltzing right outside of it with me in tow.

I have no idea where he plans to take me, and I'm not so sure I really care. My head's still spinning over everything that has happened to me since I decided to follow the moon's lead and go searching for Ryker.

Shane's thoughts seem to be on the same track as mine. Though he's quiet as we jog away from the cabin, heading toward the patch of woods that'll eventually lead me back to my Jeep, I figure he's gotta be thinking the same things as me because he opens up the conversation with a sigh before saying, "I'm sorry, Gem. For what my packmates did, and for my Alpha's lack of control. None of that should've ever happened."

I'm not even going to argue *that* one.

Still—

"Don't worry about it. It's not your fault."

"I'm the Beta. If it's not my fault, whose is it?"

"We can start with the ones who thought it was a good idea to slip me some mercury and throw me into the basement with Ryker."

I meant it to be a more lighthearted comment than it came out as. Oops. Forgive me for being more than a little pissed off at how they tricked me. It's been a couple of hours since I drank that sip of soda and I still feel *off*.

Reaching inside of my chest, I test my connection to my wolf. Nope. She's stronger than before, but I'm still not ready to shift.

Ugh.

"I will, Gem," Shane vows solemnly. "You can bet on it. I'll start with my sister and her mate."

Now, hold on a sec—

I think of Audrey's deceptively innocent expression as she offered me the doctored Coke. And the look of acceptance on Grant's face a split second before I sent him flying.

It wasn't personal. I was the target, and even I have to admit that.

"It's okay."

"Gem, you don't have to—"

"Nah. I mean it. They were just trying to help out the Alpha. We're pack, Shane. It's how we're wired. I don't have to like it, but I get it. Now I know not to come back to Accalia when it's a full moon." I give a mock salute, still trying to downplay the situation. "Message received."

An expression of concern flashes across Shane's pretty boy features for a second before he shrugs and, turning his back on me, begins to stride deeper into the trees. "That still doesn't explain why the others chained Ryker up down there. He's had no problem passing every other full moon with Trish Danvers before tonight."

I stop. Any humor I struggled to hang onto dies a quick, quick death at the mention of the other female.

"What?"

Shane looks over his shoulder at me again. When he sees that I've fallen a few steps behind him, he turns, an apologetic frown pulling on his lips. "Oh, Gem. Don't tell me you didn't know already. I mean, Ryker's never kept it a secret. And since you left... he made it clear last year that he chose Trish. It's why I couldn't believe it when I stumbled on your car and discovered you were here."

"You were at the Alpha's cabin?"

He nods slowly. "I went to check on Ryker, but I left when I saw Trish heading in. I didn't want to disturb them."

"But Ryker wasn't there."

"I know. And that's what I don't understand. He's always there for her visits—"

There it is again. Not as strong—thank you, mercury—but there's that sour stink again. Almost like curdled milk. I thought I caught a whiff of it before, but now I'm sure of it.

Shane is lying to me.

Which, yeah. He has to be. I mean, Ryker admitted that he's spent the last twelve full moons locked up inside of that basement because I was hiding *too* well. He didn't go to Trish to help him with his lust because she wasn't the one he wanted.

He wanted *me*.

Wants me.

And... Shane's still talking.

Still lying.

"—once I heard that Audrey and Grant rounded up some of the pack to take you to Ryker, I knew I had to step in. He's my Alpha, but no one deserves to be forced into a mating they don't want. No matter what the moon says."

Surprisingly, *that* part is true.

What the fuck is going on here?

I decide to test it. So even though Shane gestures for me to keep putting distance between us and the cabin, I stay where I am.

"How did you know I was even here?"

There were so many wolves in the woods when they caught me leaving Audrey's house, but Shane—

Audrey's brother and the pack's Beta—wasn't one of them. Interesting, now that I think of it.

"Told you. I saw your car."

"And you knew it was mine?"

When I first arrived in Accalia last year, I was careful not to let anyone know that I had my own car. Most shifters rely on traveling by foot, though there are a few pack vehicles that they share. Maybe it's because I'm an alpha, but I always need to know that I have my own escape. No one knew I had a car until I drove out of Accalia that night. Now it's a year later. How can he know the Jeep's mine?

"Of course. It has your scent all over it."

Really? Because I distinctly remember tossing Aleks's charmed fang inside of the Jeep before I left with Audrey. And while the magic couldn't hide my scent since I wasn't wearing it, I'm pretty sure it's powerful enough to shield the car.

Even if I didn't know how the charm worked, how it did something to conceal my shifter scent—one of its secrets that Aleks shared from the beginning, even if he neglected to mention it made me smell like *him*—I nearly snuffle when the stink of Shane's lie reaches me.

Ah-ha!

I point at him. "You're lying to me."

I don't know what I expect. Did I think that Shane would try to deny it, or maybe cover his ass with another lie? I'm not sure. But when he just looks at me, his eyes narrowing as he rubs the back of his hand along his jaw, I'm ready to admit that I wasn't expecting *that* sort of reaction.

Especially when he chuckles and softly says, "So it's true."

"What?" I'm immediately on my guard. "What's true?"

"That part of an alpha's power comes in knowing if someone's lying to you."

"What—"

"I'm not an alpha. Not yet. But, please. Don't insult my intelligence by denying what you are. It nearly killed me to watch you pretend to be an omega when you first came to me. I think we're beyond that now, don't you?"

My jaw drops.

Something happens after that. Or maybe it's been happening all along and I was too stubborn to pay attention to the warning signs.

He changes. It's subtle, and I can't really put my claw on what's different, but I can tell that he's changed. It's in the way he stands, the way he takes a step toward me as he looms, his dimples disappearing into his taut cheeks as he smirks.

Shane's right. He's not an alpha, but that predatory look in his eye? I've seen it before. In my memories, and in the few photos that my mother kept as warning.

At that moment, Shane reminds me of Wicked Wolf Walker.

He reminds me of my bio-dad.

My reaction is pure instinct. I flex my fingers and, thank the Luna, my fingernails extend into razor-sharp claws. My canines burn, begging to lengthen. I can't shift, not fully, not *yet*, but at least I have a partial shift working for me.

I'll take it.

"You don't want me to insult your intelligence?" I toss back. "Do me the same favor, alright? You didn't break me out of Ryker's basement because you're worried about me. You know I'm an alpha? Then you know I wasn't in any danger. So what's going on here?"

An arrogant sniff, and a smile that doesn't quite touch the increasingly dark look in his eyes. "It's simple. I thought we had more time to ease you into a new arrangement, but it's still very simple. I want you, Gem. I want you for my mate."

You've got to be kidding me.

"Oh, fucking Luna." I roll my eyes. "Don't tell me that you're in love with me, too."

Shane looks momentarily puzzled. It's an improvement over his false sympathy and his suddenly alarming posture, but not by a lot. "Love? Who said anything about love?"

That knocks me back a few steps. "Um. You did. Just now."

The puzzled expression vanishes. "Oh. That. Not even close. Love? Please. This isn't about love. This is about a partnership."

"What do you mean, a partnership?"

"Again, it's very simple. You take me as your bonded mate and make me your Alpha. We rule our own pack together, the most powerful Alpha couple in the East, and you'll never have to worry about me rejecting you. I don't have to love you to be loyal, Gem." Shane sniffs, throwing a look over my shoulder back the way we came. "Can Ryker say the same?"

Oof.

I don't know what hurts worse. The reminder that Ryker rejected me *twice*, that I still don't understand his thing with Trish, or that my only worth is a strange quirk of my birth.

Shane only wants me for what I can do for *him.* Just like I've always been warned.

How could I *forget*?

Pretty easily, actually. Because Ryker has spent the last few days insisting that my alpha status doesn't mean anything to him, and Aleks could never be affected by such a shifter concern.

Oh, boy.

I fucked up.

I fucked up big time.

"All you have to do is say yes," Shane tells me. As he takes a step closer, a stray moonbeam lights up his face, showing his absolute certainty that I'm going to agree to this insanity. "The moon will bless us if you agree. We can mate right here, be bonded right now."

As an alpha, it goes against everything I am to retreat. Then again, I'm not pure wolf. I've got a human half that knows when to cut and run.

I move back. I just need to find the opportune moment to get the hell out of here.

Keep him distracted, Gem. Then *go*.

My instincts warn that pretending to be sweet— pretending to be an omega—will probably tick him off, so I just give him a disbelieving look of my own. "Yeah? What about Ryker?"

"What about him? He might not have taken the bait any time I sent her his way, but he'll settle for Trish when he has no other choice. An Alpha needs a mate, and he can't stay locked in the basement for another year. Who knows? If you hadn't shown up tonight, he might not have survived this one."

I blink.

A low laugh, one that sends a shiver down my spine. Huh. Looks like I'm not the only one who's been hiding just what they are from the rest of the pack.

Here, just the two of us, Shane's finally showing me who he is.

And I *hate* the dickhead.

"You didn't come to the basement because you

knew I was there, did you?" Luna, I hope I'm wrong, but... "You were going to do something to Ryker, but you couldn't."

"Plans change. They change all the time. I've spent years working toward this moment. You think I was going to let *fate* stop me? Ever since Wicked Wolf Walker promised to ally with any alpha who tamed his wayward daughter, I've been planning on how I'd make you mine. No one's gonna stand in my way. Not the Mountainside Pack. Not its lovesick Alpha. Not even you."

Forget Ryker. Forget Trish.

"Wicked Wolf Walker," I say dully. "What do you know about the Wicked Wolf of the West?"

For almost twenty-five years, my mom and I have been hiding out from the bastard who sired me. I always knew that any male shifter who discovered my secrets would want to be my mate—and, look at that, Shane's living proof right here—but if Jack Walker found out that I was an alpha *and* that I was alive? He wouldn't stop until I was at his mercy.

And Shane's telling me that my sperm donor *knows*?

"The better question, dear Gem, is what does he know about you?" Luna, I want to slap that cocky grin off of his face. "He knows Ryker rejected you. He knows you're a lone wolf. And he knows that you're a threat to us all unless you have a mate willing to tame you. It has to be me."

"Like hell it is."

"You weren't supposed to run," he says, as if I didn't snap back at him. "Last year. When I finally arranged with the Lakeview Pack to let you out of their sight, you weren't supposed to run when I finally pushed Trish to get in the way of you and Mr. Perfect Alpha."

Oof. That *sneer*.

Go on, Shane. Tell me how you really feel about Ryker.

Hang on—

"Pushed Trish? What do you mean, pushed Trish to get in our way? Hang on." I've just remembered something. "You're the one who told me not to worry about the rumors that Ryker chose Trish. I don't even know if I would've known anything about her if it wasn't for you!"

All those times when Ryker was "busy" and Shane kept me company... I wouldn't have known about Trish at all if Shane hadn't said anything at first. Then, after her snarls, her snotty comments, and the evil eye she gave me as she told me that I wasn't worthy of the Alpha...

He nods, a hint of a gleeful smile making his dimples pop again. Damn it. Those fucking dimples fooled me, didn't they? "I had to. It would've been so much easier if you rejected Ryker first. You could choose anyone. Another Luna... you would be wasted with Ryker. Mate me, Gemma. Be mine."

All it takes is me accepting his offer and, by pack law, he can force me into doing whatever he wants—including a lifelong mating I'd never be able to escape form.

No fucking way.

"No."

There.

Simple.

Effective.

Try to twist that into a *yes*, asshole.

"Just like an alpha." Shane's grin widens. "Because of Ryker?"

No point in denying it. "Yes."

I'm not his mate, not yet, but my heated *never* from last year has cooled off some. He was right to refuse me when I offered to mate him earlier, but does that mean I won't offer again? I don't know.

One thing I do know for sure, though? I might not be Ryker's mate, and my sitch with Aleks is complicated... but I definitely don't want anything to do with Shane.

"That's a shame." Shane closes the gap between us, quicker than I thought he would. "Will he still want you if you're not so pretty, Gem? 'Cause I will."

What the—

Turns out that I'm a fucking moron after all. Because only an idiot would stand there after the bad guy makes a quip like that and not realize what was going to happen next.

CHAPTER 18

Before I can react, Shane lunges at me, hand swinging toward my face.

It's my fault. I never expected he'd lash out like that. And if he did? I'm a predator myself, one who was trained by an Alpha. Even if I didn't think he'd turn on me, I was ready for him to go for something vital if he *did* attack. My heart. A lung. Maybe even a kidney if he snuck around my back. But my face? I never thought to guard my face.

His claws rake down my cheek. It's only pure luck that he misses my eye.

The rusty, tangy scent of my blood fills the air. I gasp, part in shock, part in agony, before I push the pain aside and fight back.

Either he's faster than I've ever given a beta wolf credit for or I lost a step or two living as a lone wolf. Hell, Shane was there during that fateful council meeting. Maybe he picked up a couple of pointers because, no matter how quick I am when I go for his heart, he dodges me easily.

Which just means I have to try harder.

Since I had to pretend to be an omega, I couldn't train with some of my other packmates. Mom was the only one who knew that I was an alpha, but as a true omega herself, she didn't have the training and the skills I needed to learn and flourish.

Paul, on the other hand, did.

Mom didn't trust her new mate right away—thanks for her lingering trust issues, *Dad*—but when she finally confessed that I was different, my adopted father did everything to prepare me to protect myself. He took care of my training himself, and there's no one better than a pack Alpha to teach fighting to a young pup.

Too bad Shane seems to have had just as good of a teacher.

He's toying with me. He let me get in a few good hits—before long, his blood perfumes the air alongside mine—but nothing to compare to the slash marks on my face. My skin feels like it's on fire, and I have to spit out the blood that gets in my mouth. From the taste, I know it's mine, and that just makes me angrier.

Angrier, and more reckless.

I see an opening. He went for my knee, trying to knock me under his right side, but that left his other half wide open. I dig my claws into the meat of his chest, just like I did to Ryker last year.

I want that heart—but I *miss*.

In the fury of our fight, my aim is off. I scrape his ribs, tearing through muscle, but I can't find his heart.

In response, he backhands me.

It's such a vicious, cruel sort of slap. Cowardly, too. At least with his claws, he fought like a wolf. But maybe that's the beta inside of Shane, throwing all of his strength into a backhanded hit that sends me flying. I'm sure I took a chunk out of his chest with me, but he's still standing when I crash into the ground with so much force that I nearly snap the tree I hit with my back.

By the time I can recover, popping back up to my feet, all I see is a pile of tattered, blood-stained clothes in the dirt.

Shane's gone wolf, and he's already disappearing into the forest.

I'm bloody. Aching. My body is still trying to fight off the effects of the mercury, and now I have countless injuries to heal.

But Shane is escaping, and I call desperately on my wolf.

With a keening howl, she responds.

Fucking hell, I can finally shift again.

Yes!

I don't even hesitate before I tear off after him, adding my shredded clothes to the pile.

In my wolf form, I'm faster than Shane. It's part of being an alpha. My sight is keener, my instincts sharper, my pads more sure as I fly across the terrain.

Plus, I want it more.

Forget the way he slashed at me like that. I'm a shifter. Unless I want the scar, or I accepted his offer of a mating—ha, yeah, *right*—my face will be back to normal come morning. I'm a big girl, and despite acting like an omega for nearly my whole life, I'm still a wolf. I've been in worse scrapes than this one.

But for him to threaten Ryker?

To admit that he's responsible for Trish coming between us?

To bring Wicked Wolf Walker into this?

I have to get to him before he escapes.

I almost do. At one point, I get so close to him that I get a mouthful of fur when I lunge at him and snap my jaws on the tip of his tail. I misjudged his speed and he turned it on right as I pounced. If I'd waited for another second or two, I might've got my fangs in his flank, but I missed.

He spun around, tongue lolling as he turned his snout toward me. His wolf's eyes glittered before he changed direction, a quick yip letting me know which way he's gone.

I dig my paws into the dirt, stunned.

That crazy bastard actually thinks we're playing some kind of a mating game!

Ha. I bare my fangs at him as I arrow my body, loping after him. My wolf mimics his yip, inviting him to let me catch him. Only, unlike what happened when I let Ryker catch me down in Muncie, Shane's not going to like what I do to him if I tackle him.

I'm so focused on my prey that I don't realize that we're not alone until Shane slips between a gap in two towering trees and I'm blocked from chasing after him. Four wolves cut me off, forming a line that separates me from Shane.

No!

I snarl but, for the second time tonight, I find myself being surrounded.

No!

Now that there are intruders in our little game, Shane's not going to stick around. He might've been playing with me, but it was obviously a game just for the two of us. While I'm blocked from chasing after him, he's tearing off as fast as his wolf will let him.

Oh, come *on*.

I reach out with my senses, but the four wolves prowling toward me are the only ones I can pick up on. So either they're the advance guard, or they were just together when they caught the scent of my fight with Shane and they came to check it out.

One thing's for sure: they never expected to find me in my wolf form.

Four wolves. One with a black coat, one that's brindled, and two grey wolves. They're all regular packmates. Deltas, though, instead of gammas since they're all younger; no elders in this quartet. I outrank them easily, both as a born alpha and the sweet, pure omega I've always pretended to be.

If they're still convinced that I'm an omega, their instincts will be to separate me from the threat and herd me back to the heart of pack territory. But if they've finally accepted that I truly am an alpha, this could be trouble. Their loyalty is to Ryker, and Shane's their Beta. I'm covered in Ryker's scent and wearing Shane's blood.

Either way, I'm screwed if they think I'm a threat to their Alpha or their Beta.

Unless—

Pack lore says that the Luna's howl can control any packmate. Now's probably not the best time for me to see if mine will do the same, but I can't let these wolves get between me and my prey. Their snarls and their posture makes it pretty clear: they're not just going to let me continue after Shane unless I force them to.

Here goes nothing.

I throw back my head and howl. A deep, guttural howl that rips out of my wolf.

As one, the four wolves in front of me drop to the

dirt. Front legs straight in front of them, bellies to the ground, they lower their muzzles and they lower their gaze. They might've been yipping and snarling moments ago, but my howl has turned each of them submissive.

Holy shit. It *worked*.

I wasn't so sure it would. I've never used my alpha status against another shifter; not on purpose, at least. For too long I let my packmates believe I was an omega like my mom, and this last year nearly everyone I've met has been convinced I'm human. I was always too afraid to really tap into my alpha side for so many different reasons—

Because Mom made me swear I wouldn't.

Because I was afraid my bio-dad would come after me.

Because I never wanted to take advantage of something I couldn't change even if I wanted to.

—but after twenty-six years of hiding who I am— who I was born to be—there's no point in hiding any longer. Wicked Wolf Walker knows about me. Shane has betrayed both Ryker *and* me all for the promise of becoming an alpha himself. I only got one real good swipe in, but he's leaving enough of a trail for me to track him down.

The other wolves are waiting for me to do something. My howl put them under my sway. As the only alpha around, they're waiting for me to give them instructions.

They're confused. I don't blame them. Even if they believed I was an alpha before now, none of the Mountainside Pack has ever seen me in my fur until a few moments ago. Without the blonde hair, pretty honey-colored eyes, and petite shape to fool their senses, it's undeniable that I'm a born female alpha. Add that to the scent of blood and sweat in the air—mine and Shane's—and they know that their Beta has been here.

I can't just take off after Shane. I might be an alpha, but I'm not their Alpha. These wolves are devoted to Ryker, and not in the sneaky, slimy way that Shane was. Right now, they're listening to me because of my howl. If I go back to chasing Shane, these wolves will come after me.

I recognize their scents. That brindled wolf is Jace. The oversized grey wolf is the big shifter who carried me earlier tonight. The black wolf over there is Dorian. Each one is a part of Ryker's inner circle, and they were all there tonight to present me as a kind of sacrifice to their Alpha. I don't know if they'll hunt me down because they'll want to drag me back to Ryker's basement, or if they'll try to shield Shane when I go for his throat, but I can't just run off.

There's only one thing I can do. Shifters can communicate basic thoughts and intentions to each other when we're in our fur, but nothing beats shifting back to human when you want to make sure there are no misunderstandings.

So that's what I do.

I grew up in a pack. Nudity's nothing to be ashamed of when it involves shifting. There's no intimacy involved. It's just my body, and I don't even think about how I'm standing bold as brass in front of four wolves with my tits hanging out.

I point in the direction that Shane has gone. "I'm hunting your Beta," I announce, my voice husky and raw as I put as much alpha power into it as I can. "He's betrayed your Alpha. He's betrayed the pack. He's sold us all out to the Wicked Wolf of the West."

Jace snaps his fangs at the mention of my sperm donor. Or maybe it's because he's gotten a good eyeful of my ruined face.

Yeah.

Same, Jace. Same.

"I'm going after him. If I have to drag him back to the Alpha myself, I will, but his fate belongs to Ryker."

It's true, I admit to myself. As pissed off as I am that Shane worked with Trish to come between me and Ryker, and how skeeved out I am at the idea of choosing to mate with him so he can become Alpha, even I know that pack law puts Shane's fate in Ryker's claws. By interfering with his mating and working with another pack's Alpha, he's challenged Ryker—and only Ryker can answer to the challenge.

But Ryker is still chained up in his basement, sure that his Beta is trustworthy and that I'm safe.

Okay. So Shane is a lying prick. But I'm doing just fine, and I'll be doing even better once I get my claws in Shane again.

I flash my gaze over the wolves, my shifter's eyes flaring to the molten lava color that tells them that my alpha wolf is in control. "You can come with me to run him down, or you can return to the pack. Either way, no one is stopping me."

The massive grey wolf—I really have to learn the big guy's name!—is the first to pull himself up to his paws. His lips pull back from his muzzle, showing off his canines, but his drawn-out rumble of a growl tells me that while he's pretty fucking pissed, it's not me he's pissed off at.

That honor belongs to the former Beta.

I flick my eyes over the other three. "You in? Jace? Dorian?" A flash of recognition hits me. I'm pretty sure the smaller grey wolf is another Danvers. Trish's younger cousin. "Bobby?"

Bobby yips. Dorian echoes it, while Jace stretches out his front legs before resting on his haunches. His head cocks in an obvious, "We doing this or what?"

I can't keep the smile from tugging on my lips. I might've spent a year convincing myself otherwise, but hell if I didn't miss being part of a pack.

I leap forward, already shifted to wolf by the time my four paws hit the dirt. The other wolves give way, letting me speed right past them before they form a line at my back.

———

I WISH I COULD SAY THAT WE FOUND HIM. WITH THE FIVE of us hot on his tail, I wish I could say that we surrounded him and took him down.

But we didn't.

Because I'm in the lead, I'm the one who first notices when the trail goes dead. I was following the scent of Shane's blood mingling with his wolf, and I stop short when I get a snout full of exhaust. The blood trail disappears right when the exhaust starts and it doesn't take an alpha wolf to figure out what went down.

Two wolves dart past me when I stop, the other two staying at my back.

A soft rumble has Dorian and the larger grey wolf returning. The big guy cocks his head as he comes clomping back to where the rest of us are crowded around a visible tire mark left in the dirt.

I know this path. We took a roundabout way to get here, but this is one of the mountain roads that leads straight into Muncie

In case the other two haven't caught on yet, I paw at the dirt, drawing their attention to the tracks.

Jace nods, then lets out a soft growl. I know what

he's asking and I use my front paw to swipe the nearest wheel mark away.

Do I want them to chase after the vehicle into Muncie? Not even a little. After a year of living in the vamp town, I know just how lucky I was to meet Aleksander my first night. Without the protection of the Cadre, the Nightmare Trio would've torn me to shreds just because I'm a shifter—and that's if I didn't slaughter them first, inevitably starting another Claws and Fangs war.

I've made contacts. Friends, too. Aleks's fang kept me safe, and my reputation as someone not to fuck with has made it so that I can still walk around Muncie even without the charmed necklace.

But that's just me. With Ryker in town, things were getting a little more dicey, and only the fact that he's Mountainside's Alpha—and, thanks to Roman's suspicious peacekeeping measure, made untouchable by the Cadre—stopped the local vampires from going after him.

These shifters wouldn't have the same protections. If I invited them into Muncie, I'd be a naive fool to believe that all four of them would be walking out again.

Here's hoping that a hungry vamp solves my problem for me. A car hadn't saved me from being caught, and only Aleks's inexplicable urge to claim me at first sight kept me from becoming a vampire's late night snack. There's always a chance that one of the vamps on the outskirts will get to Shane before I do.

If not, then I'll get *my* chance.

Not now, though. I won't risk Ryker's packmates just because I have a personal vendetta against his Beta. I'll track him into Muncie myself as soon as I can.

But first—

With the others waiting for my next command, I swing my muzzle back toward the mountain. A soft whine escapes my throat, echoing in the still night's air as I pad away from the tail end of the tracks before opening up my legs and sprinting for the path.

As one, they all follow me back toward pack territory.

CHAPTER 19

At some point I'm probably going to have to go back for my Jeep.

I'm not so worried about my car right now. It's probably safer in Accalia than I ever was, and once Ryker gets past the worst of the moon's pull, I have no doubt in my mind that he'll arrange for it to get back to me. For now, it can hang out in pack territory.

Me? I just want my bed.

I had to use another alpha howl to convince the four wolves—Jace, Dorian, Bobby, and... oops, I forgot to ask—to stay behind in Accalia. If I wanted a retinue of bodyguards at my back as I head home, I could've chased Shane's car into Muncie.

No. I need them on the mountain. Someone has to spread word about Shane's deal with Wicked Wolf Walker, and maybe I'm wimping out, but I don't want to be there when Ryker finds out that his Beta betrayed him.

It's about the pack, I tell myself. To any Alpha, the pack has to come first. And, sure, I know Ryker's gonna have something to say about me being the reason why Shane turned on him, but I'm way too tired to deal with that right now.

The sun's coming up as I slink my way up the fire escape. I was careful on my return trip to the apartment. From a distance, the humans might see my blonde wolf and think I'm just a suped-up dog or something. Vampires will know, of course, and without Aleks's fang to shield me, they'll think it's open season on me for daring to stalk through a notable Fang City in my fur.

Better to be cautious, even if it takes longer.

And if I'm hoping that maybe Aleks turned in for the day and I can avoid discussing anything about last night, well... yeah. I totally am.

Claws crossed.

I throw my shoulder into the balcony door. For a moment, I'm a little frantic. The door doesn't give and all I can think is that Aleks saw that I hadn't come home last night. Instead of leaving me a way inside in either form, he locked the door and—

The door pops inward on my second shove.

Oh. I just didn't push hard enough.

Phew.

Tiptoe. Tiptoe.

I navigate the living room, heading toward the hallway. Though my stomach is grumbling, I ignore the kitchen. I want my bed. Well, no. First, I want a quick shower. Then I want my bed.

Tiptoe—

Aleks's bedroom door opens right before I can sneak past it and hide in mine.

Ugh. So close!

Like the other night, he sees me padding down the hall, but it's obvious that this is no walk of shame. His curls are tousled, flat on one side; if he hadn't been sleeping, he was at least laying down. He's barefoot, but he's still wearing street clothes. Waiting up for me then?

Probably.

As a vamp, no doubt he can smell the blood on me, too. Most of my wounds have healed, but I didn't think to find a stream or a puddle to try to wash off the streaks of blood that stain my blonde fur. It's mostly mine since I was still bleeding when I shifted, and that's not taking into account all of the mud and shit I've got covering my paws.

Good thing I tried to wipe as much of it off as I could before I came inside. Last thing I need right now is to track that all over Aleks's floor.

Actually. No. The *last* thing I needed was for Aleks to catch me sneaking in when I was planning on taking the next couple of hours to wash up, get some rest, and make sense of... of everything.

I let out a soft whine. It's the most I can do while I'm in wolf form, and while I had no problem being naked in front of the Mountainside wolves, it's not the same with Aleks these days and we both know it.

He nods, like he understands. And, honestly, he probably does.

"I'll put a kettle on," he tells me.

Aleks and his tea. With a soft yip, I continue to my room.

Once inside, I shift back to my skin. A quick cursory look reveals that I was right: I'm coated in blood, but apart from a few faded scratches and a nasty bruise on my ass from where I hit the tree hard, I'm okay.

Physically, at least.

Mentally? Emotionally?

Yeah, not quite.

My bare feet slap against the tile as I slip into the bathroom. I know my roommate is waiting for me, but I have to shower. First, though, I brace myself before peering in the mirror hanging over the bathroom sink.

A soft sigh of relief. Though my cheek still feels tight, there isn't a single mark left on my face. No bruise from where Shane backhanded me, and no claw marks from where he ripped me open like a present.

Aleks can already sense that something's up. If I

walked out there looking like some other wolf's chew toy, I don't even want to think about how my overprotective vampire will react.

I take as quick a shower as I can, standing under the spray until my muscles relax and the water stops running pink with the washed-off blood. Then, knowing that Aleks is probably on his second cup of tea by now, I throw on a fresh outfit, toss my wet hair into a ponytail, and hope for the best.

I know that this isn't going to end well when, as soon as I ease into the kitchen, I see that Aleks is standing next the counter, an untouched mug sitting at his elbow. No steam, which means I took longer than I meant to, and his gorgeous face is pulled into a worried frown.

His pale green eyes light up when he sees me, though his brow furrows.

And then, as if on cue—

"You took off your necklace."

It feels like a lifetime ago when I asked Audrey to take it for a second so I could see something.

I nod. "Yeah. I did."

"An accident?" he asks hopefully.

"Not this time, Aleks."

He exhales. A year after I met my first vamp, and it still startles me when he does that. Mainly because he doesn't need to breathe so when he makes the obvious gesture, there's a reason behind it.

I brace myself.

I knew this was coming. Some part of me knew this would be coming from the moment I made the decision to go after Ryker during the full moon. One way or another, I made a choice. It's time to own it.

"You're not going to put it back on, are you?"

"Now that I know what it really means?" At his nod, I shake my head. "I can't. I... you know that, right? It's your way of claiming me as your mate. I could wear it when I thought you were protecting me—"

"I am protecting you, Gemma. The only way I know how. I can't fight your battles for you." Again, Aleks huffs. "Do you know what it does to me, seeing you walk in here wearing blood? *Your* blood? I want to use my fangs on anyone that would hurt you, but I know *that* would hurt you more."

He isn't wrong. Though vampires don't have a hierarchy the same way that the packs do—there's the Cadre and the vamps they rule, that's it—Aleks has always sensed that, as a shifter, I was only comfortable hiding because it's what I've always known. Not because I was scared. Not because I couldn't protect myself. But because it was easier.

The more I let out my alpha side, the more I have to admit that Omega Gem is gone and buried. I don't want a mate who will stand in front of me. I want one who will stand at my side, an equal.

Alpha, Beta, vamp... it never mattered to me *what* my mate was. Only *who*.

And, for the last eleven years, I've always known it was supposed to be Ryker Wolfson.

Regardless, no matter how much it hurts him to hear it, I have to tell Aleks the truth.

"I can't wear your fang," I try again, "because I'll never be your mate."

"Why? Because of that wolf?" Aleks pushes away from the counter, his Polish accent growing noticeably thicker as he lets his temper get the better of him. I don't have to ask what wolf he means. In all the time I've known him, Ryker's the only one who could ever get him *that* riled up. I used to think it was just another part of his protective side. Now? Now I know better. "I could make you so much happier than he could."

True. I'm sure he could. I've been happy living with Aleks this past year, but only because he's my friend. Even when he mentioned turning our relationship into something else, something more, I've always shut the subject down.

I don't see him like that. After these last few days with Ryker, I don't think I ever will.

"Aleks, I'm sorry."

"You're the one who told me it's who you choose that matters."

That's also true. After I left Accalia the first time, I told any supe who would listen that fated mates are a crock of shit. What did Fate know? It's who you pick that counts.

I said that to try to justify Ryker's choice. A mating had to be accepted on both sides. If I wanted him, but he wanted Trish... well, why shouldn't his choice count as much as mine?

"I know."

"So why can't you choose me?"

"Aleks..." I don't know how to answer that. My life would be so much easier if I could forget all about pack life and go back to embracing being a lone wolf in Muncie with a powerful vampire mate at my side. "I wish I could."

"Yeah? Ja też mały wilku."

Oh, boy. Aleks rarely speaks in his birth language around me since he thinks it's being rude when he knows I don't understand it. Except for the last part: *mały wilku.* I know what that means because Aleks told me once ages ago when I asked him why he always called me that.

Mały wilku.

Little wolf.

Ouch.

———

I'M OUTSIDE, MY FOREARMS RESTING AGAINST THE railing of our balcony, a can of ginger ale dangling from my hand. I take a sip every now and then, hoping it'll do something to settle my queasy stomach.

It's been two full days since I went back to Accalia. The last of the mercury has got to be out of my system by now, but I can't shake the nausea. I kept thinking I was going to hurl when they were carrying me to Ryker's place, and though my wolf is fully recovered, I still don't feel right.

Of course, that could have something to do with how rough the last couple of days have been...

Hailey took one look at me when I went down to Charlie's last night and, though I *appear* fine, my human friend told me to get my ass back to bed. Maybe humans are more perceptive than I thought, or else she knows me better than I expected, because I didn't bother arguing with her.

Even if I hated the idea of returning to an empty apartment...

I've got work in a couple of hours. I'm not letting Hailey cover for me for another night, and I already texted her so she knows that it's her turn to have a break. I'll probably pick up the next couple of shifts to make it fair, but tonight's a start.

I'm just thinking that maybe I could go in early, show Charlie that I still want this job, when my wolf perks her ears up. She's been resting ever since I had her running up and down the side of the mountain, and for the first time in days, she's alert.

A moment later, so am I.

My nose is working better than ever; I can deal with the queasiness so long as my other senses are back. Breathing in deep, I catch that familiar scent—of pine, of musk, of spice—on the breeze a moment before a moving target comes loping toward the back-side of my apartment building.

Almost as if he knows where to find me—and when I tug on the bond stretching between us and get an answering tug in return, I have to admit that he does.

I watch his approach, a little bit curious, a little bit apprehensive, and a whole lot of turned on.

Luna, can he run. Even from a distance, I can see his bare arms ripple with his easy speed. And all that delicious tanned skin... unh.

I don't want to know where he got those black pants from. No shoes, no shirt, so he was definitely walking around Muncie in his fur before he shifted to skin. A tentative sniff confirms that he's not carrying any other scents, so they're his. A shifter stash? A spare change of clothes around town? Maybe.

I guess I should be grateful that he's at least got his bottom half covered even if my eyes are glued to his sweat-slicked chest.

Oh, mama.

Don't stare, Gem. Don't—

Holy shit, look at him just about fly up the fire

escape. The pitted steel doesn't tickle against the pads of my paws, and I can only imagine what they're doing to his bare feet as he takes them two at a time, but yeah.

He's on some kind of a mission all right.

There's just enough time for me to relax against the balcony door, as if I haven't been waiting two days for him to make an appearance.

Me? Worried that Ryker was staying in Accalia?

Nah. Couldn't be.

Ryker's head pops up from the hole in the fire escape, squeezing his broad shoulders through the gap as he suddenly takes up way more space than I thought he would. His dark gold eyes brighten when he locks on me, but he doesn't say anything right away.

Instead, his nostrils flare as he takes in a deep breath. "Where's the bloodsucker?"

Of course that's the first thing he asks me. "His name is Aleks, you know."

Ryker gives me a look.

I ignore it, taking a sip from my can.

For two days, I couldn't stop thinking about what I would say to Ryker when I saw him again. I didn't know when I *would*; considering everything he had to be dealing with as an Alpha, I expected it might take a while until he could come back to Muncie. Before the next full moon, definitely, but I thought I had a little more time than this.

I'm not ready.

I lift up my can. "Thirsty? I've got a couple of more cans inside. Just ginger ale, though."

A dark look flashes across his face. "No Coke for you for a while, huh?"

"Got that right."

Ryker shakes his head. "Don't blame you. And I'm good. Thanks for offering, though."

I shrug, going for careless. "It's called being a good host."

"It's called providing for your mate," he argues. "But we can put a pin in that for a minute. How are you? You okay?"

"In one piece, so yeah, I'm okay. You?"

That dark look of his turns feral. "Be better if I didn't have to deal with my Beta trying to claim my mate out from under my nose."

The ginger ale can crinkles as my grip tightens. "That's not my fault. None of that was my fault."

He exhales roughly. "That's not what I meant. I know it's not your fault."

"Damn right it's not." I wait a beat. "And I'm not your mate."

"Yes. You are."

Welp, I knew this was going to go down eventually. Between what happened the last night we were together in Muncie and the full moon, I knew I was going to have to try to explain myself.

But how?

I want him. I'd only be lying to both of us if I tried to deny it. I want him, and my feelings for Ryker Wolfson might've been buried this past year, but there isn't a grave deep enough for me to try to get rid of them now. I love him—but does that mean I'm willing to tie myself to him for life without knowing how he feels?

I have no doubt that he wants me just as much as I want him. When it comes to sex, we're a match. But, despite its name, a mating is so much more than the physical act. Shane was cold-blooded in his approach, but he got one thing right: a mating is a partnership.

And I need an equal. If I accept him as my mate because I love him, and he only accepted me because of my rank—if he's as ruthless and cunning as Shane turned out to be—it really will kill me this time, no vampires necessary.

But he's watching me closely, waiting for me to say something, so I do. "Okay. You want to do this? I've got a couple of hours 'til work—"

Ryker's laugh is hollow. "So kind of you to squeeze me in."

"Do you have to be an asshole?"

"Do I have to be? No. Am I? You know me better than anyone else, Gemma. What do you think?"

Honestly, I think he's fucking with me. If he honestly believes that I know him better than anyone

—and he does, because I don't scent any deception on him—then I don't know what that says about either one of us that I kind of, sort of feel the same about him.

Maybe it's an alpha thing. I don't know. Most of the time, he just gets me. Like now. Like asking me what I think.

What *do* I think?

"I think I deserve the truth. Too many people have lied to me—"

"I never lied."

No. He didn't. I'm beginning to think my ability to tell when someone's lying *is* an alpha thing because, no matter how hard it was to hear, Ryker *never* lied to me.

But he's also very good at not telling me the complete truth.

"Alright. Prove it," I dare him. "When did you decide that you were going to go after me? When I slipped up and everyone realized I was an alpha?"

"I covered that up," retorts Ryker. "The council guessed, but no one else knew you were an alpha."

At least that explains how the other packmates treated me when I went looking for Ryker. They guessed, but only Ryker and Shane knew for sure— until I went and used an alpha howl to control Jace, Dorian, Bobby, and... huh. I still don't know the big guy's name.

I think about asking Ryker, realize that that can

wait, then say, "You didn't answer my question. When did you decide I had to be your mate?"

"I didn't answer you because I thought you already knew." After a moment where I stay quiet, he shrugs. "Same as you. When I fully accepted that you were my fated mate."

My heart drops.

That didn't work the way I expected it to, did it?

CHAPTER 20

"So the night you rejected me, huh?" That's what he said when I asked him about the scars. He fully accepted his side of the bond just in time for the marks to be made permanent—right after I showed off my alpha side. "Funny. You weren't so keen on mating me when you were telling me that you had no intention of going through with the Luna Ceremony. Then, surprise. Gem's an alpha, and you have to have her."

His dark brows draw together. "You don't honestly believe that, do you? That I could be so cold? So ambitious?"

Why not? It worked for Shane.

"What's that you told me?" I flick my free hand toward his sculpted chest. "Those are your marks now, right? Proof's right there."

Ryker glances down at his chest as if only just realizing he's not wearing a shirt. "It's the first time you marked me. Of course I kept them." He looks back at me. "What's it you said to me? Back in the basement?"

The moon fever isn't just affecting you...

Oh, I was wondering how long it would take before he threw *that* in my face. Some part of me was holding onto the hope that we could pretend that moment of pure insanity didn't happen. Ryker was chained up, I'd just been poisoned... we should get a pass, right?

One look at the determination etched into every line of his gorgeous face tells me quite simply: *wrong*.

I shake my head. "Know what? Forget it. I'm not doing this right now. Not with you."

"Gemma—"

"I think you should just go."

"I'm not going anywhere."

Oh?

"Fine."

He can stay out on the balcony all night if he wants to. See if I care.

Moving away from the balcony door, I throw it open. I stalk back inside the apartment, slamming my half-drank can of ginger ale onto the nearest surface.

Just my luck, the sticky soda sprays out everywhere.

Grumbling under my breath, I start to storm toward the kitchen to grab a wet paper towel when I hear the predatory footsteps follow me inside. I cast my eyes toward the moon, then spin around.

Ryker's leaning with the bulk of his shoulder against the now closed door. His arms are crossed low, highlighting his muscular form, with the whisper of a daring grin on his soft lips.

Luna, help me. Can't he take a hint?

"Get out."

"No."

"This is my territory." My claws come out with an audible *snick*. "Don't push me, Ryker."

"Did you know? When you go alpha, there's nothing sexier." His eyes flash, a come hither look lurking in their depths. "Come here, sweetheart."

Why? So he can use my undeniable pull toward him against me?

It's my turn to refuse him. "No."

A soft exhale. He straightens, using the opportunity to step further into the apartment. "You're wrong, you know."

I quirk an eyebrow, careful to stay on my side of the room. "Yeah? About what now?"

"About when I decided to accept you. You think it was that night last year."

"Of course I do."

"Wrong."

I'm not. "Ryker—"

"Gemma. I've always known who you were to me. Just like I've always known what you are."

I gulp. "I don't know what you're talking about."

"You recognized me as your mate when we first met, didn't you?"

Suspicion has me squinting over at him. "How did you know that?"

He holds out his hands, offering me his palms. "You're like me in so many ways. We're probably too alike, and it's made me wonder if we'll work. But I figure the good Luna wouldn't match us up if we wouldn't. And we fit. Luna knows we fit."

Don't blush, Gem. You have a half-naked Ryker Wolfson in your living room talking about 'fitting'. Don't you dare blush.

Clearing my throat, I look away from the heat in his gaze. Of course my eyes land on his bare chest—his bare chest and the five perfect scars I gave him.

The scars he stubbornly kept.

My hand slides up to my cheek. The marks were gone before I made it back to Muncie, but I can still sense them.

He glares at my cheek, almost as if he can sense the wounds that were there, too. And maybe he can because, with a strangled snarl, he tells me, "I'm an alpha wolf. A protector. Until I was sure you were safe, I couldn't let myself have you. Not last year. Not two nights ago."

"What about now?" I interrupt. "What's so different about now?"

"I did a lot of thinking in that basement. If you

couldn't be safe from me, I have to accept that you might never be safe. At least not as safe as my overprotective wolf demands. But that's okay. The world's not a safe place, but I still know that there's no better place for you than my side. You're mine."

"Excuse me?"

You think Ryker would've figured me out by now, especially since he's convinced that I know him so well. That's not a polite 'excuse me' where I'm asking him to repeat himself, and it's not an incredulous 'excuse me' that's giving him the chance to think about what he's saying to me. No, it's a warning that maybe he wants to stop right there before he goes any further.

He sets his jaw, the last glimmer of his humor fading as he turns his gaze into high beams. "You don't want to hear this—"

Damn right. "Ryker. It was just sex."

Because that's what this is all about, isn't it? I know. He knows, too.

Giving up any pretense that this isn't an alpha fight —just different than any I've had before—Ryker strides the rest of the way into the apartment.

"What did you say?"

The hairs on my arm stand straight as a shiver courses down my spine. My wolf rises from her cozy slumber again, completely alert and paying sudden attention as his quiet question triggers my own alpha instincts.

Only, I'm not angry, like I was when I stormed inside earlier.

I'm burning up.

I can't let him know that, though. He already chose placating Trish for some reason over telling me the truth once before and, despite everything that's happened between us since he stalked back into my life, I can't help but expect it'll happen again.

"It was the pull of the moon," I tell him. A couple days early, but the run and the chase with Ryker definitely hadn't helped. "If it wasn't me and it wasn't you, it might've been someone else."

Might've been, though I doubt it. The underground room with the chains proves that Ryker has his own way to temper the need that came during every full moon. Maybe it's worse for male alphas since I've always been able to deal with my libido with some brainless TV, a turn with my vibrator, and a gallon's worth of Breyer's.

Or maybe I want to believe it because, if I accept that he really stayed away for me, that Trish might've been as much a pawn in this as I was thanks to Shane... then I have to really begin to think that I don't have a choice.

That we really are fated to be together...

Suddenly he's right in front of me. Ryker grabs my hand, pulling me into his space. His territory. His warm skin is a furnace against mine, his breath tickling the tiny hairs framing my face. My head is tilted back, though I don't even remember jerking it that way. It's as if I can't help but meet his dark gold eyes.

Before I can avoid him, his mouth is slanting over mine. I gasp, and Ryker takes full advantage of my open mouth with a kiss so deep, I swear he's licking the back of my throat.

Then, almost as quickly as the kiss began, it's over and the only thing keeping me up is his hold on me.

"It wasn't just sex," he growls.

I shiver. Whether it's from the heat of his embrace, his demanding kiss, or his growl, I don't know... hell, it's probably from all three. "It—"

"No. It's my turn. And I'm going to tell you that it's never been just sex to me. Mating is for life. That's what I want from you, Gem. What I've always wanted from you. Forever."

Forever... forever... forever.

It echoes in my ears.

Forever...

"You can't mean that."

"Oh, but I can. You see, you're my first. My last. My *everything*. Nothing will ever change that, and I'm done with letting you try to pretend it will."

I blink. "But Trish—"

Ryker lets loose a rumble deep in his chest. "What about her?"

Am I really blushing now? As the blood rushes to

my head, I can't help it. "I'm sorry. I... I don't know what to believe. I thought you and Trish—"

Saying it out loud, I feel ridiculous. I went into a prospective mating with Ryker a virgin because that was *my* choice. I never blamed him for bedding someone—Trish or anyone else—because that was *his* choice. My issue had to do with Ryker bringing me to Accalia while still fucking Trish on the side.

But he said something about me being his first that morning after we were together. I ignored him then.

Something tells me that I can't ignore him now.

"Me and Trish *what*?" Then, before I can answer, he nuzzles the edge of my jaw. "Let me make this as easy to understand as I can. There has never been, nor will there ever be, a 'me and Trish'. It's my fault for ever allowing you to think so. You won't have to worry about her anymore. She's gone."

All I get out of that is: *she's gone*.

I had to have heard him wrong. "What did you say?"

"She's gone. I've kicked her out of the pack."

"What? Why?"

He pulls back enough that I can look him in the face as he explains, "It was always coming. I would've done it after that the night you marked me." Ryker takes my hand, sliding it between our bodies, laying it on his chest. "I thought I was the only one who knew you were an alpha. I didn't care. I don't care,

Gem," he says, cutting me off when I start to argue. "Alpha, beta, omega... if you were a gamma, I'd still want you. Because you're mine. The moon only confirmed what I knew from the moment I first laid eyes on a scrawny fifteen-year-old kid and freaked out because she made me harder than I'd ever been before."

"You were only seventeen," I point out. "Everything had to have made you hard."

"It was different," he insists. "And when you're seventeen, looking at your forever, it's a little scary that she's so small, so delicate, and, well, fifteen."

"I might be small," because, *duh*, "but I'm not delicate. And, in case you haven't noticed, I'm not fifteen anymore, either."

A long, lazy look as he leans back and takes me in from head to toe. "Oh, sweetheart, I noticed."

He thrusts his hips just enough for his erection to bump into me.

I swallow my moan before reminding him, "And you're not seventeen."

"But you still make me hard."

You know what? It would be so easy to let him seduce me. To continue with this heated tease until I'm half-naked like Ryker and then, whoops, we're both naked. Ryker asked me where Aleks was, and I purposely side-stepped the question. My roommate took off after our awkward conversation in the kitchen and he hasn't been back since he explained that he needed to take some time to be by himself.

Translation: he needed to get the hell away from me.

With my luck, he'll decide to show up again in the middle of me and Ryker fucking like bunnies in the apartment.

That, if nothing else, has me shoving him in the chest.

Like Aleks, I need some space. Just a little.

I know how to get it, too.

"You were telling me about Trish. Please," I murmur. "It would be so easy for you to kiss me again and make me forget. But I have to know. Please, Ryker."

It amazes me how different things are. I remember when, once upon a time, I choked out a *please* and Ryker accepted it as his due.

Now?

He just nods, and says, "Trish knew. She knew you were a born alpha. When she told me a few months before my Alpha Ceremony, I pretended I didn't know, then I acted as if it was impossible. She had proof, Gem. It caught me off guard, and when she said she'd tell everyone if I didn't keep my distance from you, I thought I could keep you separated until I could figure out where she was getting her information from."

"And then you became Alpha," I guessed. "And you had to take a mate."

Ryker sighs. I get it, too. The only way an Alpha gets the gig is by taking over for the last one. He could've challenged his father for the position, or he could've waited for him to die. And then his dad had his accident, and suddenly Ryker was stuck.

"Right. And the whole pack thought it would be Trish because she was obvious that that's what *she* wanted. Even after the moon said otherwise, even after I made my choice, she kept pushing. I had to keep her quiet until I could figure out how she knew the truth."

Obvious is an understatement. Up until Ryker told me that he didn't actually *choose* Trish, I was convinced he had.

Even then, I was having a hard time believing he really wanted *me*.

I still do.

At least we both know now how she learned the truth about me. That was Shane, the same bastard who kept throwing Trish at Ryker, hoping he'd take her and leave me available for Shane to swoop in and steal me away.

As if.

"I don't get it, though. Why did it matter what she threatened to do?" Hell, after a lifetime of guarding it fiercely, I gave up my own secret for Ryker's sake. "She blackmailed you over nothing."

"Not nothing," Ryker responds fiercely. "Do you think I don't know what would happen if it got out that you were an alpha? How many challenges I'd have to fight to get you? I'm a calculating bastard, sweetheart, and I didn't like those odds. I had one thing on my side. I knew you were meant to be mine. I always knew. I was hoping you knew it too, since it's an alpha thing. I was hoping our bond was strong enough that, if I was forced to reject you to keep your secret, you'd forgive me eventually."

Right. And what did I do instead?

I almost tore his heart out of his chest, and then I bolted. Thanks to Aleks's fang, I managed to hide from Ryker for over a year.

Whoops.

I duck my head, pressing my lips to his chest. I kiss the nearest mark. I think it's from my pointer finger.

Looking up at him again, I give him a crooked grin. "Aren't you glad that I didn't rip this out when I had the chance?"

"Why? It's yours, Gem. It's always been yours. Take it if you want. I gave it to you a long time ago."

I blink. "Ryker—"

A shadow darkens his ruggedly handsome features. "I know where Shane is."

My jaw clicks shut. Okay. After that solemn declaration, I didn't expect him to change the subject so quickly. But, yeah, he's definitely got my attention.

"What? Where?"

Ryker lifts his hand, smoothing the top of my hair.

"You want to know why I kicked Trish out? For the same reason that I'm gonna need a new Beta. He's been two-timing me, just like she's been using her jealousy to turn her against our pack. Shane wanted you, and she wanted you gone. It's why she's been sneaking around my cabin when I wasn't around, and why Shane broke you out of the basement the night of the full moon. Someone else was giving the orders."

"You don't mean..." I can't even finish my thought.

All the same, he nods. "They both gave their loyalty to a new Alpha long before you came to Accalia for the first time."

My stomach sinks. I don't have to ask, I can already guess I know the answer, and still—

"Who?"

"Wicked Wolf Walker."

Luna *damn* it!

"I fucking hate that guy," I mutter.

"Yeah, well, get in line. I don't know how he knew about you"—wait, he doesn't?—"but he's the one who told Shane about the rumors that the Lakeview Pack was hiding a female alpha. He figured out it was you somehow, and he passed the intel onto Trish. He pushed me to mate her, knowing that I didn't want anyone but you." Ryker's eyes shift, more of a deep amber this time. His canines lengthen just enough that his fangs bite into his bottom lip as he grins. "When I get my claws in him, he'll understand why

Betas don't interfere when it comes to the Alpha couple."

He said *when I get my claws in him...* "I thought you know where he is."

"I do. He made it through Muncie," he tells me, "and he's now the acting Beta of the Western Pack."

My birth pack.

With my sociopath of a sperm donor.

Shit.

I sag. I didn't mean to, but this is just too, too much. It was one thing to know that Shane was out there plotting against us; I figured since there weren't any rumors of another wolf getting caught by one of the local vamps. But to hear that he's actually with my sperm donor, working with him?

Not even Ryker's confession that Trish got the boot makes this any easier to swallow.

I might've sagged into him, but Ryker's strong enough to support us both.

"I won't let them get you, Gem," he promises me. "Just like I know you've got my back. We're in this together. You and me."

Seriously?

"I—"

With his hand a possessive brand on my back, his erection still a hard length of steel against my belly, Ryker dips his head to steal another kiss before I can get another word out.

Which is a good thing since, as soon as he starts kissing me, I completely forget what I was going to say. He even manages to knock Shane and Trish and my monster of a father out of my head if only for a few seconds.

Whoa.

I'm out of breath, eyes bright in a mixture of affection and need, when Ryker breaks the kiss. With his free hand, he cups my chin before running the edge of his wolf's claw against my bottom lip. It's probably swollen—it's definitely tender—but the gentle caress has me just about creaming my poor panties.

"Ryker..."

"You're mine," he whispers. He rests his forehead against my hairline, forcing me to meet the possession in his molten lava gaze. "I want you, and I won't let anyone have you. You're strong, sweetheart, but we'll be stronger together. So make it easy on me, would you? Will you accept me as your mate? Will you say yes?"

"No," I tell him. And then I give him a coy smile as I throw my arms around his neck, dragging him even closer to me so that I can kiss him this time. "But ask me again tomorrow."

AUTHOR'S NOTE

Thanks for reading *Never His Mate*!

This book is the first in a planned set of three featuring Gem and Ryker, though the series will continue after that with another hero (who you've already met, *hint hint*). So while things end on a more hopeful note for these two, they still have a bit of a journey ahead of them—though I do want to assure readers that they will end up together.

When I had the idea for this series, I always knew that he had "reasons" behind rejecting her, especially in front of the rest of his council. Like Gem, Ryker had his own secrets, so this is the sort of "rejected mates" story where the fated couple works things out instead of going against "fate"—though that doesn't quite mean that the next featured couple will end up the same way. It's just the way these two stubborn alphas' story will be told, and I can't wait for what's up next!

And if you liked this story? I have another book —*Season of the Witch*—that utilizes this same trope. In it, the wolf shifter hero keeps rejecting his fated mate bond with the empathic witch heroine before he finally pulls his head out of his ass and realizes that fate got it right and they belong together—now if only he can convince *her* of that. The first three books in that fated mates PNR series are also available as a box set—and part of Kindle Unlimited!

Not only that, but I'm about to release a prequel for this series, featuring Gem's mother Janelle: *Leave Janelle*. It tells the story of how she found the courage to escape Jack "Wicked Wolf" Walker, and how she met —and mated—Paul, Gem's adopted father. It's a little darker than Gem & Ryker's story, but it's another type of rejected mates story, and will give readers more insight into Gem's background.

For now, keep reading for a peek at the cover and the description for the next two books in the series —*Leave Janelle* (#0.5) & *Always Her Mate* (#2)—both coming out in July, as well as more information on the *Claws Clause* series.

xoxo,

Sarah

AVAILABLE NOW

ALWAYS HER MATE

I've always known that Ryker is my fated mate. What I didn't know? Was that he's always known he's *mine*...

Ryker Wolfson.

Strong. Sexy.

Powerful.

Irresistible.

For as long as I can remember, I've been waiting for the Luna Ceremony that would make him my bonded mate. Though it's not supposed to be possible, I've known since I was a kid that the future Alpha of the Mountainside Pack was fated to be mine. I figured my knowing had something to do with me being a rarity: a born female alpha.

Turns out that I'm half right. It's not the female

part, but an alpha thing. Because Ryker? For the last eleven years, he's known exactly who I am to him.

Worse? The rejection that had me hiding out this past year was as planned as everything else he has his claws in. Ryker might've thought he was protecting me, but all he did was push me away—all because he forgot for a moment *what* I am.

Omega Gem is history. Long live the Alpha of Muncie.

Only I'm in a bit of trouble these days. He might've spent years keeping my secret for me, but it's out now. An unforeseen betrayal in his pack has Ryker reeling, and me walking around with a big ol' target on my back.

As if dealing with my infatuated roommate wasn't bad enough. Now I have a powerful wolf chasing after me, desperate to claim me during the next full moon.

Not to mention the summons from my birth pack —and my old life. My sperm donor has discovered just how valuable I am, and since I've been "rejected" by Ryker, he wants me to go home for the first time since I was a pup.

Yeah? Well, I want him to drop dead.

And while I'm used to getting out of tougher scrapes than these, I'm beginning to see that—once again—I'm left with basically one option, and it isn't running away.

It's *Ryker*.

Maybe it's time that I accept that he's *always* been my mate...

———

* **Always Her Mate** is the second novel in the *Claws and Fangs* series. In a case of "better the devil you know", Gem realizes that Ryker is her best chance at avoiding being forced into a mating she doesn't want. It's tough, though. Because while she's always wanted *him*, her pride still can't get over his rejection...

Out now!

AVAILABLE NOW

LEAVE JANELLE

Sometimes fate gets it wrong.

When the Luna announced that I was fated to be the mate of the Western Pack's Alpha, Jack "Wicked Wolf" Walker, I knew that I would never survive him.

I'm an omega. Gentle by nature, all of my packmates thought I could temper his cruelty—but they were way wrong. As it is, it's all I can do to avoid being marked by him and tied to him for life. Luckily, my brute of a mate has a taste for females, and fully bonding me to him means that he won't get to hop from cabin to cabin while I pretend like I'm happy to be called *his*.

For three years, I walked a thin line between being

Jack's plaything and his bonded mate. When I gave birth to his pup, I thought he might change, but I did the one thing that he considered unthinkable: I gave him a daughter.

Worse, I gave him the first female alpha since the Luna herself.

Not that he knows that. I manage to hide her true nature, passing her off as an omega just like me—until Jack discovers the truth, and I'm left with no choice but to leave.

I know he'll come after us. My mate is psychotic, he's vicious, and he's cruel. He thinks he owns me, and he'll kill my daughter if he can get his claws on her. And while I may be an omega, I'm also a wolf. I'll protect her, no matter what, and when I pass into the territory of a neighboring pack, I attack the first wolf I see.

Who just so happens to be the Alpha of the Lakeview Pack...

———

* *Leave Janelle* is a prequel novella (35,000+ words) that is set approximately twenty-five years before the events of *Never His Mate*, and it's the story of Gemma's mother.

HUNGRY LIKE A WOLF

SNEAK PEEK AT ANOTHER
FATED MATES NOVEL

Maddox had spent the entire time trying to work up the nerve to ask if she was free for dinner—while trying not to think about how ludicrous it was to have to ask his *wife* out on a dinner date in the first place—and recognized that his window of opportunity was quickly shrinking. Because, all too soon, the conversation started to dry up. He was just trying to think of a way to stretch it out when Evangeline's lips suddenly thinned. Maddox recognized the look of annoyance that flashed across her lovely features.

He was willing to bet he knew what caused that expression. An annoying buzz had been going off almost non-stop for the last ten minutes. It wasn't his phone—Colt was the only one with the number and he knew better than to bother him—which meant it had to be hers.

And she'd finally caught on to the fact that it was ringing.

"Something wrong?" he asked, keeping his tone light.

"What? Oh. No. I just—" She picked her purse up from its place on the floor and propped it on the edge of the tabletop. After fishing around inside of it for a few seconds, she pulled out a cellphone. It was vibrating loudly. "I thought I heard something," she murmured, more to herself than to Maddox. She glanced up at him. "I'm sorry. I... I should really take this call."

Evangeline kept the screen angled toward her. He didn't know if that was on purpose or not, but it didn't matter. Maddox couldn't see who was calling her and, while he didn't want to share, he had to remind himself that he didn't have a real claim to Evangeline.

Not yet, anyway.

"I understand," he lied. He choked down a sip of his cold coffee, acting as if it didn't bother him one way or another that she was choosing to talk to someone else.

And then she answered the phone.

"Hello?"

"*Eva.*"

Maddox's hand shook so hard that he spilled half of the mostly untouched coffee onto the tabletop.

A man's voice. That was *a man's voice.*

Evangeline looked up at him again, her eyebrows raised as she caught sight of his mess. "Hey. What's up?"

"Where are you, babe?"

And there went the other half of his coffee. Babe. That faceless bastard just called *his* mate 'babe'.

Evangeline leaned over and grabbed a handful of napkins from the dispenser. Covering the mouth-piece of her phone with one hand, she murmured, "Clumsy," and handed Maddox the napkins before getting up and taking a few brisk steps away from their table. As he made a half-assed attempt to mop up the spilled coffee, he was focusing on every word she exchanged with the mysterious man on her phone.

Thank fucking Alpha for shifter hearing.

"I told you what my plans were for the day," she said softly. "I'm getting coffee right now. Then I'm going right back to work. Remember?"

She might have been keeping her voice down. Maddox thought her words were clipped. She was clearly annoyed. Evangeline had always hated it when she felt she was answering to someone else which made for quite a few arguments early on in their courtship. Possessive shifter versus headstrong human, it had taken Maddox some time to learn how to care for Evangeline without smothering her.

This dumbass certainly hadn't.

"I tried calling you a couple of times while I was taking lunch. Then just now. You didn't answer."

"The coffee shop is loud. I must not have heard it. Is anything wrong?"

Maddox thought of the way Evangeline's eyes had strayed toward the floor a few times during their conversation. He had heard the vibrations before and ignored them, so intent on listening to what she was saying. It made him a little bit happier to know that she might have done the same.

His happiness deflated like a balloon when the man started to speak again.

"No, nothing's wrong. I just called because I wanted to remind you that it was Friday. You seemed a little iffy about the days yesterday. Didn't want you to forget about date night."

"Yes, Adam. I remember. I'll be ready by eight, like usual."

"And maybe we can head back to your place after for some coffee."

"We'll see, okay?"

"Okay." There was a pause. *"You sure you're feeling okay, Eva? You sound a little... off."*

"I'm fine. I was just getting ready to leave. I've got a couple of pages to proof before I get ready for tonight. Then I'll be free."

"I'm looking forward to it. Eight o'clock... see you then. Love you, babe."

Maddox was stunned.

He could hardly believe what he was hearing.

No. No, that wasn't true. He *could* believe it, except that didn't mean he wanted to. Or that he *would*.

Sure, his mate was sitting there, having coffee with him, smiling at him—*bonding* with him—but only for this one moment in time. For a few precious minutes he had been able to pretend she was his again before reality smacked him in the face.

There was no bond. His Evangeline didn't know him from Joe Schmoe down the street.

And she was going out with some bastard named Adam.

Eight, as usual. There was a *usual* involved. This Adam fucker kept insisting on calling Maddox's mate 'babe' like he had the right. No. He refused to believe it. Something might have happened to break their bond, but it was going to come back stronger than ever.

It *had* to.

Keeping one ear cocked for the rest of the conversation, Maddox had been writing Adam's obituary in his head, already figuring out where he could hide the body if he ever got his claws on the bastard, when he heard Adam clear as day: *Love you, babe.*

Yeah, not if he knew what was good for him.

Maddox stopped breathing, waiting to see how his Evangeline would react. If she said it back...

And that's when she did something that made the

fur sprout along the back of his hand in a total loss of control. After a small, almost imperceptible sigh—imperceptible to a human, not a shifter—Evangeline brought her phone's speaker up to her mouth before she smacked her lips softly into it.

Kissy noises.

Fucking *kissy* noises.

To another man.

It didn't matter that she rolled her eyes as she did it, or that she sighed again as she ended the call and slipped her phone into her bag. The damage was already done.

Because that little display meant one thing to the jealous wolf she'd unwittingly just provoked.

It meant that, despite her eye-rolls and tight voice, Evangeline wasn't being forced into another relationship. She was choosing to be with Adam when she'd already made her choice years ago to marry Maddox. To mate with him. To *bond* with him.

Except what the fuck did that mean when she obviously didn't remember?

Before any of the Ants in the coffee shop saw, Maddox jammed his furry claw-tipped paws into the pockets of his jeans an instant after he shoved away from the table and climbed to his feet.

Sure, it could have been worse. She could have said "I love you" back.

But *kissy noises*?

That did it. No more Mr. Nice Guy. No more lovesick puppy dog gazes, hoping she would throw him a bone. No more sitting and waiting and hoping she would remember and the bond would come back.

It wouldn't come back until he *made* it.

Without a word, and leaving a sopping mess of napkins and a visibly startled Evangeline behind him, Maddox stormed out of the coffee house. His borrowed turtleneck was already pulling at the seams as he fought his body's urge to shift. Because even his beast knew what was going to happen next.

Evangeline had sealed her fate the second she answered that phone. From there on out, she wouldn't be facing off against the man he'd been pretending to be.

Nope, she'd be dealing with the big, bad wolf...

AVAILABLE NOW

IF YOU LIKE THE SHIFTERS IN
CLAWS AND FANGS, CHECK
OUT THESE POSSESSIVE
HEROES...

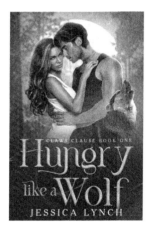

In a world where paranormals live side by side with humans, everybody knows about Ordinance 7304: the Bond Laws. Or, as the Paras snidely whisper to each other, the Claws Clause— a long and detailed set of laws that bonded couples must obey if they want their union to be recognized.

Because it wasn't already damn near impossible to find a fated mate in the first place. Now the government just has to get involved...

I remember—

Three years ago, Maddox Wolfe lost his mate. Since there's nothing more dangerous than a bonded shifter on his own, Ordinance 7304 gave him three choices: voluntary incarceration until he's no longer deemed a threat; a lobotomy-like procedure performed by government-employed witches that would dissolve his bond; or, most final, a state-sanctioned execution so that he could be with his mate again. And while death held a certain appeal in the hazy days following the tragedy, Maddox had his family and his pack to live for. So, refusing to give up his memories of his sweet Evangeline, he chose to spend the rest of his days in the Cage.

I forget—

There's a hole in Evangeline Lewis's memory. The doctors tell her that it's normal, that she'll recover fully in time. After all, it's only been three years since the accident that nearly killed her. They never thought she'd wake up; a nagging, annoying sensation that something's wrong is the least of her worries. Especially since she has so much going on: a new apartment, a new job, her mother's well-meaning attempts at match-making... but tell that to her wayward psyche.

By day, she can't shake the feeling that something's missing. And, by night, she can't escape the dreams of a shadow man with glowing golden eyes...

It's entirely by chance when Maddox's brother follows that familiar scent to the beautiful brunette with the haunted smile. But Colt knows immediately what he's found: Maddox's mate, alive if not altogether well.

Once he learns the truth, Maddox will stop at nothing to get her back, even if it he has to follow every twisted, convoluted letter of the ridiculous Claws Clause to do it. And when that doesn't work?

Sometimes a wolf has to do what a wolf has to do. Stalking his mate, taking her captive until she remembers him... if it works, he'll have his mate back. If it doesn't, he's dead. Even worse, Evangeline will probably hate him forever.

Maddox is desperate enough to take those odds.

Hungry like a Wolf is the first novel in the *Claws Clause* series, featuring a determined alpha wolf shifter who goes a little dark without his mate and the woman who cheated death to find her way back to him.

Get it today or check out the 3-book collection, featuring 1,000+ pages for one low price!

KEEP IN TOUCH

Stay tuned for what's coming up next! Sign up for my mailing list for news, promotions, upcoming releases, and more!

Sarah Spade's Stories

And make sure to check out my Facebook page for all release news:

http://facebook.com/sarahspadebooks

Sarah Spade is a pen name that I used specifically to write a series of holiday-based novellas (and, now, a rejected mates series that's set in a different universe from my other PNR shifter series). If you're interested in reading some more books that I've written (in a variety of genres, including: romantic suspense, Greek mythology-based romance, shifters/vampires/witches romance, and fae romance), check out my primary author account here:

http://amazon.com/author/jessicalynch

ALSO BY SARAH SPADE

Holiday Hunk

Halloween Boo

This Christmas

Auld Lang Mine

I'm With Cupid

Getting Lucky

When Sparks Fly

Holiday Hunk: the Complete Series

Claws and Fangs

Leave Janelle

Never His Mate

Always Her Mate

Forever Mates

Hint of Her Blood

Taste of His Skin

Stolen Mates

The Feral's Captive

The Beta's Bride

Claws Clause

(written as Jessica Lynch)

Mates **free*

Hungry Like a Wolf

Of Mistletoe and Mating

No Way

Season of the Witch

Rogue

Sunglasses at Night

Ain't No Angel **free*

True Angel

Ghost of Jealousy

Night Angel

Broken Wings

Lost Angel

Born to Run

Uptown Girl

Printed in Great Britain
by Amazon